FEB   1998

By Jake Page:

Mo Bowdre mysteries
THE STOLEN GODS
THE DEADLY CANYON
THE KNOTTED STRINGS
THE LETHAL PARTNER
A CERTAIN MALICE

Science fiction
OPERATION SHATTERHAND
APACHERIA*

Nonfiction
WILD JUSTICE: The People of Geronimo vs. the United
  States (with Michael Lieder)

*Forthcoming

A CERTAIN MALICE

Jake Page

BALLANTINE BOOKS • NEW YORK

A Ballantine Book
Published by The Ballantine Publishing Group
Copyright © 1998 by Jake Page

http://www.randomhouse.com

Library of Congress Catalog Card Number: 97-94064

ISBN 0-345-40539-0

Manufactured in the United States of America

First Edition: January 1998

10 9 8 7 6 5 4 3 2 1

For Susanne, as usual,
and for Frank Stone

What's life? Life is an applecart.
                                    —Mark Twain

meditation

After midnight in March in the high country of northern Arizona, the bright eyes and sweeping tail of the constellation Scorpio dominate the southern sky. To the north the Great Bear has wheeled high off the horizon and an orange star called Arcturus is directly overhead. Light from Arcturus has taken a mere forty years to arrive in the icy thin atmosphere of the mesas where the Hopi Indians have lived for a millennium. The light from Arcturus is, therefore, the freshest, newest light to arrive from the firmament, and an unimaginably small fraction of it shines straight down through the rectangular entrance in the roof of an underground chamber the Hopi call a kiva. There, the starlight mingles with the urgent orange of a fire that flickers below the overhead entrance. Some of this fire's light, in turn, passes upward through the hole in the roof, along with smoke that dematerializes in the cold night air the way a prayer disappears into the world of the spirits.

In March, a time in the year's cycle that the Hopi call Angk-wa, the annual rebirth of the world has already begun.

For three months now, the spirits of life and nature called katsinas have been making appearances in the Hopi villages, and on this night in March some of them have already appeared in the kiva, bringing gifts of food and dancing before moving on. More will come soon. At the bottom of the ladder, an old man with a red headband tends the small fire and waits for them. Also waiting, some twenty women sit wrapped in brightly colored shawls in chairs at one end of the underground chamber, while men sit on bancos along the three other whitewashed walls.

Among the Hopi men along the walls, a huge man with blond hair and a blond beard sits erect as a post, thick forearms folded across his chest, unseeing eyes shielded behind sunglasses. This white man, this *pahana*, is a welcome and familiar guest in the kiva. (His long-time companion sits among the other Hopi women.) As with many blind people, the big man's hearing is especially acute, and he hears the low hoots of katsinas approaching well before the Hopis in the kiva do.

Soon, from above, a rattle sounds, and the old man in the headband calls out a welcome, just as a father welcomes his children. One by one the spirit beings descend the ladder, emerging from the black night outside into the warm, firelit chamber. One by one they take up their positions. A rattle sounds again, and a drum, and they dance. The kiva fills with sound: the identically clad katsinas sing, the drum thunders rhythmically, bells and turtle shells tied to the dancers' legs jingle and clack. All is a swirling repetition of motion, shadow, color, and sound, over and over, over and over, commandeering the rhythm of human pulses, freeing the people there in the kiva from the constraints of time, allowing their minds to journey. . . .

. . . The blind man sees no color, nor does he understand the words being sung, but his mind also floats free. He finds himself descending into a familiar mountain, in a dank poorly lit tunnel, one of many honeycombing the earth. Fifty-three miles of underground track, drilled and blasted out of the mountain for molly-be-damned. Molybdenum. Greasy gray molybdenum. Steel wheels roll over steel track under wet ceilings, and occasional sparks crackle from the high voltage wire, fifty-three miles of it, powering the Toonerville trolley and a few naked lightbulbs. The place smells of ozone and dynamite and fractured rock. And muck. The flumes are filled with muck and spring runoff, the mountain leaking like a sponge. Far off, down the tunnel, men with lights on their heads are digging the muck out of the flumes, over and over.

Directly overhead is a rectangular opening through which he now climbs, ascending into another dimly lit tunnel, just a short one with a gray rock wall at each end. At one end, he and the other man unwind the yellow fuses and make the other preparations. These are dangerous rituals, especially when left in the hands of greenhorns.

It's time to retreat, to scrabble over loose rock, get around the corner, get your feet out of the yellow tangle.

A brilliant white flash comes too soon, and even before the pain and the blackness can follow it, he knows his eyes are gone, he's lost his vision. He knows he'll have to create a new world for himself because the old one is gone.

But something else has been lost as well. What? What is it he has lost? There's nobody to tell him of this other thing he has lost. In that same instant, he knows he'll have to keep coming back to this place of tunnels where maybe one day he'll remember. . . .

. . . Now, in the kiva, over the din, a rattle sounds. The dancers stop and the kiva falls silent. One after the other the katsina spirits mount the ladder and leave the warmth of the kiva to emerge yet again into the night where Arcturus and the other stars crawl across the sky. Soon it will be dawn, time for feasting, for welcoming the blessings of the new season.

one

Frazier always served white wine at these events, a good white wine and plenty of it, but T. Moore Bowdre would have preferred beer, or maybe even some hard stuff. He didn't like these openings, not a damn bit, standing around with a stupid grin on his face, sipping white wine and listening to what seemed to be thousands of voices all at once—indistinguishable, all babbling courtesies and self-conscious commentary that swirled and eddied in the huge room, echoing off the walls, the high ceiling, the sculptures, merging in his superacute ears as a single loud hum of audio overload.

The big man leaned over and stage-whispered to his companion. "Connie, this is just pure cochlear chaos."

"What are you talking about?" said the broad-shouldered woman with a coppery, round face and long black hair.

"All this noise," Bowdre said.

"What?"

"All this noise."

"Huh?"

"Connie, you stop that. I know these things are important.

Doesn't mean I can't complain. I got a constitutional right to complain. It says right there in the First Amendment that nothing shall abridge the right of a citizen to complain that art openings are a pain in the ass. Hah. Hah. Hah." T. Moore Bowdre's version of laughter erupted in separate, staccato bursts. "The founding fathers," he resumed, "knew about this kind of thing. I mean, just think of all them minuets and the powdered wigs and lacy duds those boys had to wear, drive a man straight into the soothing arms of demon rum."

Bowdre's voice had been rising from a stage whisper to a highly audible bray, and many of those standing nearby in the huge gallery stopped talking to stare at the source of the noise—precisely what Bowdre had had in mind of course. His companion, Connie Barnes, looked heavenward and smiled weakly at the people standing nearby, many of whom she knew.

They in turn applauded politely, and one—a tall woman whose gaunt frame managed nonetheless to support a bushel or two of turquoise and silver beads—said: "Yes, a word from the artist. Speech, speech." Her voice was a menopausal croak.

Mo Bowdre reached up and with a beefy hand pulled his black cowboy hat down a notch over his forehead. Thus perched, its rim only an inch above his dark glasses, the hat looked a size too small. He grinned broadly through a blond beard, white teeth shining.

"As I was saying to Connie just now, it's a real honor being here—hah, hah—and I'm seriously grateful to you all for comin' out to see all these new pieces. Of course you all know there's a partnership in doing this kind of thing between a sculptor and the foundry. So if you don't already know him, I hope you'll go up to Hank Adams from the foundry and shake his hand. He's the tall skinny guy with his eyebrows singed off. Occupational hazard. He's around here somewhere."

Bowdre reached out and rested his hand on the forehead of a mountain sheep, a bronze ram peering down from a crag. It consisted of bronze fragments, curls, and chunks of bronze joined haphazardly like shrapnel that somehow had been induced into coming together in the form of a ram. Its neck was arched, and the head, flanked by smooth swirls of horn, peered down with elegiac grace. The animal stood poised for flight.

Around the room, two dozen more sculptures rose up from the polished oak flooring, spirited creatures in bronze bespeaking great weight, gravity, but somehow airy as well, as if glimpsed for only a moment. The overall effect was of two dozen silent explosions of matter, all stopped for an instant in animal form before disappearing into formless chaos.

It had begun to dawn on many of the people assembled for this opening that not only was this a new style for Bowdre, the noted wildlife sculptor, but a major statement as well. In the course of a year in the more than one hundred art galleries that compete for attention in Santa Fe, New Mexico, which (it is said) is the third largest art market in the world, major statements by artists are not at all uncommon. Indeed, a growing number of people make a living of sorts by winkling out these major statements and explaining them to an awestruck public. In these endeavors, they are often aided substantially by the artists themselves, who earnestly speak of such things as "the whereness of the near," or "a shaman's descent into the beast." On the other hand, when it came to explaining his art, Mo Bowdre was always, as now, taciturn to a fault.

"I don't have much to say about the pieces themselves," he said. "Once these things are done, I figure they gotta speak for themselves, like grown children you've let loose in the world."

He patted the ram's forehead and let his arm fall to his side. "As I said, I'm real grateful to you all for coming." He executed a small bow from the waist, touched the rim of his hat, and stepped back as the buzz of conversation again arose around him. Now, he thought, I can ease my way over to the door real slow, real polite, tugging my forelock, smiling, yes ma'am, thank you, that's nice of you to say, and then . . . *home*. Sleep for a week.

He felt long thin fingers encircle his wrist, smelled a wave of perfume enveloping him like a cool mist, and knew it was Rhiannon Sharp before she once again uttered her basso croak in his ear.

"Now, Mo," she said, "*dear* Mo, you can't leave us hanging like that. This work is all very new, very . . . protean. You're saying something here about the fragility of life. Isn't that it?" Her fingers squeezed his wrist. "The momentary spark."

"Well now, Rhiannon . . ." Mo began. The woman owned two Bowdre bronzes, a life-size sleeping bear and one of his few equestrian efforts, a quarter-life-sized study of a mustang mare poised alertly for flight. The bear dozed in the adobe-walled courtyard of the Sharp hacienda several miles northwest of the city, while the little mare presided nervously over the Sharp dining room from a huge mahogany sideboard.

Rhiannon Sharp had arrived in Sante Fe from Virginia horse country in the early 1980s, newly divorced, well-moneyed, and with the name Frances. She had eagerly steeped herself in all the local cultures, particularly Hispanic and Indian, but also the burgeoning and many-faceted realm of self-awareness. She had also judiciously patronized the Santa Fe art world—and changed her name to Rhiannon, a Celtic goddess whose talents evidently included bringing the dead back to life.

A small local publisher, Adobe Press, published her memoir of her first year in New Mexico, a slim volume entitled *Refractions* that the *New York Times* had taken brief but approving note of, conveying upon her a great deal of local repute and solidifying her position as a mover and shaker in the City Different.

Several years after she arrived, she married a widower two years her junior, a man named John Franklin, whose stolid, single-minded devotion to breeding Arabian horses stood in sharp contrast to Rhiannon's ebullient interest in virtually everything. Indeed, just what she, an extravagantly good-natured liberal, saw in John Franklin, a fourth-generation Republican so stodgy and close-mouthed that many took him for a mute, had been a source of local wonderment for years. Now in her late fifties, she was on the board of two local museums and an organization that sought to preserve indigenous languages around the world, and for all three she was an indefatigable fund-raiser.

"Never mind," she said now to Mo Bowdre. "I know

you're not going to talk about it. Not even to me, one of your beloved benefactors. But there's something I urgently want to talk to you about. Connie, could you bring him out to see me tomorrow? I promise you, Mo, you'll be fascinated." Her fingers tightened on his wrist like the talons of a hawk, and Mo knew there would be no escaping.

Frazier's invitation had been a study in elegant understatement—a black and white photograph of a detail from Bowdre's mountain lion, its face seen in a three-quarter view, almost an abstraction. It had been printed with three black plates, giving the image a nearly electric dimensionality, and inside, the words had been simple:

Frazier Gallery
invites you to see
new work by
T. Moore Bowdre
Saturday, June 6, from 4:00 to 6:00 P.M.

"That's awful damn dignified," Mo had said when Connie described it to him. "You think Frazier's gonna tell me I got to wear a suit? You know that fella Thoreau, lived in a cabin by himself back East? Henry David Thoreau. He said to beware of any enterprise that requires new clothes. Good man. Strange as a snake with three ends, but a good man."

Connie had reassured him that no one would suggest such a thing, and Mo had gone grumbling to the opening

wearing his usual black cowboy hat, jeans, and a voluminous calfskin vest; but instead of the blue workshirt that
was also part of his signature apparel, she persuaded him
to wear a teal-colored silk shirt he had gotten a year ago
for a wedding and hadn't worn since.

By six-fifteen he'd managed to escape Frazier's
gallery and stood on the sidewalk on San Francisco
Street a half block west of the plaza, with Connie at his
side. A tall woman stood with them. She wore her red
hair pulled severely back from her face and woven into a
complex series of knots on the back of her head, and she
was sheathed in a long, loose-fitting dress of multiple
tones of purple that ended a few inches above a pair of
elaborately beaded moccasins. She was Phyllis Lodge,
proprietor of a local herbal shop and a happy warrior in
all of the environmental battles that constantly arise like
weeds in the fragile soil of northern New Mexico. Now
she rested a long-fingered hand on Mo's forearm.

"Fabulous, Mo!" she said. "Fab-yoo-lous stuff. You've
really outdone yourself this time. One of each. I'd like
one of each. If I had any money I'd buy it all. Pile it all
into my backyard and just sit there hugging myself.
Aren't you just thrilled? I mean, *thrilled*! Connie, isn't
Big Sweetums here pleased with himself?"

Mo smiled broadly through his blond whiskers. "I
could use a beer," he said. "All that white wine makes
your mouth feel like cellophane."

"Beer?" Phyllis said. She poked a long forefinger into
Mo's protruding stomach. "You don't need any more
beer, honey," she said. "Not with this."

"I suppose you've got a flask of sauerkraut juice or

some awful stuff you people drink to promote healthy mucous membranes. No thanks. Beer's what I need. Two beers. Maybe three. Come on, Phyllis, I'll treat you to some V-8 juice. They tell me it's good for your gums."

Phyllis stood up on her toes and gave Mo a loud smooch on his cheek. "Thanks, but no thanks. I've got to get back to the store. Come and see me one of these days, guys." She turned and strode down San Francisco Street in a long-legged gait, cheerful as a cloud of negative ions.

"We should do something to celebrate," Connie said. "Maria's maybe?"

"Haven't been there in—what?—three days?"

"Green chili stew."

"And posole."

"Sounds real good," Connie said. "Let's go."

Her lineage was impeccable, as was her bearing. The blood of legendary forebears stretching back in time to the grandest estates in Victorian England and thence further back to the ancient sands of Egypt, coursed through her regal veins and arteries. She stood quivering, alert, nostrils flared, large and luminous deep brown eyes watching the horizon where the sky, now beginning to turn the palest orange, met the rounded purple haunches of the Jemez Mountains. Between her and the mountains the land rolled westward, clad in piñon pine and juniper that cast long shadows over the sandy ground. It was new, unfamiliar, and the shadows were latent with omens only she could perceive. She shifted restlessly on her feet.

She was a two-year-old by official reckoning, but in actual passage of time two and a half, and John Franklin was deeply pleased with her. She had manners and courage. A breeze had suddenly whipped through the surrounding scrub, ruffling her mane, and a lesser creature might well have shied, even bolted. Even now, barely broken to the saddle, she would fetch at least $35,000, but he had no plan to sell her. The life course ahead of her was already thoroughly planned with prospective genealogical precision. She would be one of the queens of Kokapelli Arabians.

Franklin felt her mouth under the reins and pressed lightly with his calf. She turned, as if following his gaze, and stepped down the incline into a shallow arroyo that led crookedly into the larger dry gash called Canada Rincón a half mile away. They were now almost a mile from the tailored pastures and white pipe fences of Kokapelli Arabians, her maiden foray out of the familiar oval training ring and into the wild geometry of the high desert northwest of Santa Fe.

John Franklin, of course, knew this was an ill-advised venture. No one in his right mind would take a green, just-broke Arabian filly, however highborn, off alone on an excursion into what amounted to a wilderness where anything—the sudden flight of a raven, even the wind— could spook her and send her wildly careening. These Arabs were all taut as the strings of a viola, always on the alert for a horse-eating rock, a horse-eating shadow, a predatory branch. But Franklin knew this animal, knew her with his hands and his heart, and he smiled now, pleased with himself for the confidence he had in her and the trust she in turn had in him.

Comfortable in his hands and within the circle of his legs, she picked her way genteelly down the slight incline between two piñons into the narrow sandy ribbon of a dry streambed, and they made their way east toward home.

Thirty feet farther ahead, some improbably large yellow boulders lay alongside the streambed, and Franklin idly wondered how they had arrived here. The long-dead stream could never have been great enough, even in its heyday, to have transported them. Drawing nearer, he noticed that the low angle of the sun lit up what looked like petroglyphs on the boulders. The old Indians must have seen these rocks and felt the strangeness of their presence here—

Suddenly, the world quaked, sank violently beneath him, heaved up and hit him like a trip-hammer, and the Arab was six feet up the bank.

He tightened his grip and marveled that she was standing still now, deep breaths heaving in her chest, ears pointed like radar screens at the boulders. He remembered to breathe, patted her neck with a gloved hand, and urged her with his calves the rest of the way up the slope, where he brought her to a halt.

Distracted from whatever had terrified her in the streambed, she reached down to tear a mouthful of sage from a bush, and Franklin pulled her head up awkwardly.

"Uh-uh," he cautioned quietly. "None of that." He looked back at the boulders in the streambed, wondering with amusement what it had been about this inert presence that spooked his future queen, when he saw the feet.

Two pairs of feet, bare feet, toes upward, in the shadows behind the boulders.

Youthful feet, no signs of wear. A young couple? In the wrong place. Franklin knew he should look closer, go back into the streambed, and he knew the filly would balk at that. He knew now what had terrified the filly in the first place. Perhaps the insect sound, the buzz. But certainly the smell of rotting flesh assaulting his nostrils now, too. He didn't want to look any closer.

He turned the horse and guided her along the edge of the arroyo, headed upstream. A hundred feet or so and he crossed the streambed and circled widely through the piñon and juniper trees, returning to the arroyo upwind of the boulders, and on a high embankment. The filly reached down again, tearing at a sage bush, and he let her misbehave while he looked down the embankment at the boulders.

In the shadow, two people lay faceup, male and female side by side, naked and relaxed in death, livid in the purple shade, but some of the flesh grotesquely bruised. Where eyes had once looked out, there were now four black holes where flies swarmed frantically. Below the angry, bloated abdomen, more flies swarmed over gashes where the blood had turned black.

Franklin's gloved hand went to his mouth. He gagged and turned away, wheeling the horse. Sensing that they were now turned toward home, the filly fell into an eager trot, and Franklin let her break this rule as well. He

gagged again at the picture he feared was now lodged
forever in his mind's eye.

Two Tylenol caplets had done their work, and Sergeant
Anthony Ramirez, homicide detective with the Santa Fe
Police Department, was pleased to say goodbye to the
dull ache that had hounded his eyeballs all afternoon. He
wondered again if he should be in a job that gave him a
headache so often. Usually, he knew, it happened when
he was trapped in the office doing what they used to call
paperwork. Now, all the records were done on the bright
screen of a vintage computer that hummed and occasionally wheezed on his desk and created bright little letters
in bright little boxes, summing up the criminal activity of
the day or the week, all the details of human degradation
flickering into cyberspace.

So maybe it was the computer that gave him the
headache. Or maybe it was the building. He'd read somewhere about buildings making people sick, something to
do with the air circulation, vents. Foreign Legion disease,
or something. Well, the hell with it. The headache was
gone and he felt fine now, and was enjoying the sweet,
citrus, salty infusion of a margarita at his usual table in
the bar of Maria's Restaurant on West Cordova Street.

Except for one DWI, a guy from Oklahoma who had
plowed into the wall of the Norwest Bank on Cerrillos
three nights ago, there had been no homicides in Santa Fe
for eight days, and Ramirez had the next three days off.
Three whole days.

The big wooden door to the bar opened and his
mood brightened yet further. Connie Barnes, the broad-

shouldered Hopi woman, came in out of the late afternoon light, the big sculptor in tow. She smiled when she
saw Ramirez across the room and leaned up to say something to Bowdre, who grinned in turn. A few heads in the
bar turned as the couple made their way through the
tables, the Indian woman in a tailored gray suit and
Bowdre in his usual redneck attire and solidly opaque
dark glasses. One beefy hand lightly holding Connie's
elbow, the sculptor moved smoothly across the floor like
a great ship coming into a mooring, and no one who
didn't already know could have told he was blind.

His old friends made a strange, even outlandish couple,
Ramirez thought fondly, even in a town given to idiosyn-
cratic pairings.

"Tony," Mo Bowdre said, pulling out a chair. "I'm
glad you're here. You can help us celebrate. That is, if
you're not in one of your gloomy Iberian snits about
mortality and all that."

"Hi, Connie," Ramirez said. "So what are you celebrating? Oh, yeah. You had your show. How was it?"

"It's over. That's what I'm celebrating."

"I got to get over there, see it," Ramirez said. "I got
three days off. Maybe tomorrow I'll go."

A waitress, a young woman named Viola, made her
way to the table, and Bowdre ordered an ice tea for
Connie and a Negra Modelo for himself.

"The criminal class taking a break?" Mo said.

"There's always something," Ramirez said. "Hey, get
this. You know that big cop Gutierrez? He and another
uniform, guy named Sanchez, they were driving through
that trailer park out near Rufina, you know? This

afternoon. Heard this woman screaming from one of the trailers. 'Help, help,' she was screaming like a stunned pig—"

"It's stuck," Mo said.

"What's stuck?"

"The pig is stuck. It's stuck pigs that scream."

"Do want to hear this story? I'm trying to tell you a story."

"Boys," Connie said menacingly.

Mo put his hands up.

"Okay," Ramirez resumed. "So Gutierrez and Sanchez stop outside and bust in and there's this naked woman spread-eagled on the bed, tied to the bedposts, screaming, 'Help, get me out of here.' She's hysterical, man. And on the floor, there's this pile of something covered with a blue cloth, like a tarp."

A shrill sound interrupted Ramirez.

"*Merde,* it's my beeper. I got to go to the phone."

"Tony, you can't just—"

The policeman stood up. "Okay, get this. What the pile on the floor is is a guy out cold, wearing nothing but a Batman mask and a cape. See, he was evidently up on the bureau in this Batman cape. He dives for the bed where the woman is all tied up and waiting, and knocks himself out on the chandelier. So there he is, out cold on the floor, and the woman tied to the bed screaming for help. I'll be right back."

As he left, Viola arrived and put the two drinks down on the table.

"What's so funny?" she said.

"How do I love thee," Mo intoned. "Let me count the

ways." He picked up his mug of dark beer and drank mightily. "Ah, now that's as good as it gets."

"Is he all right?" Viola asked.

"So far," Connie said, and the waitress swayed off through the tables, shaking her head and passing Ramirez on his way back to the table. He was fishing his wallet out of his back pocket.

"I got to go," he said. "Here's for my drink."

"Keep it. What's up?"

"What else? Homicide. Two kids. Out near Canada Rincón."

"Where the hell is that?"

"Over west of Tano Road. Out where they're building all those estates." The policeman turned to go.

"Isn't that where Rhiannon Sharp lives?" Mo said to Connie. "We're going over there tomorrow."

Ramirez stopped and looked back at the table. "The call came in from her husband. He found 'em. Small world. Well, thanks for the drink. See ya."

Connie watched the policeman leave, and looked around the room. The eight tables were filled with people loosening up, enjoying themselves. Maria's margaritas were dissolving whatever cares had been brought in the room. The waitress bustled through with her tray. Connie scanned the room idly and her eyes fell on a young woman sitting on a stool at the end of the bar. Something about her was familiar. Her hair was brown and hung half-way down her back like a silky waterfall, covering whatever message had been silk-screened on her T-shirt. She wore jeans almost white from wear and a pair of dark brown cowboy boots, equally worn. She was studiously ignoring a man in a new straw cowboy hat and a rodeo shirt who was leaning toward her, cajoling her.

The young woman turned and said something—a word or two—and the man in the cowboy hat startled and turned away as his face reddened. He finished his beer, plucked his change up, and moved stiffly down to the other end of the bar, his squared shoulders saying "I didn't want that cookie anyway."

As for the young woman, she finished her beer and said something to the bartender, who gestured with his head toward the rest rooms. The woman reached down and hoisted the strap of a spruce-green canvas bag over her shoulder. Watching her stride into the back of the restaurant, it came to Connie where she had seen her—at the gallery. On their way out, she'd been standing in front of Mo's mountain sheep, staring at it intently, the green bag hanging from her shoulder.

"Homicide," Mo said. "That sure puts a damper on this here celebration of ours. I guess we'll be finding out about it tomorrow."

Connie sighed. Small world, Ramirez had said. Too small sometimes.

Several years earlier a consortium of real estate investors led by a prominent Santa Fe gallery owner had bought up a former ranch of slightly more than one thousand acres that lay north and west of the city proper. The ranch had belonged to an old New Mexico family which, like so many such families, had finally spawned a generation more interested in pursuing the high life that throbbed out there in places like San Francisco, L.A., the Big

Apple, than the drudgery of a rural life in New Mexico, no matter how astonishing the sunsets. It had been years since any livestock dwelled there, and the ranch buildings were easily razed, clearing the entire spread to be carved into twenty- to forty-acre lots, each with a spectacular view of the Jemez Mountains to the west.

A set of architectural and other covenants were carefully drawn up which, along with the sheer expense of the new properties, assured that nothing but very large, very tasteful, one-story Santa Fe–style haciendas would be built, none within sight of another, allowing each supernally wealthy resident to imagine himself sole proprietor of the entire American Southwest before humans set foot in it.

The onetime ranch was now lightly laced with a few well-hidden dirt roads, each bearing the name of a member of Coronado's expedition in the 1540s. The gallery owner had intended that none of the roads be named at all, the ultimate in classy estate culture, but the city insisted not only on street names, but numbers as well, for the benefit of the fire department and other parts of the city's emergency apparatus. But the consortium had won one battle with the bureaucrats: if the city insisted on calling this elegant tract a subdivision, at least it had no pretentious name. It was simply there.

John Franklin and his wife Rhiannon were among the first to buy in, purchasing forty acres at the northern extreme of the onetime ranch, and built a sixteen-room solar home of real adobe bricks all stuccoed an old-looking dark brown, as well as stables for twelve Arabian horses, along with outbuildings, riding rings, foaling stalls, a small office, and other equine necessities. Three twelve-hundred-foot wells, drilled at fabulous expense, supplied water ample to their needs, and two gasoline-powered generators provided a backup system in case the electricity (carried along underground cables) failed.

Not only could Franklin and his wife Rhiannon sit on one of two west-facing patios and fancy themselves the first white people to set eyes on the landscape. They could also imagine themselves to be totally self-sufficient.

Through a corner of the forty acres ran a shallow arroyo that twisted prettily among the piñon-juniper forest, debouching aridly into the northern end of Canada Rincón, where, at seven o'clock that night, the disfigured corpses of two young people still lay rotting—among other things, a staggering rebuke to the fantasy of perfect serenity and elegance implicit in the covenants.

Upon reaching home early that evening, Franklin had called 911 from the phone in the stables, hurriedly fixed himself a vodka martini on the rocks from the refrigerator that hummed quietly in the office, and only then tended to the young princess who had worked up a fine sweat trotting home. Armed with his second martini, Franklin went through the carefully xeriscaped garden toward his house, seeing a plume of dust making its way toward him about a half mile off. Too early, he calculated, for the police, and then he caught a glimpse of his wife's maroon Suburban before it dropped out of sight behind the trees.

Most of the residents in this brave new wilderness drove Range Rovers—and one sported a four-wheel-drive Mercedes-Benz—but Rhiannon tended to snort about such ostentation. Who in their right mind, she wanted to know, would take a $50,000 automobile off the road in the first place? She was a wonderfully direct, no-nonsense woman, Franklin thought, as supple and strong in character as a tall oak.

The martinis, slipping icily down his throat and gently pooling with silver heat in his stomach, had calmed his nerves to an extent, but he dreaded having to explain to Rhiannon what he'd come across on the far corner of their property. He went in the house, poured her a glass of red wine, and waited.

"Good God!" Rhiannon said, and spilled her wine on the tiled floor. "Conrad ..." She referred to her step-son, Franklin's seventeen-year-old son from his second marriage.

"No, no, of course not," Franklin said. "The boy out there had blond hair. The girl was dark. Conrad's still in Taos. His pickup's not here."

"That's a relief," Rhiannon said. The unspoken cloud descended on them again. Conrad was a moody and often sour boy, what Rhiannon picturesquely thought of as a black-hole personality, sucking up troubles and confusion from the universe around him. One always dreads that the worst could happen to such people, and that Conrad could even have gotten himself killed was not unimaginable.

"You called the police, of course," she said, a note of command returning to her deep voice.

"Nine one one. That must be them now." They heard two vehicles pull up outside the walled patio.

"We'll have to lead them out there," Rhiannon said.

"You don't . . . You shouldn't . . ."

"Of course I'll come, dear. It happened on our property, didn't it? Answer the door while I change into jeans. God, what an awful thing. And how horrible to have found it." She patted him sympathetically on the arm and strode out of the room.

two

In the high country of northern New Mexico, to which Santa Fe is a preeminent gateway, the sun gives up each day slowly, as if out of some kind of reluctance, especially with the onset of summer. As a consequence, sunsets are not just spectacular, but long-lived, and even after the sun drops below the horizon, the western sky remains lit for more than an hour. Along with poets and artists, the state motor vehicle department has taken note of this, decreeing that motorists need not turn on their headlights until exactly one hour past sunset.

State troopers and other police in the state often disagree with the motor vehicle department and the other state agencies that have responsibilities for one or another aspect of public safety, but still cling to some of the West's notions of rugged individualism. Less drawn to such fantasies and myths, the cops generally would prefer, for example, that drive-up liquor stores be banned, that speed limits on major highways be lowered, not raised, and—a relatively minor matter to be sure—that motorists be required to turn on their headlights at or before the moment the sun drops out of sight.

As if to set a good example, and almost as a matter of habit, police headlights are early to go on, and noting this in his rearview mirror, John Franklin switched on the lights in his wife's Suburban as he set out cross-country toward the dry arroyo and the two corpses, with two white police vehicles in tow. One was a four-wheel-drive Bronco, the other what appeared to be a remodeled RV—a mobile crime lab, they had explained. A homicide detective, Sergeant Anthony Ramirez, sat in the Suburban's passenger seat in plainclothes—a blue blazer and a crisply ironed pair of twill pants.

He had arrived a few minutes after the others in a standard squad car now parked outside the patio walls in the graveled driveway, and introduced himself with lugubrious courtesy. With a frown, he listened to Franklin's terse, efficient account, establishing that the two corpses were no one Franklin had seen before. Now he sat silently, arms folded across his chest and staring ahead through the windshield, his suggestion that Rhiannon Sharp need not accompany them having been summarily brushed aside. She was in the backseat, peering forward intently as the vehicle bumped and bucked over the rough land among the darkening piñons and junipers. Far off where the Jemez Mountains rose up, a shaft of saffron light lit up the foothills, causing them to glow as if from within.

"Sergeant," Rhiannon Sharp said in her croaky voice, "my husband says the bodies appeared to have been mutilated."

"Well," Franklin said, "I really didn't look that hard. Once I saw they were, uh, dead, I left."

"John, you said their eyes were gone and it looked like their crotches had been . . . torn. It sounds like some kind of horrid ritual to me."

Ramirez stirred and cleared his throat. "Some very unattractive things happen to bodies that are left in places like this. Animals, you know. Scavengers have their own preferences in such matters."

They lapsed into silence again and the Suburban began to climb a low rise. Ramirez craned his neck around to peer out the back. He smiled at Rhiannon Sharp.

"Just checking to see if that old RV's gonna make it," he said.

At the top of the rise the land fell away abruptly and Franklin stopped the car. "They're down there, Sergeant, about fifty yards down the arroyo behind some large boulders."

"Very good, Mr. Franklin. Thank you. You and your wife can go home now. We'll be several hours here, perhaps all night. I'll want to talk with you this evening. An hour or so, after everything is set in motion here. I'm sorry for the inconvenience." He opened the door and stepped out.

"Good heavens, officer," Rhiannon said. "We want to do anything we can to help."

The detective nodded, smiled distractedly, and began to walk off, his head bent. Then he stopped and turned around.

"You stopped here on your horse?" he asked.

"Yes, I think so."

"The horse's tracks stop here."

"Oh," Franklin said, and watched the detective begin

his descent. He waited until the other two vehicles had come to a stop alongside, and then backed up, swinging the Suburban's back end between two piñons. He heard a branch break off behind him.

"Christ," he muttered, and his wife sighed loudly. He looked over at her. "Damn it, who cares about a piñon tree?"

"That's not what I was thinking about, dear."

Ramirez elected to walk back to the Sharp-Franklin house, using a small but extremely bright flashlight to keep the car tracks in the sand in sight. He looked at his watch. It was nine-thirty. The forensics had established their arena around the two D.B.'s and would be delicately picking over the scene like ants for several more hours. Ramirez had stood staring at the two bodies—the guess was that they were late teens and had been there at least since the night before. The male was Anglo, with hair light brown to blond. The female's hair was black, and her skin, to the degree one could read it under the horrid discoloration of both death and the activity of the sun, was brown. The guess was she was an Indian.

Something about them had made him profoundly sad. Normally he could banish such emotions. Even before his arrival, some switch in his mind, like a smoothly functioning light switch on the wall, altered the personal human horror of a murder scene into a collection of impersonal items strewn in what would surely turn out to be some kind of pattern. But these two ... from two races, of course. Kids trying to bridge the awful gap? Or maybe it was the precise way someone had laid them out, absolutely parallel. For some reason they struck Ramirez as more innocent, more undeserving of the finality of death, than the usual homicides he had to deal with. He found that a strange thought: Who deserved death unbidden? He groped in this inappropriate darkness for the switch.

They were bloated, baked in the sun for what appeared to be a full day, and by the time Ramirez left, which was before the forensic people turned them over, a probable cause of death had yet to be established. There had been little blood from the wounds inflicted on them, meaning that something other than the visible wounds caused their deaths.

The Sharp woman had jumped to the conclusion that they had been ritually mutilated, and surely she was imagining a case of Satanism. The tabloids loved to flash Satanism in everybody's face, even little kids in the supermarket line, and there had been some local talk recently of cattle mutilations, plenty to stoke up the popular imagination. Some ranchers up in Rio Arriba County had found a few cows out in the National Forest, various organs carefully excised. There was the inevitable dark talk of Satanist cults, and also some dark talk about cow-hating environmentalists becoming vigilantes. In some minds up there, to associate environmentalists with pagans and the Antichrist was no great leap of the imagination.

Even to a homicide detective with more than a decade's labors behind him, the world seemed to be going mad.

Madder.

He remembered a seminar the previous chief had forced him to go to a few years back where a bunch of East Coast cops took over one of the meeting rooms in the Holiday Inn in Albuquerque. The cops specialized in cult crimes and explained that there was a huge Satanic conspiracy in the country, responsible for the death of fifty thousand vagrants, young people, and babies specifically bred for sacrifice. As part of their presentation, the cops—they called themselves "cult consultants"—flashed some symbols on the screen, including the flower children's peace sign from the Sixties. They termed it the Cross of Nero, the Satanists' way of mocking the Christian cross.

One of them held up a book by one of those weird self-appointed prophet types that spring up from time to time, a guy named Crowley. The cop said it was one of the "bibles" of the Satanists, and you could only get it from one occult bookstore in Pennsylvania. He said mysteriously that he couldn't reveal how he got his copy.

Ramirez had wondered how one bookstore in Pennsylvania could have gotten this bible into the hands of enough people to ritually murder fifty thousand people around the country and start a nationwide baby-breeding industry. A few days later he came across the same book in a Santa Fe bookstore with a metaphysics and occult section. It was called *The Book of the Law*, published by a New Age publisher, and it was readily available, the bookstore clerk told him. Sensing a phony, Ramirez had looked into all this a bit more, finding among other things that the hippies' peace sign, the ominous Cross of Nero, had been invented in the 1950s, combining the semaphore signals for N and D, which stood for Nuclear Disarmament. He went on probing and finally took great pleasure in reporting to the chief that the cult cops were themselves fundamentalist evangelicals, the kind that see the horns of Lucifer in every blade of grass.

Not that there couldn't be real loonies out there holding nefarious rites, Ramirez admitted. But those cult cops were loonies, too. He heard later that they were on *Geraldo*, waving their mysteriously obtained copy of *The Book of the Law* around and all that.

Geraldo was not one of Ramirez's favorite Hispanic celebrities and role models.

As best Ramirez could tell at this point, the D.B.'s in the arroyo had been assailed by scavengers. Ravens and vultures usually go for the eyes first, coyotes and dogs go after tender flesh first. The forensics were looking for animal tracks, among other things, but the place was rocky with a thin layer of sand over the rocks, and the wind had been blowing in the afternoon. Somebody had done those kids, though, maybe there in the arroyo, maybe somewhere else. They'd know soon enough.

Nearing the house now, Ramirez saw that the lights were on in what had to be most of the rooms. Off to the northern end of the house he could barely make out some white pipe fences and a barn or stables or whatever. A horse whinnied off in the dark. He made his way around the south end of the long, rambling building thinking that it looked like a small pueblo, thinking also that a lot of people, when touched by death, tend to turn on all the lights.

On the gravel driveway, with its spacious area for

parking and turning around, he saw the Suburban, his own unit, and behind them a large shiny black pickup that hadn't been there when he arrived. From the round snout he guessed that it was a Dodge Ram, a big one. It was the kind with a little backseat in the cab, probably cost thirty-five thou new, and it looked new. Ramirez didn't keep up much with automobile prices, and when it came to matters mechanical, he happily turned them over to the mechanics.

Approaching closer, he smiled, seeing that he'd guessed right. It was a Dodge Ram 1500. It bore a lone bumper sticker: SHIT HAPPENS. Inwardly he winced. He hated that bumper sticker under any circumstances, and here was someone with a new $35,000 pickup, with a rack of highly polished chromium searchlights on the cab roof and probably two thousand dollars worth of sound equipment inside, and he was driving around saying SHIT HAPPENS.

To who, dickhead?

Ramirez put his hand on the back of his neck and twisted his head from side to side. Then he took ten deep breaths and looked up at the stars. Shit does happen, he thought, and it's getting to me.

The walled patio was lit with several artfully placed floodlights, and, among the cacti and other desert plants with which the area was landscaped, Ramirez noted a bronze bear sleeping peacefully, a Bowdre. The Sharp woman evidently saw him coming through a window, because she opened the ornately carved wooden door before he raised a hand to knock.

"Come in, Sergeant." She ushered him through a

dimly lit hall into a long room with a high ceiling of wooden vigas, white walls plastered by hand, and curved archways leading to other rooms. The floors were an ocherish orange-colored tile, and the room was filled, almost cluttered, with comfortable-looking puffy sofas and chairs all in different flowery patterns—a kaleidoscope of bright color. Highly polished tables here and there, large vases with flowers, three exceptionally large Navajo rugs, mostly lavenders and peaches and oranges, on the floor. Most places, people hung these rugs on the wall. They cost a small fortune.

On the wall opposite, a gold frame held a large oil painting, maybe four feet by six, of a boiling, sun-shot yellow sky, or was it an ocean, or both? In the left-hand corner of the painting he saw what was evidently part of an old sailing vessel—did they call it a bowsprit?—looking storm-tossed. He glanced around the room again. None of the earth tones so favored in Santa Fe were to be found here. None of the familiar icons these people were so fond of, like old Spanish saddles sitting in the corner. Just lots of color, flowers, light. Ramirez had never been in so welcoming a room. He glanced down and saw to his dismay that he had accumulated a film of dust on his shoes.

From one of the puffy-looking easy chairs at the far end of the room, John Franklin rose up, still in riding boots and those skintight riding pants, holding a glass in his hand, a martini glass. His face looked a bit flushed, and Ramirez checked his watch, wondering how many martinis this guy had consumed in the two hours since the three of them had driven off in the Suburban. He was about six feet, and looked to be in good physical shape—an athlete. Not an ounce of fat on either of these people, Ramirez thought.

Rhiannon Sharp was almost as tall as her husband, and couldn't weigh more than one twenty, if that. Either she was anorexic, which you didn't see too much of in women in their fifties and sixties, or she had one of those blast-furnace metabolisms that burns everything.

She was standing next to him, observing him observe the room. She wore a flowing green shirt, probably silk, and a lot of excellent turquoise and silver around her neck—what they called liquid silver and turquoise chunks and tiny heishi beads, probably from Santo Domingo. Faded jeans and blue velvet slippers that looked like they came out of Arabian Nights.

"This is real beautiful," Ramirez said. "That painting over there, it's not one of our locals, huh?"

"It's a Turner," Rhiannon Sharp said. "My grandfather bought it years ago in London."

"Turner," Ramirez said. "Right."

"Something?" Franklin said, gesturing minimally with his martini glass. "Coffee?"

"No, thanks," Ramirez said. "Our people are going to be out there for some time, I'm afraid. Probably most of the night. I hope they don't disturb you later when they go. It's going to take a lot of time, collecting things, all that, before they can remove the bodies."

"How awful," the Sharp woman said in her deep, gravelly voice. "Do we know . . . ?"

"Nothing really yet, Miz Sharp. They been there maybe since last night. No identification. No probable cause of death yet. As I say, there's a lot of poking around before you can move them. Well, anyway, I was wondering who else is here. The pickup out there."

Franklin had resumed his place in the puffy chair and set his glass down on the table beside it. "That's my son's pickup. Conrad. He was in Taos."

Ramirez nodded. "Taos," he said.

"Musician friends," Franklin said.

"He's a musician?"

"That's what they call it," Franklin said, with the trace of a smile. It struck Ramirez that he had not seen any expression on the man's face until that moment. The trace of smile vanished and Franklin's square face returned to its normal expressionless state.

"Perhaps I should call him?" Rhiannon Sharp asked.

Again Ramirez nodded. "There are some routine questions I have to ask. Procedural stuff, really. Might as well have you all here."

"I'll go, John," the woman said, and walked in long, graceful strides through one of the arches and out of sight. In a few minutes she returned, with Conrad a few paces behind her.

Conrad, Ramirez noted, had the sullen, almost angry look so many young people adopted. His temples were shaved almost clean of dark brown hair, but a patch on the top of his head had been carefully tended until it was long enough to be tied in a small bunch in back. He wore the baggy black pants and overlarge black T-shirt so many of his age also adopted—the universal uniform of defiant individualism. The shirt's sleeves had been cut off and it sported a purple death's head along with a message in illegible gold script. Maybe IN YOUR FACE in Russian, Ramirez thought.

Conrad Franklin was a slender kid, perhaps seeming all the more so because of his oversized clothes and his naked temples, and he had not inherited the athletic look of his father, or his father's prominent, even aggressive chin line. Conrad's features were soft, his chin a bit underslung. Generally speaking, Ramirez thought, he was stuck with at least a few more years of being a geek.

The boy looked directly into Ramirez's eyes as he walked in and sat down. In this room full of color and pattern, Conrad, in his dull, severe black costume, looked as appropriate as a turd on the breakfast table. And that, Ramirez reflected, was obviously, even tiresomely, his intention.

"Conrad, this is Sergeant Ramirez. He's in charge of the investigation."

"Hi, Conrad," Ramirez said affably. "Just back from Taos, huh?"

"Yeah."

"Doing some music?"

Conrad stared at him. He had the same dark brown eyes as his father. "You're asking me? Or telling me what my stepmother told you?"

Ramirez's eyebrows danced upward. "Conrad," he said, "I'm just trying to be polite. You know?"

"Christ, Conrad," his father said.

"It's okay," Ramirez interrupted. "We'll get along. I just have some routine questions here. I know guys like this—what are you, Conrad, seventeen?—guys like this don't feel comfortable around cops. Teachers. All that. I didn't when I was his age."

Conrad glanced up at the ceiling briefly, and Ramirez nodded, grinning.

"See?" he said. "Conrad, I know this is an imposition, but it's probably not as big an imposition as what happened to those people out there, so why don't you just pretend you're almost an adult here for a few minutes, and then I'll be out of your hair. Okay?"

Conrad looked down at the floor and his shoulders softened.

"So when did you leave for Taos, Conrad?"

"Yesterday. In the afternoon. Around four o'clock."

"And these friends up there can tell me that you were with them the whole time?"

"Yeah."

"Good. I'll get their names from you later. It's just routine, Conrad. I don't think you're a number one suspect here."

"What happened to them?"

"We don't know yet. Just that they're dead."

"My stepmother says they were, uh, messed with."

"We don't know that yet, either. Or what killed them."

The kid continued to look down at the floor. Ramirez took a long narrow notebook and a Papermate pen from his inside jacket pocket. Poised to write, he said: "Who were you with in Taos?"

Conrad gave him a name and a telephone number, and Ramirez wrote them down.

"Thanks. Okay, you can go if you want, Conrad."

The boy stood up and began to move toward the archway.

"You play an instrument?" Ramirez asked.

"Bass guitar," Conrad said, standing still in the arch.

"Conrad?"

"Yeah?"

"Shit happens, pal." Conrad looked back over his shoulder and the corners of his mouth twitched into a fleeting smile. Then he disappeared through the arch.

"I always wanted to be a musician," Ramirez said. "Tone deaf. Not a prayer. Well, I'm sorry about all this, but I'll have to ask where you were last night, too, and this morning. Routine. We'll have to ask all the neighbors out here if they saw anything, heard anything, all that." He sighed.

"Last night we attended an opening at the Gerald Peters Gallery," Rhiannon Sharp began. "And from there, at about six-thirty, we went to dinner with the Halsteads, Philip and Margery Halstead, at Julian's, that marvelous Italian place. We came home about ten, I'd say, and went to bed. This morning, after breakfast at about seven, I went into Santa Fe for a hairdresser's appointment and then went to an all-day meeting of the board of IPOLA. This afternoon I went to the opening at the Frazier Gallery—"

"The Bowdre show? I see you got one of his bears out there."

"Yes," the woman said, her eyebrows raised a notch. "And another in the dining room. And then I came home."

"And you, sir?" Ramirez said, thinking that if the Sharp

woman was fifteen, twenty years younger, and twenty-five pounds heavier, she'd be a knockout. He knew he wasn't supposed to think things like that. . . .

Franklin looked peeved in his puffy easy chair. "Played golf all morning and into the afternoon. Came home around three. Went riding. D'you want the names of my golfing partners?"

"I can't imagine that will be necessary, sir."

The man nodded. Ramirez put away his notebook and pen and turned to face Rhiannon Sharp. He had to look up slightly. "I'll leave you folks now. Thank you. I'll probably be talking to you again." He turned to go.

"Let me walk you out," she said, falling in beside him. They passed through a wide arch into the entrance hall. "Our son," Rhiannon said. "It's such a troubled age."

"You don't need to apologize for him, ma'am. It's a terrible time to be growing up."

She put a bony hand on his arm and stopped him at the heavy wooden front door. She smiled, almost mischievously.

"I have to say, Sergeant, I admired the way you talked to him. A very nice application of pressure."

Ramirez grinned widely. "Miz Sharp, I have to tell you. For us cops, leaning on these kids a little is irresistible." He pulled open the door and stepped out into the night.

"Good night, Sergeant," she said, and he heard her chuckle as the door closed behind him. It was like the sound of water falling over a gravel river bottom. The moon, nearly full, sat halfway up the sky above some dark clouds hanging over the Sangre de Cristo Mountains.

Old devil moon. There was some song about that. An
old song.

*Look at this place, it's like a foreign country, one of those
South American places, with these old beams sticking out
through the walls, old porches stretched along the street,
expect some fat old guy to waddle out in a sombrero. All
these brown buildings, houses with walls around them,
people living behind walls. What do they do behind those
walls? Sit in big chairs counting their money. I've got
money. Enough. Not enough for these big hotels, look
like something out of an old movie. Where am I? Oh,
back at that big square. That guy's asleep on the bench.
Homeless. Like me. It's right over there where the gallery
is, down that street, yes. That's where he was, standing
on the sidewalk with those women. I didn't think he was
going to be that big. All those rich people, whew. Look
at all this stuff in the windows, these dresses here must
cost hundreds. Rich people's clothes. And here, look at
all this stuff, pots, and those rugs! Intricate designs on
these rugs, like a headache. Rich people's stuff. I'll be
rich. Don't know if I'll want to get this kind of stuff when
I get rich.*

How am I going to do this?

*Here. Turn here. Look how narrow this sidewalk is,
hardly room for one person to walk straight. Turn here.
Uh-oh, what's that over there in the shadows? A man
over there in the shadows. Leaning against that wall in
there. Did he move? Keep walking. Head up, shoulders
back, not the kind of person to take any crap from*

anyone. Look at that. The guy's pissing on the sidewalk. That's disgusting. These homeless people are disgusting.

I don't want anyone near me. Touching me. But I got to find a place to stay. Not around here. Not where all the rich people go. God, another one of these monster hotels, looks like one of those Indian villages you see in books. Turn here, keep walking. Oh man, look at this. No, keep the head up, eyes front. Car's got tiny little wire wheels, sitting on the road like that, an inch off the road. Oh, man, I hate this. Spanish guys.

"Hey, you. Hey, baby, you with the big tits, you wanna fock?"

"Sure, but how you gonna do it with no balls, little man?"

There, Chicano bastard. Don't mess with me.

Go ahead, laugh, you jackasses. I hope you get herpes.

God I miss . . . I miss . . . I got to do this, got to. I hate this place. I need a shower. I want to go to sleep. Why did it happen? Back home. Home, sure. All that coughing. Coughing all the time, smelly in that old bathrobe, coughing, disgusting, feet swollen like that, red. No more. No more of that anyway.

I hate this place. Guy pissing on the street in front that fancy store, all those rich people's clothes in the window, Chicano shitheads in cars from hell, leering. All these shadows. Don't touch me, you. Don't touch me. Is that me yelling? My head is yelling. It's my head yelling at me. Shush.

I hate this place. Head up. Walk. Put the bag on the other shoulder. Walk. There's the weapon in my bag. I can blow 'em off. Jackasses. I'm okay, they're gone.

Oh, all that yelling, coughing. The old bitch in her smelly bathrobe. Yelling at me. Coughing. Turn on the lights, for God's sake! Turn on the lights in here, won't you? Open a window, for God's sake. This place stinks. You stink, old woman. Old, old, old woman, hear that? You stink! You! You did this! Screaming those words . . . those words.

Shush. Keep walking. Be quiet. Please be quiet. You've got to leave me alone. . . .

I don't know how this is going to work. Oh man, not another one of these . . . Jeez, a cop.

"Excuse me, miss. This isn't a real good place to be walking around alone."

"I'm okay."

"You want some help, a ride somewhere?"

Oh sure, man. Get in that car with you.

"Where are you headed, miss?"

Fat old guy. Looks harmless. If he touches me, I'm out the door.

"To my motel."

"Where's that, miss? Which one?"

"Well, I'm looking for one."

"There's a Motel 6 down on Cerrillos. Get in, I'll take you there. Where you from?"

"Colorado."

"Long way from home."

"Yeah."

This is my home now.

The imperious jangle of the telephone pierced Mo Bowdre's dream and he woke up with a sense of dread.

Phone calls in the night. It's either bad news or some imbecile with the wrong number:

"Is Millie dere?"

"No, goddamn it. You got the wrong number, and what the hell are you doing calling Millie in the middle of the night anyway, you moron?" *Slam.*

And then try getting back to sleep.

The phone jangled again and he felt Connie roll over toward it, heard her pick it up.

"Yes?" she said, her normally alto voice a few notes deeper. "Oh, yeah, hi." He felt her body tense and put a big hand in the silky valley between her rib cage and her hip. She listened, and replied in Hopi, which he didn't understand. She talked rapidly, then listened, talked again.

Trouble at home, Mo thought. There's always trouble at home on the Hopi Reservation. Some of it self-inflicted. Some of it imaginary—at least to his way of thinking. And of course, at Hopi, his way of thinking could be totally irrelevant. And a lot of the troubles that are always arising out at Hopi are just the standard lousy turn of the wheel of fortune. He wondered which type of trouble it was now. Connie continued to converse for a few more minutes, then hung up. She rolled onto her back and sighed.

"What's up?"

"Eeeeee," she said, a Hopi sound signifying trouble, a sound much uttered in Hopi history. "It's my father. He had a heart attack."

Mo's still groggy mind spun like an engine revved up while the car is in neutral. Her father? Her father was a white guy named Barnes who'd disappeared when she was two years old, never seen again. Had he suddenly showed up and keeled over?

"Marvin," she said, referring to an old Hopi man, Marvin Tongvaya. It was one of those clan things, Marvin being some kind of clan uncle, which meant he was, like all the other members of that clan, Connie's father. Everywhere Connie went, she ran into fathers, old ones, little kids, all fathers. It had been explained to him several times—how all this clan stuff worked—but he couldn't keep it straight in his mind, any more than he could comprehend what anyone meant by the term *second cousin once removed*.

Mo rumbled a sympathetic noise. "Oh, man," he said. "That's terrible." He heard the antique clock in the hall begin to chime wheezily, and with part of his mind counted the hours: eleven.

Marvin was a short little guy, about seventy years old, with a face lined like a 3-D map of the canyonlands, and a perpetual twinkle in his eyes. He always wore a trucker's hat—maroon—that said BIG SHOT, and he rarely wore the teeth the Indian Health Service had supplied him with a few years back, when the last of his own gave up this life.

Marvin had taken his paternal connection seriously, Mo knew, apparently helping to raise the little Connie on a weekly if not daily basis. Until a few years ago when Marvin had taken on the responsibility of katsina father in his village, there had always been a katsina dancer just Marvin's size who had never failed to peer around at the crowd through its slitty eyes and then single out Connie first, handing her a katsina doll.

A month or so after Connie moved in with Mo in his house on Canyon Road, old Marvin had turned up on their doorstep unannounced and stayed for a week. He never said what he was doing there, just hung around, but Mo knew that he had come all this way—his first trip this far from home—in order to get a bead on the big white man, the big *pahana* now in his "daughter's" life.

"How bad is it?"

"He's in the hospital at Keams. They're going to keep him there. That's all my mom knows."

"Maybe it's not so bad, if they're not going to fly him down to Phoenix. He's a tough old bird," Mo said.

"It's his second one, remember?"

"Last year, wasn't it?"

Connie rolled over and put an arm across Mo's chest. "Yes, last year, this same time. He missed Home Dance. I guess he'll be missing this one, too."

"Maybe not."

"I'll call tomorrow."

Mo knew she wouldn't sleep again that night. He also knew that when he woke up, he would find Connie out in the yard, sitting on a cement bench among some penstemon beds, waiting for the sun to rise. The sun was also her father, a deity the Hopis call Dawa. Most mornings, Connie sat quietly on that bench, attending to this father.

But now they reached for each other and slowly, in the manner of a pavane, made love and comfort.

Conrad Franklin pressed the button on the side of his wristwatch and its face lit up radium-green: eleven-twenty-something. He had listened for the last flush of the toilet in his parents' bedroom suite down the hallway and knew that within minutes they would both be snoring away, dead to the world. They were both good sleepers in any event, and after spending most of the evening guzzling martinis, his father would sleep through an earthquake, snorting and gasping all the while. What did they call that? Apnea.

The jerk.

Outside, the world was silver, lit by the nearly full moon. He slid the Thermopane glass door open and stepped out onto the little patio outside his room. One of the horses whickered distantly off to his right, a reassuring sound. He loved the horses.

Conrad had exchanged his black clothes for a pair of worn blue jeans and a gray sweatshirt, the better to blend in with the moonlit landscape, and he stepped lightly and silently over the low adobe wall, imagining himself to be nearly invisible. About fifteen minutes later he saw the glow of lights from the arroyo where the cops were working the scene of the murders. He had circled around, approaching the scene not from the rise north of the arroyo where the vehicles were, but from the south, where the piñon trees were thicker.

They won't be looking for anyone out here anyway, he thought. All I have to do is be quiet. Even so, he could feel the adrenaline coursing, and his arms felt weak.

In a low crouch, he scooted from one piñon to another until he had a view of the floodlit scene and the cops, about thirty yards away. From his spot, lying under the branches of a particularly broad piñon, he couldn't see the bodies. They were behind the boulders. Six cops were poking around, and that sergeant, Ramirez, was standing off to one side, watching. One of the cops made his way down the arroyo out of the light, the beam of a flashlight lighting his way, and in a few minutes he came back, shrugging his shoulders at the sergeant.

It was weird, thinking about the two bodies lying near those boulders. This was a place he often came, to sit on the boulders in the silence and the utter stillness and the sun, to daydream. More often than not, his daydreams took the form of sexual fantasies, the movie screen of his mind filled with extreme close-ups of Sharon Stone's anatomy, to which he might adumbrate the face and voice of whatever girl had caught his fancy most recently. And, of course, he would bring himself to a happy climax as Sharon's magic groin ground wildly back and forth atop him. . . .

The air was cool now, maybe in the fifties, but Conrad was sweating, wondering if the cops would find any traces of . . . him . . . out there. He lay in the sand, watching the cops perform their extreme slow motion rituals in the illumination cast by the lights they had set up, all wearing white gloves that the floods turned a ghastly green. Conrad couldn't figure out exactly what they were finding. They were finding things, though, that was for sure. They kept putting stuff in little plastic bags.

One of them had a camera, and the others would summon him here and there to take flash pictures. There was a flash in the camera, and the guy had another he held in his other hand, and it would look like a little lightning storm in the arroyo.

They went about their business quietly, as if it was

choreographed, saying little. Occasionally he heard a low murmur, and a murmured answer. And occasionally he heard a snatch of laughter.

After an interminable amount of time—he didn't dare light up his watch—he heard a vehicle rumbling toward the arroyo from the north, and presently some men with stretchers appeared in the ring of greenish light. Conrad watched as the men he presumed had come in an ambulance bent down behind the boulders, again presumably putting the bodies in bags. Yes, that's right. He saw them hoist the stretchers up, each bearing a shiny black shape like a giant slug, and carry them effortlessly up the slope and out of the light. The cops watched them disappear into the night, and then extended the break from their search. A couple of them lit cigarettes.

After a while, maybe five minutes, the sergeant squatted down on his heels, pointed down the arroyo and said something at length. The two cops with the cigarettes leaned over, rubbed the butts on the rocks, and put them in their shirt pockets. Carrying those big flashlights, the kind with long shanks that look like they have a dozen batteries, the two cops started out, one walking north and the other south . . . toward him!

Adrenaline. Sweat. Panic. Did they hear me, see me? He slithered backward from under the tree, rose into a crouch and hustled his way south, holding his breath until his chest ached, darting among the piñons, repeating to himself: oh shit oh shit oh shit oh shit.

Wait, he cautioned himself, coming to a stop beside a shadowy cedar tree. They aren't looking for me. And if they see me, so what? What law am I breaking, walking around my own place at night?

Pressing his fingers against the stitch that had developed in his side, Conrad walked slowly home, justifying his presence near the crime scene in the middle of the night with a host of unassailably legitimate reasons—none of which, alone or cumulatively, did away with his overriding sense of guilt.

Reaching the low-walled patio outside his room, he stepped over it silently and like a shade slipped through the sliding glass door into his room, his sanctum.

three

"Whoa now, friends, that is an odor for the gods," Mo Bowdre said, leaning his thick forearms on the cool pipe fence. It was ten-thirty, Sunday morning, and the sun had not yet chased the mountain cool from the air.

"Pristine air is fine, just fine, the pure crystalline smell of wilderness and all that Sierra Club poetry, but in my book you just can't do better than a whiff of horseshit. I mean, if plain air is chicken, then horseshit is tarragon. Spice. Rich, tangy, full of promise."

"Promise?" Rhiannon Sharp croaked. "What are you talking about?"

"The ee-ternal cycle of nature—earth giving rise to grass, horses making manure out of it, manure enriching and perfuming the earth, giving rise to more grass, or tomatoes, on and on, over and over, fecund world without end . . . You know, herbivore shit is just plainly fine stuff. Carnivore shit, on the other hand, is ugly. I notice you don't keep any dogs out here. I myself am not especially partial to dogs. Allergies. Also, being blind, I can't tell if I'm going to step in one of their blessings unless I'm downwind. Hah. Hah."

"Mo," Connie said, the sound of disapproval unmistakable in her voice. She had heard all this before, and, he knew, she was impatient and nervous, what with old Marvin's heart being hammered.

"Forgive me, Rhiannon, Connie. It's just that this brings back fond memories of when I was a boy, doing the chores around my daddy's stable. He kept a couple of quarter horses he liked to race locally. The memories are fond now, anyway. So I guess what you want to talk to me about has something to do with these horses, right?"

"A commission," Rhiannon said. "John's filly, Flame Gypsy. She's the sweetest thing on legs, really. And beautiful. Typy as they come."

"Typy?"

"Arabian type. Big lustrous eyes, a fine narrow muzzle, long arched neck. They carry their tail high, like a banner. There's a lot of technical stuff. To me, they look like those old paintings of unicorns without the horn. And Gypsy, well, she's just gorgeous. When she prances around, her tail straight up, mane waving, it's a ballet. She hardly touches the ground."

"And so you want . . ."

"For John's birthday present."

"When's that?"

"Oh, not until November. That should be plenty of time, shouldn't it? He knows about it, of course. We both adore that mustang you did."

"Well, see, that was a generalized mustang. This sounds like a portrait. That's different."

Rhiannon was silent.

"I suppose I could do a likeness," Mo resumed. "It

means I'd have to spend a whole lot of time in there with her, you know, get to see her with my hands. Some horses get a bit impatient about that sort of thing."

"Not Gypsy. She's as friendly as a puppy. You'll see. John's just brought her out. He's going to let her go without her lead. You watch." Rhiannon caught herself. "Ooops."

"Hah. Hah. It's okay. Just a manner of speaking."

Mo listened to the rhythmic tattoo of hooves in dry dirt. The place smelled also of dust.

"She's beautiful," Connie said.

"Here she comes," Rhiannon croaked. "Hi, baby." The horse snorted, practically in Mo's ear, and he felt the heat from her body. Then he felt a soft, lippy plucking at his hand. Slowly, he put the back of his hand against one of her warm nostrils and felt her sniff, a powerful intake. Slowly again, he moved his hand up a few inches and touched her nose with the flat of his palm, and felt her lean her head slightly into his touch.

"We're gonna be good friends, honey," Mo said.

Rhiannon chuckled. "She prefers men."

"You can hardly blame her for that, now can you?" Mo scratched her over her eye. "I am real sorry to tell you this, Connie, but I am in love here. Do you Hopi ladies ever put up with a little good-natured polygamy? I heard somewhere that two wives can get along with each other just fine so long as they each have their own kitchen."

He heard Connie giggle. "Why don't you let that horse produce the manure?"

"As the senior of two, you'd get a lot of privileges."

* * *

A half hour later the three of them adjourned to the house, and Mo noticed that it was cooler inside by some ten degrees. Good planning, he thought.

He followed, half a step behind Connie, down a long corridor and into a room that smelled faintly of the perfume that Rhiannon had worn the night of the exhibition. It was a cool smell, like lilacs. At Connie's light touch on his arm, he stopped and slowly sat down in what was a high-backed chair, a wing chair. He heard a wooden chair scrape across the brick floor, and concluded that Rhiannon had sat down behind a desk before him. Connie sat down to his left into another easy chair.

On the way back to the house, Rhiannon mentioned a large dollar figure that Mo found utterly satisfactory. More than satisfactory. He had made no pretense of protesting its grandiosity. False modesty was not among his sins, and bargaining not in his nature. Mo had said, without hesitation, "Done."

"I need to talk to you about something personal," Rhiannon began now, and Mo began to see why she was overpaying him for the horse sculpture. "I haven't known exactly who to turn to about this—oh, I've had the usual discussions one does, but all these so-called professionals seem so mealy-mouthed. And they don't seem to have any answers, really. You'll see what I mean—I'm sorry to start off so vaguely." She cleared her throat.

"It's about our son Conrad. You've met him."

"A while back. I remember his voice was changing. Every now and then he'd squeak. One of life's humiliations."

"Has it been that long? He's seventeen now, almost eighteen. In August. And he's troubled. I mean, more than usual. They're all so mixed up these days, and I don't blame them, with all the absolute crap that's dinned into them from every direction. I don't want to sound like an old fogey, but my God, it's inescapable, this awful culture. Drugs, violence, the anger! And the bad taste. I was part of all that in the Sixties, but this is different. Then at least some of it came from hope. People were angry, yes, but at injustice, stupidity. It was all directed at making changes. Even those silly flower children with their dirty hair and feet were saying that things needed to change. Now, what we've got is all so hopeless, so despairing, so . . . banal.

"And Conrad has . . . well, I know he's tried some drugs, I don't think very heavily. And he mopes around like a pile of dirty laundry and all that. But recently there's been a change. It's like something behind his eyes has gone dead. It scares me." Her voice had gone oddly soft.

Mo pursed his lips and let a small stream of breath escape.

"I'm his stepmother, of course, but I feel just as deeply, just as urgently about him, as if he were my own son. I've raised him since he was eight. His father—well, they don't get along at all anymore. Nothing new there, I gather. Fathers and sons. They all seem to go around like dogs or wolves, lifting their legs and marking territory. Do they ever get over it? They've always argued, but there used to be some fire there. But now John has about thrown in the towel. Just grudges him what he wants—

like that pickup. Twenty-five thousand dollars. Spoils him and disapproves of him at the same time. That's confusing enough, I suppose. And of course poor Conrad doesn't have his father's looks . . . I don't think poor Conrad has much success socially. With girls."

Mo stirred in his chair. "As for his good side . . ."

Rhiannon laughed. "Oh, yes. He's terribly smart, terribly talented—artistically. God knows I can't tell good punk rock from bad, but he's artistic in other ways. He sees beautifully. I remember when he was younger . . . well, no need to go gushing on about that. Take my word for it, there's a highly sensitive, highly intelligent young man in there. But suddenly he's gone sour, like I said."

Mo sat quietly, his big hands draped over the arms of the wing chair.

She cleared her throat again. "So I've been thinking, and it's terribly presumptuous, I know—"

"You want me to coax the bad apples out of his tree."

"I thought you might need some help with the horse to do this sculpture, and Conrad *does* love the horses, and I thought . . ."

"Rhiannon, you sound positively flustered," Mo said cheerfully. "Now when was the last time you were flustered?"

"Mo," she said. It was like a plea.

"That's a real good idea," Connie said. "He'll need some help with that horse, and he's going to be needing some help at home, too. I've got to go home for a while, back to my village. One of my relatives is sick. Maybe Conrad could come and stay at our house while I'm gone, drive Mo around, that sort of thing."

Rhiannon exhaled a long breath. "I'll talk to him. I'm sure—"

"Do you think Conrad would sit still for the minimum wage for acting as my seein' eye dawg?" Mo said. "It sounds to me like it would be better if I set out to hire him, pay him for services rendered. Like it was my idea. No offense intended, Rhiannon, but from what I'm hearing, he probably wouldn't take too kindly to a suggestion from his parents."

Mo had known, ever since talking to Rhiannon at the opening, that he was going to be trapped, but into what, he couldn't imagine at the time. So he was to play therapist for a teenage loser? Role model for a would-be punkrocker with no social skills?

Mo was pretty well convinced that kids were all infected at age twelve by some alien virus, a slow virus that lasted about eight to ten years. He knew, of course, that people attributed the inexplicably stupid behavior of teenagers to the fact that they were drowning in hormones, but that rationalization seemed weak to him. He had his own teenagerhood as an example, after all, and there was more to it than a sudden flux of testosterone. Such a total regression of brain power couldn't be explained by testicles alone. Or ovaries. It had to be a virus that settled somewhere inside the skull that turned teenagers into the equivalent of prehuman hominids, like the ones that roamed the grasslands a million years ago, still occasionally walking on their knuckles, still banging rocks together and making whooping noises like apes.

So I'm going to be mentor for one of them? he thought. Well, hell, it could be worse.

* * *

Mo sat in the passenger seat of his old pickup, an ancient Ford 250 that had just the week before qualified for plates designating it as "classic." The man who owned it before him had done little to it except religiously change the oil every three thousand miles, and Mo had seen to it that this practice continued. So it sufficed, and Mo wasn't about to give up on it.

Connie gave Rhiannon a brief hug and came around to the driver's side.

"Is that Conrad's?" she asked, pointing with a turn of her head and a slight puckering of her lips at the shiny black behemoth parked next to them.

"That's the one," Rhiannon said.

"Mo, you're going to be the talk of the town," Connie said. "That's what they call the Rambo of pickups."

"Where'd you get that?" Mo asked, amazed.

"Us Hopis know our pickups," she said. "It's a cultural thing."

Mo shook his big head. "Rhiannon?" he said. "You haven't been totally forthcoming here."

"What?"

"My understanding is that you had a homicide out here, a double homicide, and nothing is juicier than that. And you haven't said a word about it. It must take real concentration to talk about horses and teenagers when you got corpses lying around your property."

"Oh, God, that," Rhiannon said. She explained briefly about her husband finding them, one an Anglo, the other—the female—maybe an Indian, and the apparent mutilation of the bodies, which the police said could be nothing more than predators. Vultures and coyotes.

"In fact, it was your friend, that Sergeant Ramirez, who was in charge of the investigation. He recognized your bear in the patio and I was a bit surprised, you know, a policeman knowing about art. How snobby of me. Then I remembered you two have worked together."

On several occasions in past years, Mo had found himself embroiled in police matters, and there were those in Santa Fe who called him the redneck Nero Wolfe. He rather fancied that. It all started innocently enough, from his standpoint, when some Hopi religious artifacts had been stolen and, through Connie, he'd become involved in finding them and helping pinpoint a pair of murderers. Then several other criminal affairs thrust themselves into his life—or, as had happened, too, he thrust himself into such affairs, finding the challenge something that could distract him in much the manner of a crossword puzzle when he was in a generalized funk he called Sculptor's Cramp. Locals familiar with some of these exploits sometimes came to him with strange requests.

"Anyway," Rhiannon continued, "the sergeant talked to my son last night, asked his routine questions—where he was the day before, all that. Conrad began to put up his usual sullen front, but the sergeant leaned on him in the most exquisite way, and Conrad even smiled! It was almost miraculous. I had the thought right then that what Conrad needed was someone like that, someone outside his usual circle who he was a little scared of but maybe could admire at the same time. So I thought of you."

Mo laughed his staccato laugh.

"Me? Scary?" he said.

She's got to be an Indian. All that jet-black hair hanging straight down her back. Almost to her waist. And her face, sort of round, with those black eyes and thick eyebrows that almost meet. Light brown skin but not like light-skinned black people—more reddish. Got to be an Indian. Pretty weird seeing an Indian dressed like that, silk blouse and black slacks. She must have been wearing thousands of dollars of turquoise and silver. God, that stuff looks good on skin like that. She's beautiful.

I guess they're married.

I wish my skin was that color, instead of this pale, pale color. What color is it? No color. Another unwelcome gift from the old bitch.

It didn't say anything about the Indian in any of the newspaper clippings. Or did it? No. I would've noticed that for sure. Well, the last clipping is a couple of years old. Old enough to get all yellow, even in that silk-covered box she keeps in her closet.

Man, the stuff she keeps in that box, like a packrat. High school ring her fingers got too puffy to wear, that awful little bunch of dried flowers and the dance card from her senior prom. She sat out the middle dances. Danced all the others with just two different guys, first one for a while, then another. Probably she was out in their cars the rest of the time with her crinolines up around her waist, panting and grunting in the backseat, getting porked by those pimply-faced rubes. The first guy was her date, there's a photo, this geek in a white jacket standing next to her. She was pretty then, looking like she just caught a big fish, standing in her white dress with its crinolines, holding his hand. She danced the first four dances with her geek, and then she danced with this other guy from the eighth to the end. So she did her date, is my guess, while the band played five through seven, then took up with number two. The second guy . . . maybe he didn't even know he was getting sloppy seconds from the Slut of Central City. Then again, he probably did. That's how I read the dance card.

"I was the town pump and look where it got me," she told me one night. Two years ago? No, longer than that. I was out with some guys from Salida, and she waited up. She was going to give me a lecture—me!—about hanging out with guys like that, but she was so drunk by the time I got back, all she could do was blubber on about what a mess she'd made of everything in life. The pathetic old cow. "I was pretty then. I was so pretty."

She was right. She was pretty then, and she let every swinging dick in the county see just how pretty she was. Look where it got her. Life in Leadville, toxic waste dump of the Rockies, married to the emphysemic manager of the drugstore, my stepfather, who spent his last days hacking and coughing at eleven thousand feet above sea level and wondering how many of his fellow members of the Kiwanis had popped old Millie before he got there— and maybe since, for all he knew, though she gave that up mostly after she got double pneumonia the second time and let her body go completely.

Not for me. Not for me.

Measure it out, like gold dust.

These clippings. Tucked in there with the dance card and all the other sad stuff. From the Rocky Mountain News. *She doesn't read newspapers. Someone must have sent them to her. Maybe some old classmate who made it in Denver. Anyway, there he was in the photograph, ten years ago, this big guy with a blond beard and dark glasses, standing next to a statue of an elk. The guy's blind but he did this statue and some others that the Amex company put in the courtyard outside their offices. He used to work in their mine at Climax, where he lost his eyes in an accident. Now he was from New Mexico, living in Pecos. T. Moore Bowdre. Grew up in New Mexico. Uncle was Charlie Bowdre, who fought with Billy the Kid, or so the clipping says. He's kind of cute in his cowboy hat and his big smile. Friendly looking.*

Four other clippings, a few years apart. He lives in Santa Fe. More of the statues, all animals, in galleries. One about some stuff in a wildlife museum in Wyoming. T. Moore Bowdre. Famous now. A big shot. Nothing about that Indian woman.

All yellow now, the earliest ones all dried out and falling apart. But they're safe now, in these plastic folders. Safe.

I remember when she was pretty, too. Green eyes were alive then, brown hair like mine, but cut short. Holding my hand when we took walks along the river. Watching me play on the riverbank in the wind, patches of snow in the shade but the world warming up. Nobody but us on the riverbank outside of town. She was pretty then.

"Millie," I say, walking into the kitchen. She's sitting at the table with the yellow linoleum top, wearing that *light blue bathrobe. She's stubbing out another cigarette in the little copper ashtray, and she's spilled some coffee from her cup into the saucer. She looks up and clutches her bathrobe closed. She winces. She hates it when I call her Millie, but sometimes it's the only way to get her attention. "Millie, who's this guy?" I hold up one of the clippings with a big photo of the guy, smiling his big smile, looking kind of silly in his dark glasses and that black hat perched on his forehead.*

Moan, groan, that's my private place, my private things, blah blah, cough, hack, what are you doing looking in there? Then the tears, the blubbering. "Oh, God," she says, "Oh, God," and goes on about loss, mistakes, stupidity, and—of course—poor, poor Millie.

It takes a while but I get it out of her. All of it.

And the next morning I tell her. I got my stuff packed and I'm going. I'm outta here, Millie. I'm not doing this anymore.

"Huh?" she says, sitting at the table again, putting out another cigarette, having another cup of coffee, waiting for another day to end.

"I'm going," I say. "I won't be back."

She looks at me. Her eyes are droopy, like the lower lids can't hold themselves up anymore. She blinks. Then she nods. "Yeah," she says. "Yeah." And she looks out the window.

I think she was relieved.

Anthony Ramirez had reached the point in life, or so he thought, when four hours sleep simply didn't help much. He awoke on his back, feeling no more refreshed than when he went to bed. Less refreshed, if anything. And with a strange sensation of being outside himself, like the focusing apparatus on a camera hadn't quite been turned far enough, leaving two overlapping images on the viewfinder screen.

The forensic guys had completed their tasks by four in the morning, and the small caravan had bumped and lurched back to the Sharp-Franklin place, dropping Ramirez off at his vehicle. By five he had set the timer on his coffee machine for nine, ripped off most of his clothes, and slid into bed, where he went immediately to sleep. Now he sat up, noting that the bedclothes were virtually undisturbed. He hadn't moved in four hours. He could smell the coffee, and guessed it had been the machine's familiar belching that wakened him.

Reluctantly, he got out of the bed, tugged the covers down on his side, considering the bed made, and looked out the window into the courtyard of the apartment complex two flights down, which was dominated by a swimming pool gleaming light blue in the morning sun. A man and a woman were braving the morning chill, settled in on lounge chairs with their ritual equipment strewn beside them on the ground—several tubes of windscreen, two thick paperback books, the newspaper. Each was wearing a small headset wired to the woman's canvas pocketbook, and both had expensive-looking dark glasses over their eyes. Overhead, silver-lit clouds moved slowly across a bright sky. Beyond, the green Sangre de Cristo Mountains rose above the city.

He knew the couple to say hello to. She worked for the phone company or some utility-type thing, and he was evidently an up-and-coming young hotshot in the Nor-west Bank. The scuttlebutt in the complex was that she was pregnant, and so the questions people were asking themselves were when and if they'd get married, if they would be moving to a larger place than their two-room apartment, and how long she would wear that bikini.

It's Sunday, Ramirez thought. So here is an early-bird service in the Church of the Holy Sun.

The other couple flashed unbidden into his mind, the one that had also lain intimately parallel, faces to the sky. There was little he could do about that until the forensics had some specifics for him. And he wouldn't hear from them until the afternoon probably. Until then one could only speculate, and he didn't want to do that yet. The dead couple had legitimate demands on him, but he pre-sumed that if the dead retained any qualities the living would recognize, one was patience.

Down below, the man reached out a hand and placed it on his companion's stomach. Her stomach was, in fact, a bit rounded, a bit pronounced. When was it, Ramirez wondered, that it first began to show? Three months? He simply didn't know. The young man patted her stomach and Ramirez smiled: a banker patting his nest egg.

A cloud moved across the sun, putting the couple in the shade. The man sat up and craned his head around to the east. Evidently satisfied, he flopped back on his lounge chair and the shadow moved off. Abounding faith justified, Ramirez thought, down there in the cathedral of the sun.

Coffee.

There were two bagels in the refrigerator, only two days old.

He'd cleared his desk the day before, getting ready for the three days off he now would put into the bank. Maybe he'd stop by the Frazier Gallery before he went to the station. Then he would make some phone calls. Routine phone calls. Blessed routine.

Ramirez looked at his watch as he stepped out of the gallery onto San Francisco Street. It was four minutes past eleven. He walked toward the plaza, annoyed with himself. He hadn't been able to keep his mind on the sculptures, to look at them with seeing eyes. His mind kept veering off, back to the couple in the arroyo, and his friend's sculpture had seemed inert, irritating. He would come another time.

In the plaza, some workmen were setting up a platform and speakers over near the Palace of the Governors, the ancient two-story adobe building that commanded most of the northern side of the plaza. Either some band would show up, or some outfit opposed to nuclear energy or government corruption or cruelty to animals, or whatever. There was always something in the plaza. In the shade beneath the long portal that shaded the front of the palace, the Indians had already set themselves up, blankets spread before them on the sidewalk, covered with turquoise and silver jewelry. A lot of it was *handcrafted*, which didn't mean what it sounded like. Handcrafted meant assembled by hand. A lot of the Indians who sold wares in the plaza bought previously machined parts, like earrings, and put machine-formed turquoise in them. Perfectly legit, and some of it nice stuff. And some of the stuff was *handmade*, every bit of it formed by Indian hands. You could get bargains there on the sidewalk, but like the rest of the world, Ramirez thought, the watchword was *caveat emptor*.

A few emptors were standing before the Indians and their blankets, pondering. At the eastern side of the plaza, a little circle of teenage boys in hip-hop garb like rag dolls were playing hacky-sack. Ramirez watched for a few minutes during which the kids didn't let the little bag touch the ground, each kicking and spinning and jiving with the concentration and grace of professional athletes. A few tourists were sitting on benches, watching the boys and eating ice cream; a few others were sitting on the grass, looking up at the sun.

On a bench nearer Ramirez, on the western end of the plaza, a young woman with long, shiny brown hair and a green canvas bag on her lap was sitting in the shade. She had her arms wrapped tightly around the bag, and Ramirez noticed that her shoulders were moving. She was crying. She was looking straight ahead, crying, tears running down her face.

I'll go see what's wrong, he thought.

But no, it's not my business. People have a right to sit in public and cry.

He climbed in his car, which he'd parked illegally on San Francisco Street, and turned down Don Gaspar. People were still bunched up around the entrance to Pasqual's, waiting to get in for a late breakfast or brunch. Part of the little crowd had leaked into the street from the narrow sidewalk, and Ramirez waited patiently for them to notice him and move. Traffic was beginning to build up, tourists circling in toward the plaza looking for a legal parking space on the streets, which was about as likely as a winning lottery ticket or drawing a full house with three aces.

Fifteen minutes later he was at his desk in a small cubicle off the main bullpen, dialing the medical investigator's office in Albuquerque. Some manila files had appeared in his box.

Before long, one of the assistants was on the phone and they commiserated about having to work on Sunday, particularly a beautiful Sunday. The assistant said to Ramirez that she supposed he wanted to know if there were anything he could learn informally about the two bodies they'd brought in last night, and Ramirez agreed that it was the reason for his call. The assistant then explained in an expressionless voice, which sounded like she was reading from an instructional manual or something equally innocuous, that Dr. Menendez was in the process of performing the autopsy at that very moment. She was working on the female, the male to be autopsied next, or as soon as one of the other pathologists arrived. The other pathologist on call, Dr. Freund, called in to say that there had been a fire in her apartment building which would delay her. Dr. Menendez had already determined the cause of death in both cases. Ramirez waited with teeth-gritting impatience while the assistant explained that Dr. Menendez could see why Ramirez and the others hadn't seen it out at the crime scene. The weapons, and the wounds they inflicted, had left virtually no blood that one might notice immediately . . .

Come on! Ramirez prayed silently.

. . . but on a preliminary examination, Dr. Menendez had found, buried firmly about a half inch down in the left ear of each of the D.B.'s, the head of a two-and-a-half-inch-long twelve-penny nail.

Also, the assistant said after a pause, Dr. Menendez ascertained that the female was three months pregnant.

four

Three of them, Ramirez thought. Holy Mother of God, how horrible.

His mind flashed back to his first look at the bodies and the sense he had then of something innocent about them. *Verdaderament,* he said to himself. Indeed.

Three months pregnant—he'd just been looking at a three-month-pregnant woman at the swimming pool in his apartment building. You couldn't tell. Or could you? Not from two stories up. At least *he* couldn't. But what did he know? None of the women who got pregnant in his family—nieces and all—walked around with their stomachs showing.

The guy had patted it so fondly, protectively.

Ramirez reached out for one of the manila files in his box, pulled it to him and opened it, letting a sheaf of photographs fall loosely on his desk. Ferguson had worked the rest of the night and into daylight in the darkroom. Good man. He spread them out, looking for . . . Here. Here was one where the woman's abdomen . . . No, no sign he could see with all the bloating, the disfigurement below, Jesus. He

69

set the photograph aside and stared out the door of his office for a long time.

He found that he had to swallow several times before he could look again at the photographs, and very slowly he held one after the other up and made himself look at each, eyes scanning every detail. First the shots with both bodies, lying next to that big boulder. Unquestionable, he thought again. They were laid out, carefully laid out— flat on their backs with their arms down at their sides. His left elbow was touching her right elbow. Legs spread apart but straight out. His left foot was touching her right foot. He was lying close to the boulder; she was next to him.

He had checked the angles the night before, satisfying himself that John Franklin's story could be true. From where the horse tracks ended on the west side of the arroyo and the horse turned and went upstream, he would have seen only the feet. From above, again where the horse stopped thirty yards away on the other side of the arroyo, he would have been able to see the bodies and know at a glance that they were dead. The eye holes and the wounds in the groin were visible from there, along with a few gross details, like hair color and the female's breasts. In the hastiest glance, he would have registered a dead woman and a dead man with hair that was not the color of his son's. Okay.

Ramirez kept staring at the photographs, looking for exactly what, he wasn't sure. He would be looking at these photographs again and again, he knew, and perhaps less aimlessly when the written reports came through from forensics and from the M.I.

Christ, nails in the ears. Who the hell would have thought of looking for something like that?

Who the hell would have *done* something like that? And why? Why with nails, for God's sake? It was a crazy way to kill someone. Insane. Were they asleep when it happened? Drugged? Well, he'd find out soon enough, he supposed. No point in speculating yet.

There was another why question, too. Why had they been killed? He hated the thought that had hung in his mind since the night before, and one that seemed all the more likely now, with the news of the baby. The almost baby. The fetus. The woman's boyfriend, or husband, an Indian guy, discovers the woman with this Anglo, goes apeshit. But does a guy who's in a jealous rage kill them with nails hammered in their ears?

Ramirez shook his head.

The killer—killers?—had presumably done this some-where else and carried the bodies out to this place and laid them out neatly, side by side, and . . . what? Left them there? Why there? Out in the middle of these fancy estates and in the blazing sun where someone—someone like Franklin—could easily be patrolling the south fork?

Had the killer, and not scavengers, mutilated them, too? Earlier? At the site? Again, he'd know more about that soon enough.

They had not found anything by way of tracks, either around the body or leading up to it from the nearest dirt road, which was about a hundred yards off to the south. The wind might have accounted for that. Or someone had gone to a lot of trouble to get rid of them.

No animal tracks either. No paw prints of coyotes or

dogs. No sign of buzzards scrabbling around their heads
with their naked feet.

Ramirez shook his head again, and found that he'd
shuddered slightly. He would send some men back out
there to make a wider sweep of the area.

He hated to think that this was one of those Anglo-
Indian things. Two hundred years of accumulated shit
would hit the fan again, in sharp focus. The woman could
be Hispanic, though: just as bad. Five hundred years of
accumulated shit.

He looked again at one of the photographs showing
what was left of their faces.

He couldn't tell what she was. The M.I. would.

Idly, he stared at the photograph, his glance moving
to the face of the boulder just beyond their heads, and
the petroglyph etched on it. He had noticed a few
petroglyphs on the rock the night before. There were petroglyphs all over this country. Anyplace you found rock
with a flat surface, you might well find some design,
some picture, etched into it by some Indian bypasser,
some pilgrim or priest or whatever.

Directly beyond the male's head and maybe a foot
above it on the rock face was a spiral. Real common,
Ramirez thought. See 'em everywhere. Someone had
told him it was a migration symbol of some kind. The
Pueblo people up there—Santa Clara, San Ildefonso.
Their ancestors came from somewhere like Mesa Verde,
the Anasazi ruins. Migrated here seven, eight hundred
years ago or more. All these guys left these marks, sort of
an Indian Kilroy-Was-Here deal, maybe. But sacred, of
course.

He looked elsewhere on the rock surface. Only the lower third of the boulder showed in the photograph, and it looked like there was some kind of marking—a couple of lines cut off by the edge of the photo, maybe another petroglyph—about a foot above the spiral and a little bit to its left. He shuffled the photographs, looking for one that showed more of the rock. There were several, but the rock face had been light-blasted by the flash. Featureless. He looked for one that had been shot from an oblique angle, and found it.

Above the spiral were two more petroglyphs. One looked like stairs, a little staircase with three steps, and on the top step an almond-shaped object standing upright. What the hell was that? Over to the left was what looked like a stick-figure deer, or maybe an antelope. Short little horns, anyway.

He shrugged. He knew that scholars argued with the standard bitterness of all academic disputes about these petroglyphs and what they meant. He'd once heard an archaeologist from the University of New Mexico take some amateur petroglyph hound apart for fabricating a whole lot of meanings. Guy was finding Jungian archetypes all over the Southwest that matched the marks of early man in Java or some damned thing, and the archaeologist, a guy named Binford, reduced him and his assumptions to jelly before a whole class of graduate students. It had to have been a setup, and Ramirez felt sorry for the amateur, his life's work lying in tatters around him.

Probably they ought to just ask the Indians, he thought. They remember everything else; they'd probably remember what all their ancestors were putting up on the bulletin board.

Ramirez knew exactly what he was doing, thinking about such things. He was letting himself *not* think about the meaning of these photographs, the meaning of these murders.

Nails, for God's sake. Nails in the ears.

He picked up the phone and pressed one of its buttons.

"Maria? Good. You and Sandoval go out and relieve Gutierrez, okay? . . . Yeah, he's probably asleep out there. He was up all night . . . Well, that's your problem. Take an aspirin or something. Look, somebody had to bring those bodies there, so there's got to be some sign. Find it . . . Yeah, they could of, a helicopter, but it doesn't seem too likely . . . Maria, stop screwing around and get on your horse."

Maria was a short, round cop who'd gotten her promotion a few months ago and was assigned to Homicide. She was one of those people who were always smiling, always ready with a laugh, even when she had a hangover, like this morning. He wondered how long her natural cheeriness would last.

Seven and a half hours was the usual amount of time chewed up by the drive from Santa Fe to Connie Barnes's village at Hopi. Enough time, usually, for her to knead her thoughts into a consistency better suited to the other world that lay out there on the remote mesas. Mo had once announced, during one long ride back from Hopi, that being at Hopi was like a trip into medieval times. When she bridled a little, thinking of poor ignorant peasants slogging around in the mud the way she'd seen in a few movies, he made it clear that was a compliment.

How so? she'd asked. From what he could gather, in those old medieval towns in Europe the entire universe was focused there—on the cathedral—and all the activities connected to it. It's not that the world was smaller, the universe less vast. But it was a personal universe, and everyone in town understood it pretty much the same way. Everyone knew everyone and how they were tied to each other, and how that all fit. Like a tapestry, he had said, one of those big old tapestries that told a lot of stories all at once.

Connie had never thought of it that way, and couldn't quite see what he meant. She just accepted the world at Hopi as that: Hopi. She didn't need to analyze it or characterize it. Maybe that was the difference.

White people seemed bound—both bound and determined and bound in chains by the need—to break everything down and make comparisons. To spin words describing all the little pieces and then try to build something from that. For Connie, and for a number of other Hopis she knew who split their time between the two worlds, it wasn't mental. It was visceral.

In the house she and Mo shared on Canyon Road, she could go in the kitchen and cook up a pot of corn and they would eat it and take pleasure from that. Nothing could be simpler. At Hopi, when she ate corn in the very same manner, turning the cob in her hands and moving along the rows, she accepted in some unspoken manner and from deep inside that the ear of corn was a child of its parent stalk, no different than she was a child of her parents. She accepted, too, that the color of the kernels was the direction from which her clan had come long ago, and also that the eating of it was part of a web of duties and opportunities, places, history.

She tried to explain all this to Mo, and finally said she didn't imagine a fish had to think a lot about the water it swam in. Mo thought about that and remained silent all the way between Gallup and Albuquerque—almost two and a half hours, during which he dozed off a few times.

At one point when he woke up he asked how come she could do so well out of the water. Maybe she was some kind of frog.

Connie, whose mind had long since gone on to other things, said, "A frog? Frogs are ugly." She had enjoyed it immensely, listening to Mo try to get out of that one.

Now, the old pickup strained slightly at sixty miles an hour, climbing the long rise west of Albuquerque called Nine Mile Hill. Connie thought again of Mo, standing hatless and with a big smile gleaming from behind his blond beard as she drove out of the yard onto Canyon Road.

"I'll be just fine," he had said. "Just fine. Don't you worry about a thing. Just give my best to old Marvin, tell him I said that his heart'd do fine if he'd just quit chasing all those Hopi girls up and down the mesa."

She knew he hated being left. She reached out and put her hand on his cheek.

"I'll be back in a few days."

"Sure, sure. And I'll be riding shotgun in Conrad's Rambo truck, and feeling up that horse. Don't you worry about a thing. Hah. Hah."

So she had let the clutch out and left. She hoped Mo wouldn't get involved with those two bodies they had found. Of course, he'd be pressuring Ramirez to tell him all about it, and he'd be going out there where they were found. But maybe he'd be too busy feeling up the horse and babysitting Conrad to get in trouble.

Now, as the desert opened out before her, a wide bowl of colorless scrub and sand, and Route 40 lay ahead, a shimmering ribbon in the midday sun, she began to hum. It was a song the katsinas sang in the plaza and it had many verses, and she would sing the words over and over all the way to her village.

It is common for Hopis to sing the katsinas' songs when passing long stretches of time that is otherwise idle—on long drives, or in hospitals. Connie Barnes hoped that her clan father Marvin was singing, too.

Mo Bowdre lived in an old adobe house toward the upper end of Canyon Road, a narrow street that winds uphill from the center of Santa Fe through a bewildering concentration of art galleries laced with a few restaurants. In earlier times the artists who flocked to Santa Fe lived in these very same galleries—Canyon Road was an art enclave within the greater art colony of Santa Fe. Nowadays most of the artists live elsewhere, real estate costing what it does—indeed, most of the current generation of artists and craftspeople, and in particular the struggling ones, live outside Santa Fe altogether, and most of Canyon Road's square footage is given over to the exigencies of commerce.

At its upper end, though, it is still residential, and Mo

Bowdre's house was one of the earlier residences, a low structure that had been added onto over the years with each successive owner's whimsy, resulting in something of a mazelike collection of mostly small though high-ceilinged rooms connected by arches, the floors of which were often on slightly different levels. It was hardly the sort of place recommended for people who are referred to with euphemistic sensitivity as *visually challenged*. Mo Bowdre found that phrase stupid. Blind people are not visually challenged. What is challenged are the other senses—hearing, smell, touch, and what Mo thought of as a cartographic sense. As a result of this, he knew every architectural whimsy of his house as well as he knew the contours of his own body.

The original house had been built right off the narrow sidewalk of Canyon Road on a half-acre plot that was enclosed on three sides, including the street, by a high adobe wall. Within the yard was an area of green grass and a handsome garden which had gone to weeds until Connie Barnes arrived and took these matters in hand. The gardens now were bright with irises, day lilies, and other perennials. Across the lawn was an old stone building that had once been a mill house, taking its energy from the occasional flow of what is a bit grandiosely called the Santa Fe River, a small stream that slides downhill in hearing of Canyon Road and through the city, eventually adding its waters to the Rio Grande, miles away.

A previous owner had employed a landscape designer who diverted the Santa Fe River from the old mill house to a course some ten feet west of it, and now the mill house, with its north-facing door greatly enlarged, served as Mo Bowdre's studio. It was for the most part a dark and mercifully cool place for the big man to work.

The lower end of the yard was lightly graveled and served as a short driveway, reached by opening a large wooden gate in the adobe wall. It was into this drive that Conrad Franklin had pulled his enormous Dodge Ram pickup truck at mid-afternoon on Sunday, about three hours after Connie Barnes had left for the Hopi Reservation far off in northeastern Arizona. During most of this interval, Mo had sat in the largest room in the house, a living room with a large red sofa, a huge wing chair made out of driftwood roots, which was far more comfortable than it looked, and a wall of sound equipment. For most of that time he listened halfheartedly to three one-hour programs of successively screechier ethnic music on the public radio station and felt mildly sorry for himself.

Connie was not present. Her absence was an enormous fact.

She was, of course and in a sense, his eyes, but he'd managed that aspect of life largely on his own for a number of years before meeting her. He felt Connie's absence in an altogether different way. It was she—her alto voice with its gentle Indian lilt—who first put something akin to light back into his life, colors back into his world. It was she for whom he sculpted now, used every sense and nerve ending to create physical likenesses of memories. Each of these creations he placed figuratively before her, a kind of offering, before letting them loose in the world. He was, plain and simple, addicted to Connie.

She knew this, of course, though there remained in Mo enough of the country boy not to express it in his typically windy manner, and she herself, being Hopi, also tended not to be especially verbal about such feelings. In fact, Mo was fully aware that people whose job it was to dissect human relationships and label them like butterfly specimens in a museum case might well label him an emotional codependent.

Yes, indeedy damned-do, Mo thought. He wouldn't have it any other way. How else can you love someone? And of course you should be brave and calm and proceed in an orderly, adult, and nondepressive manner and wear clean clothes and eat right and take your vitamins and all that when your partner has to go off somewhere for reasons you understand perfectly well, but that doesn't mean you've got to *like* it. That doesn't mean you've got to pretend that there's light and color in the world when there goddamn well isn't.

By four o'clock on Sunday afternoon, by which time Mo Bowdre guessed Connie was well beyond Window Rock, Arizona, he was pretty sure that his temporary seeing-eye dog, Conrad Franklin, was not the sort to shine much by way of light in his or probably anyone else's life. The boy had arrived more or less on schedule and remained mostly silent while Mo showed him through the house, finally pointing out the spare bedroom where Conrad would sleep. This was a small room with hand-plastered white walls like the rest of the house, containing a queen-size bed, a rough wooden bedside table, and a wooden chair that had been painted blue. A single small window opened to the west, and on the other walls hung three framed posters, advertisements for the gallery openings, long since passed into history, of two native artists. Thus, in this room, one's slumber was watched over by two separate katsinas by Hopi artist Dan Namingha, each emerging from and at the same time merging into the sky, and an Eskimo woman's version of a thunderbird.

Having taken a minute to glance around the room and set his duffel bag on the floor, Conrad had blurted, "Weird."

"Weird?" Mo had repeated. "Hah. Hah. It ain't La Posada, I'll grant you, but I think we got rid of the rats."

Conrad retreated into an embarrassed silence, finally saying, "No, not the room. It's—well—weird that you can't see but you don't even touch anything when you're moving around here."

"Well, Conrad, think of it this way. You can probably scratch your balls without turning on the light. This whole place is just an extension of me by now. But you put the tuna fish on the wrong shelf in the pantry and I could starve to death. Let me show you my studio out there."

It was there, at four-thirty, in the gloom of the cold mill house, amid crates of gray clay, a few large chunks of marble, and shelves laden with chisels and other tools in precise rows, that they received a visit from the homicide department of the Santa Fe P.D. in the person of Sergeant Anthony Ramirez.

He tapped quietly on the doorjamb and stood blinking in the doorway.

"I'm sorry to bother you, Mo," he said, and Mo heard

the official tone in his friend's voice. "Official business. I have to talk to Conrad here."

Mo heard the boy swallow, and thought he could feel the heat rising in his face—no doubt a surge of panic, guilt, fear, and other common teenage afflictions. If the kid didn't have acne anymore, he would likely erupt with a whole new array. Maybe he was too old for acne.

"Your mother said I'd find you here with Mr. Bowdre," Ramirez said. "You're working for Mr. Bowdre, she tells me."

"She's my stepmother," Conrad said in a near whisper.

"Very good, Conrad," Ramirez said, his voice now smooth as velvet. "I want you to be precise. Miz Sharp wanted to come, to be here, by the way, but I told her no. I have some questions, and you would be very smart to answer them truthfully."

"You want me to go?" Mo asked.

"It's up to Conrad here," Ramirez said. "You want him to go?"

Listening, Mo assumed that Conrad shook his head.

"It's not like you're under arrest or anything," Ramirez added. "So Conrad, tell me. The place where your father found those bodies. Were you out there in the past few days? Like two nights ago?"

"No, no. I was in Taos, like I told you."

"So when was the last time you were out there, Conrad?"

"Uh—"

"You were lying under a tree about thirty yards away from those corpses. When was that?"

"Last night," Conrad whispered.

"When last night, Conrad?"

"Around midnight. When you guys were—"

"Why?"

Mo heard the kid fidget, scratch himself somewhere.

"I was, well, curious."

"Conrad, why don't you just tell me the whole story here. If I have to ask you every single obvious question and drag it out of you piece by piece, I'm going to get real impatient. You know what I'm saying, Conrad?"

Mo reached out a hand and touched the boy's arm. "You can be straight with Sergeant Ramirez, Conrad. Go ahead."

Conrad swallowed again. "Okay. I was just curious. I never saw a crime scene or anything like that. So I went out after they—my parents—were in bed, and took a look. I watched you guys picking over the place, saw the ambulance guys come and take the bodies away. Then one of the cops, the policemen, started coming toward me, so I got up and went home. I figured, well, it's on my property, so what was wrong with going out to look?"

"If nothing was wrong with it, then how come you were sneaking around in the dark watching from a tree, and ran most of the way home when a cop started in your direction?"

"I—I—"

"You left a nice trail for us, Conrad. You go there often? Is that a special place for you or something?"

"I go there, yeah. Sometimes. I go there and, you know, think. It's quiet there. Indians used to go there. They left all those marks on the boulders."

"And you think about Indians," Ramirez said.

"Yeah."

"And girls, maybe?"

"Well, yeah."

"And that's where you . . . ?"

"Ohhh," Conrad exhaled.

". . . Leave *your* mark on the boulders, sort of?"

Conrad was silent, then murmured, "Uh-huh." Mo was surprised by how relentless Ramirez was, like he'd given free rein to a cruel streak.

"Okay, Conrad, okay," Ramirez said. "It's no crime doing that. When was the last time you were there? Before last night, I mean."

Conrad took a deep breath and said, "Today's Sunday? It was, like, Friday. Friday afternoon. Before I went to Taos."

"And nobody was there, right? No dead bodies. You would've seen them right there next to the boulder."

"Yeah. Nothing."

"And you sit on this boulder here, in this picture?"

"Uh, yeah." There was a long silence, during which Mo could hear the boy breathing through his mouth. He had suddenly developed a slightly asthmatic rattle in his throat somewhere.

"What are you looking at, Conrad?" Ramirez asked.

"This photograph."

"What about it?"

"This petroglyph. That one there. It's not . . ."

"Not what?"

"I never saw it before. It's new."

"Conrad, are you sure? Maybe you just never noticed it."

"No, no. There's the migration symbol, this spiral. And this deer. But this thing is new. I swear."

Mo waited in the silence, hearing only Conrad's phlegmy breathing.

"You're going to be staying here, Conrad? With Mr. Bowdre?"

"Uh, yeah. For a few days."

"Good. You do just that. I'll want to talk to you again."

"He's staying here," Mo said, "while Connie's gone. Driving me back and forth to his parents' place. I'm doing a piece for them."

"Good," Ramirez repeated. "You know, Conrad? You've been very helpful to me."

"Uh . . ."

"Mo, I'll see you. Sorry to bother you."

Mo heard Ramirez walk out of the studio, and listened until he heard the sound of his engine starting up out on Canyon Road. Conrad remained silent but for his asthmatic breathing, and Mo felt sorry for him. It had to have been excruciating, mortifying, making his grubby little confessions before a couple of strangers. Adults to boot.

"Well, Conrad, think of it this way. You might've just spotted a clue in a murder investigation. Tony sure did perk up his ears about that petroglyph. What did it look like? Here, you take this awl and draw it on this little slab of clay. Sort of like Braille."

"Oh, okay," Conrad said. After a few moments, during which Mo heard the rattle in the boy's throat subside, he said, "Shit. I messed up. Can I use the other side?"

"Sure, go ahead."

Asthma gone, Mo said to himself. This boy must find the world a terrifying place.

"There," Conrad said. "That's it."

Mo put his hand out and his fingers moved lightly over the clay slab, fluttering like an ant's antennae along the etched lines, and somewhere in his brain he became aware of this shape:

"Now what the hell do you suppose that is?" he said. "You ever see one like that?"

"No."

"Me neither," Mo said.

I never saw so many galleries in one place, so much stuff—all those paintings, jewelry, all those Indian things, weird landscapes, crazy sculptures, like, is that really a sculpture—that old toaster with the neon tube coming up out of it? The guy's got to be kidding, two thousand dollars for an old toaster with a neon light. Now that gold jewelry—that looked worth the money. Here's another of those paintings, an Indian turning into an eagle. Who is this guy Schwartz kidding?

Why am I huffing and puffing? It's uphill but this is nothing—maybe seven thousand feet. At home it was eleven thousand.

No, not home. Not home. Just where I stayed—with . . . I don't want to think about it.

Look at that! A blue wolf with purple eyes, Day-Glo eyes, peeping out from behind the grass. What is it, chalk? Yeah, chalk on black paper. Cool. But twelve hundred dollars? For a kid's drawing? And here's another one, the same wolf, but it's wearing a dress, holding a rattle. Look at those eyes. Creepy. This place is like a toy store for rich adults, this whole street. Canyon Road. This is where he lives. It must be up here farther.

Okay, houses with walls around them, everybody living behind walls here, too. Keeping the world out, keeping surprises out. But not this surprise. There, there's his number. On that big wooden gate. Gate must be a hundred years old. What's inside? Go ahead, take a look. Oh jeez, look at the flowers. They're beautiful. But what's that truck in there, big black pickup, must be brand new, one of those Dodge Rams. Lights on the top. If he's got this, how come he drives that old wreck of a Ford? And where's that? Maybe I should just go in. Go in the yard and look around and say hi.

No.

There's a door up the sidewalk there. Is that the door to his house? I should just go up and knock.

No. Not yet. I wish I knew how to do this.

Uh-oh, here he comes. Standing on that porch with the overhanging roof, wearing that hat like in the pictures, dark glasses. Now who's that coming out? A kid. Look at those pants, like they're ten sizes too big. Dumb-looking hip-hop crap. What a jerk. A son? Does he have a son?

Duck. Get back across the street.

He could have a son. Why not? Kid about sixteen, why not? Doesn't look anything like him, though. Chinless wonder, dark hair like mine, skinny guy.

Okay, here they come, out of the gate. They're walking.

He can't be a son. I don't want him to have a son. Maybe he's a stepson. But not from the Indian woman, he couldn't be hers, either. Not with skin like that.

I need to get him alone, talk to him alone. Maybe he never is alone. What do I know about blind people?

He doesn't walk like a blind man.

The jerk's looking back at me. Hey, give him a little smile, a little jiggle. Look at him, looking away, turning red.

Don't you wish, huh?

five

At six o'clock Sunday evening, Dr. Mirabelle Anjou answered the chime at the front door of her house, which was perched on one of the many little wooded hillocks in the valley between Old Taos Road and Bishops Lodge Road in an expensive residential neighborhood a mile or so north of Santa Fe. The neighborhood had sprung up essentially all at once a decade or so ago and consisted of what could be called decorator Pueblo-style houses sprinkled along lanes that twisted through the hilly terrain.

Dr. Anjou was wearing a pair of flowing black slacks and a black blouse of silk, adorned with a simple gold chain with a pendant of Australian opals, and a pair of opal-and-gold earrings to match. She was the director of a private institute devoted to research into the Indian cultures of the Southwest. The institute, located on a private road off the Old Santa Fe Trail in town, was the onetime mansion of a man, who, in the late Twenties and Thirties, had become wealthy writing children's stories and books that shamelessly romanticized cowboys and Indians. Out of guilt feelings, it was widely assumed, he had bequeathed his house and fortune to start an institute whose researches would truly reflect the Indian past and present, and over the years it had gained the reputation of doing just that. Dr. Anjou, a naturalized French scholar, was the institute's fourth director and by far its most successful fund-raiser. She was also considered one of a handful of top scholars in the realm of Pueblo Indian symbology.

She opened the front door of her house and, as expected from an earlier phone call, found what she took to be a policeman standing under the portal that shaded the entrance from the sun. He was an Hispanic man—attractive, she thought, with an intelligent-looking face. He was in plainclothes—a blazer and sharply creased tan slacks.

"Dr. Anjou, I'm Sergeant Ramirez. Thank you for seeing me on such short notice. And—uh-oh, I see you're dressed to go out somewhere."

"Come in, Sergeant. Actually, I have some people coming here for dinner. But not for another half hour or so."

She led him through a living room furnished with European antiques and out through a sliding glass door onto a patio that projected like the bow of a large ship out over the piñon trees around the house. Beyond, over the rooftops of several other houses, the skyline of the Jemez Mountains to the west was visible.

"Beautiful view," he said.

"Please sit down," Dr. Anjou said, smiling graciously and gesturing to a group of white wrought-iron chairs near the patio's wooden railing. On a matching table was a glass of red wine. "Can I get you something?"

"Oh, no," the policeman said. "No, thank you. I just need your help for a few minutes here. Then I'll be gone." He sat down, and she sat in a chair facing him and crossed her legs. Ramirez had dark brown, almond-shaped eyes and they were fixed pleasantly on hers.

"As I said on the phone, we're investigating a homicide—a double homicide. The bodies were found in an arroyo out where they're building those big estates west of Tano Road." He gestured in that direction with his head. "One of the things we have to do is put together as complete a picture of the crime scene as possible. You know, check out everything we can. And out there, on a boulder next to the victims, we noticed some petro-glyphs. We thought you might be able to tell us about them."

Dr. Anjou nodded. Ramirez fished a photograph out of a manila envelope he had carried into the house under his arm. He held it out to her, an eight-by-eleven color print of a yellowish rock face, with the light slanting across it, highlighting three petroglyphs. She bent her head over the photograph and studied it for a moment.

When she looked up, Ramirez's almond eyes were still fixed on hers and she felt a tingle of excitement. Was it being involved in a police investigation?

"Can you tell me about those things?" he asked.

She smiled and looked down. "This one," she said, pointing to the spiral, "is a migration symbol. They're very common. The old people left them all around, marking their journeys. Just why they used a spiral, nobody knows for sure. You hear a lot of silly speculation, of course. This one over here is either a deer or a—what do you call it?—a pronghorn. It's a bit hard to tell which. Most likely, a hunter pecked this into the rock—and fairly hastily—to help his hunt along."

"And the other one? That one?" Ramirez said, leaning forward and pointing.

She turned the photograph a few degrees in each direction. "Yes, very unusual," she said. "Very unusual. This looks like a set of three stairs. It's like a symbol for clouds the old Hopis used on their pottery, Palatki and other abandoned villages, and it's been revived since then. They use it on their pottery, and their jewelry. You must have seen it. But here it's upside down." She looked up and smiled at him. "That's why I was tilting the photograph. But of course, the photograph is right side up.

"Usually," she continued, "the narrow part is at the bottom. Or sometimes you see the same thing but on its side. I've never seen it upside down. It's not just a Hopi symbol, by the way. You see the same cloud symbol here in New Mexico as well."

Ramirez nodded. "And then there's this thing on the top stair. Like a nut or something. What do you suppose that could be?"

"I've seen something like this, again on Hopi material. It's a seed, a squash seed. Except it usually is just two curved lines forming the seed. This one has a little line going partway up the center. I've never seen that."

She studied it again, turning it one way and then the

other. "I wonder," she said. "You know, Sergeant, it could be something else altogether. An altar perhaps."

"An altar?"

"It's just a thought. Not even a guess."

"The Indians have altars like that?"

"No, not that I know of. But these steplike lines, they remind you of Aztec structures, you know, the pyramids where they made their horrible sacrifices. And some of these people here originally came from there long ago. Some of the old things, symbols, meanings, could be buried deep in these people's psyches."

Ramirez frowned.

"Altars could change in form over the centuries," she explained, "but the symbol for altar could remain unchanged. Like shorthand. An artistic convention."

Ramirez frowned again.

"We use artistic conventions," she explained. "A balloon with words in it in a cartoon means that Doonesbury is speaking out loud. But if there are little dots, like puffs of smoke, going from the balloon to the character, we all know he's thinking those words, not speaking them. That's an artistic convention. You see?"

The policeman leaned back and held his chin in one hand. "Then what about that seed thing?" he said.

Dr. Anjou shrugged.

"Would it make any difference," Ramirez asked, "if I told you that petroglyph might be new?"

She shrugged, pursed her lips. "These things are very difficult to date. That's one of the problems with them."

"I mean a few days old," Ramirez said.

Dr. Anjou looked up sharply at the policeman, her eyebrows arched high.

"Someone who's familiar with this place says he never saw this petroglyph there before. Says it wasn't there a few days before the homicides. Could it be one of today's Indians did it?"

Dr. Anjou frowned. She was not pleased to have been placed in what seemed a trap by this almond-eyed policeman.

"Of course, it could be an Indian, Sergeant," she said with a new snap to her voice. "But it could be someone of Spanish origin as well. As I am sure you know, the coming-of-age ceremony many Hispanic families still perform harks back to the Aztecs as well. Anyone can make a petroglyph."

She stood up and smoothed her slacks. "Now. I am afraid that . . ."

Ramirez stood up as well. "Yes, ma'am. Thank you. You've been very helpful." He turned to go, then stopped. "Just one more thing. This seed thing. Could it be a flame? Like fire?"

"It could be almost anything, Sergeant. A flame. A seed. And if it is so recent, it could even be a football." She gave a shrug, full of Gallic indifference. "It's like a Rorschach ink blot. You can read into it almost anything you wish."

She accompanied the policeman to the front door in silence and saw him out. Through a narrow vertical window next to the door, she watched him climb in his car and drive off, leaving a fine cloud of dust rising in the driveway. She was still angry with him, but she was also angry with herself. Of course it wasn't Hispanic. Hispanics had no tradition of making petroglyphs that she knew of. She had misled the policeman out of pique.

She wondered if there were a penalty for that.

Conrad Franklin followed the huge blind man up to the wooden porch that extended the entire length of the long, low wooden building. They had walked about a quarter of a mile down Canyon Road, and Bowdre seemed to know when they'd arrived. The building itself looked like it could fall down any minute. It was called El Farol. Bowdre said the word meant *lantern*, and eating there would be a great adventure.

Conrad did not especially relish the thought of adventure when it came to food. A lot of what people ate he considered gross, and he hoped this wasn't the kind of place that had only stuff like octopus. Once, he'd watched his father eat these little tiny octopuses, about an inch long and they had all their arms and all, and he almost threw up.

Tapas is what Bowdre said they served, lots of little dishes like appetizers. Conrad was not reassured.

The big man paused at the porch and said, "Conrad, you go ahead of me a little, will you? Right through that middle door." Conrad heard the flooring of the porch creak under Bowdre's boots just behind him, and he led through the middle of three doors that were open to the cooling evening air. Inside, Conrad saw a cavernous dark room with a bar that appeared to be sunken below the floor and a lot of junk up on the walls, old hats, crap like that.

The place swirled with noise and people, a lot of them walking around, some sitting at the bar, some at tables. A couple of big bikers were leaning their elbows on one of the little wooden tables nearby and they turned to glare at Conrad, then looked back into their beers. A waitress—about six feet tall, skinny as a rail and black as coal—swept by with a tray full of stuff balanced on one hand. She spun around, somehow managing to keep the tray in the air, and smiled, a brilliant white smile.

"Hey, Mo! You not been in for weeks. Where you been?" She had a funny accent, like African.

"Hey, Fred," Mo said. "This here's my friend Conrad. You got a table some quiet place, away from all these rowdies you attract?"

"Hello, Conrad," she said ceremoniously, looking down at him from a few inches away. "Follow me." She sailed off, nearly pirouetting through the people, lowering the tray to pass through a low, narrow door that had long since given up any pretension of being a collection of right angles. The floors all seemed to be at different angles, too.

"She's from Ethiopia," Mo said. "Nobody can pronounce her name so they call her Fred."

Fred proceeded at a breakneck pace through a tiny crowded room, through another narrow door into another small room and, in a third room almost as small as the others, stopped at an empty table with four chairs.

"I'll be back," Fred said with another big smile and swept off.

"See," Mo said, once they were seated and Conrad had opened up the menu. "There's all kinds of stuff there.

Grilled cactus. You ever had that? And there's something they call *gambas al ajillo*. It's shrimp they cook in sherry, lime, and garlic. Fantastic. One thing we don't need to have is those grilled snails."

Conrad shuddered.

"Snails, bleh," Mo said. "Snails are mollusks, and a man just has to draw the line somewhere. Don't you agree? I'd have to be damn near death from starvation before I'd put a damn snail in my mouth. They got ordinary stuff here, too—like little pork balls, eggplant. Now what do you want to drink? A beer? I'm gonna have me a Negra Modelo and I highly recommend it. The trick here, Conrad, is you order up a whole bunch of this stuff 'cause it all comes on these tiny little plates, hardly enough on each to satisfy a jackrabbit . . ."

Within an hour or so, during which the man did almost all the talking, Conrad had let his guard down a bit. He knew, of course, that all the talk, all the stories, were this blind man's way of making him feel included, one of the boys, not just a dumb kid. But he wasn't about to be completely taken in. His antennae were too sharp when it came to adults not to recognize when they had unspoken motives. They never did anything just for itself. They always meant more than they said. Like that cop, Ramirez, the prick—going after him like that, making him . . . Even this deal with the sculptor, helping him with the horse, driving him around, all that. Make a little money, spend time with a real artist, his stepmother had said. Sure. And maybe you'll learn something, shape up, become a better person. That's what she really thought, wasn't it? Why don't they just say it?

Even so, knowing all this, Conrad had to confess that he was enjoying this with another part of himself.

The big sculptor had ordered about fifteen different things for them, and Conrad found several that he liked, including the grilled cactus pads and an olive sauce called tapanade. Mo had ordered three Negra Modelos in all and split them with Conrad, a bit of felonious intimacy. Fred had stopped by on two occasions to chat amiably, standing with her hip shot out and a long slender hand resting on the back of one of the empty chairs, and Conrad felt comfortably included by her. The tall black woman had grown increasingly beautiful in Conrad's eyes, and he longed to touch her—maybe her hand or her arm—to see what black skin felt like. As for anything further that he might have imagined—well, she was deliciously unattainable, an angular, ebony goddess.

Eventually, a guy in a white shirt and black pants with long black hair tied back in a shiny ponytail cleared the last of the little plates and the two beer bottles from the table and Conrad leaned back in his chair, the rich food beginning to make him sleepy. Then someone else, he noticed, was standing in front of the table. He looked up and saw that it was a woman with long brown hair, in a T-shirt and jeans. Hey! It was the woman who'd been outside on the street, near Bowdre's house. She was looking at Bowdre, who was, at the moment, draining his glass, and her hands were fidgeting, fingers crawling over each other. Her face looked tight.

"Uh," she said. "Um . . ."

Bowdre set his glass down and looked up, his eyebrows dancing above the black lenses of his glasses.

"Are you Mo Bowdre? T. Moore Bowdre?"

"That's me."

"The sculptor."

"Right again. What can I . . . ?"

She put her hands on the back of one of the empty chairs and gripped it tightly. Like she was trying to keep her hands still, Conrad thought.

"I'm . . . I'm your . . ." She stopped. Took a big breath. "I'm one of your fans," she said, and the words tumbled out like running water suddenly undammed. "I've seen your work up in Colorado and I was down here, passing through, you know, and was at the opening yesterday, I was walking along and saw it in the window, and . . . well . . . I thought . . ."

The big man was smiling through his blond beard. "It's real nice of you to say hello," Bowdre said. "But you got me at a big disadvantage here. You know who I am, but who are you?"

"My name is Annie. Annie Harper."

"Okay. Hello, Annie Harper." He stuck out a big hand and she shook it. Conrad guessed she was in her twenties, maybe young twenties. "This here is my friend Conrad." She nodded, but didn't take her eyes from the sculptor.

"Could I . . . ?"

"We're just finishing up here," Mo said, "or I'd ask you to join us. Not every day a man meets a fan."

"Oh, no. No. I was just wondering . . . well, this sounds dumb, but could I get your . . . ?" She went silent.

"My autograph? Hah. Hah. Sure."

The woman fished a piece of paper, a pink slip of some sort, out of her green canvas bag and put it on the table.

"Oh, here," she said, and fetched a ballpoint pen out of the bag, putting it beside the pink paper. "There."

Mo's hand found the pen, scrawled his name in big slanted letters on the paper, and set the pen down. She snatched both up from the table.

"Oh, thanks. Thank you. This is . . . this is great." She stood undecided. "Okay, well, I guess I'll go. Thanks."

She turned and walked quickly away, slinging her green bag over her shoulder. Like she was running away almost, Conrad thought.

"Wow," Conrad said.

"Brush 'em away like flies, Conrad," Bowdre said conspiratorially, then laughed his loud staccato laugh. "Let's go." He sat up. "Just kidding about that," he said. "I don't get all that many doting admirers tuggin' at my sleeve. Still puffs me up terrible. Just out of curiosity, would you tell me what she looked like?"

Conrad looked over his shoulder, but the woman, Annie Harper, was long gone.

"Well, she was kind of tall. Not like that waitress, Fred, but tall. Brown hair. Long brown hair. She had blue eyes, I think."

Bowdre laughed. "That's pretty basic, Conrad. What else?"

"She was wearing blue jeans, a black T-shirt," Conrad said. And she had a great figure, Conrad thought, and that T-shirt was pretty tight over it, too. But he didn't know how to say that to Bowdre. In fact, she was a real piece of ass. He had gotten a better look at all that out on the street, up near Bowdre's house where she was on the sidewalk.

"She was . . ." Conrad began, but decided for no particular reason to keep her earlier appearance to himself.

"Okay," Bowdre said, leaning forward with his thick forearms on the table. "Just between us, would you say she was pretty? Plain-lookin'? Or was she plug-ugly?"

"She was pretty, I guess."

"You guess?"

"She was all tense, you know, her face. So it was hard to tell."

Bowdre nodded his head and sat back. "Okay. You see Fred, wave her over. We'll pay up and go home."

Sergeant Anthony Ramirez threw some red chili sauce into the pot that simmered on his stove. It was half full of black beans and rice he'd poured from a package into boiling water. He'd added some Italian sausages he'd found in the refrigerator and cut up into small pieces. Ramirez was not an enthusiastic cook. His imagination ran elsewhere. Normally, all he used the kitchen for was making coffee. He sipped from an icy cold can of Tecate beer, wiped his mouth, and sighed.

An altar. Suppose the petroglyph was an altar. What did that mean? An altar with a flame on it, maybe. Or maybe a football. He snorted. That Frenchwoman, Anjou, suddenly went all taut, all snippy. Like okay, Sergeant, it's time for you to fuck off. No one in his family had any Aztec coming-of-age rites. What the hell had she been talking about? Never mind.

So, maybe an altar.

He thought again about those evangelical cops, the ones with all their ominous talk about Satanism, occult symbols, mocking the Cross. Those guys had been out-and-out phonies, Ramirez was sure of it, running some fundamentalist hang-ups like it was criminology class. Those fundamentalists saw the goatman everywhere: Hey, you don't believe what we believe? Satan's got you, that's why.

But still. An altar with maybe a flame on it. Maybe it was mocking the real altar in some way. Some nut's idea of . . .

Tomorrow they would have to make some kind of statement to the press about all this. He would tell his boss, Lieutenant Ortiz, they shouldn't say anything about the petroglyph. Right now it didn't mean anything. Hell, they only had the word of a kid that it hadn't been there earlier. A sneaky kid's word, what was that worth? And what had the Frenchwoman said, you could read anything into these things. Like a Rorschach test. And God knew the loons in Santa Fe would grab on to something like that. They were already talking about the millennium, the universal *odometer*, taking it's big turn, and the flowering of Aquarius and God knows what. Sure as hell, they'd see an altar there, and the flame, and someone would shout "Satan!" like shouting "Fire!" in a theater, and all hell'd break loose, with the freaks running around, carrying on about demons and evil and witches, fire, brimstone, smoke . . . oh *shit*!

Ramirez smelled smoke, saw smoke. It was billowing up into the room, filling his kitchen. From his beans. His goddamned beans and rice . . .

He dropped his beer on the floor, lunging for the stove.

* * *

I could kill myself. I could really . . . kill myself. I mean, there I was and there he was and I chickened out. Mumbled and stuttered like some little teenager—oh, can I have your autograph?

Jesus.

Christ!

Him and that jerky kid sitting there with all those plates, it must have cost a hundred dollars just for that dinner.

What am I going to do now? Run up and say, oh, sir, I made a mistake. I'm not just a fan of yours. See, I was too embarrassed to . . .

And start mumbling and stuttering again?

Why did you do this to me, Millie, you shit? You old bag of worms. Shut up! Shut up, do you hear me? Don't say that to me, don't say that, don't.

Why don't you listen to me? You never listen, never really listen to me. I'm trying to tell you. Something important. To me. Something important to me, Annie. Me.

I'm trying . . . What do I care? What do I care if you don't listen, you disgusting bag of worms. What do you know, what do you know, what do YOU know? Ohhh, stop. Stop.

Please.

A few miles behind the point where U.S. Route 264 enters Arizona, it passes through Window Rock, the capital of the Navajo Nation. Along its course in Window Rock are two traffic lights, several fast food joints, a motel, and a few other urban signs. It is a dusty place, and much of the land around has been bulldozed of any vegetation, so that large arrays of look-alike government housing could be built for employees of the Navajo government. Once past all this, the two-lane highway begins to rise, passing through a long high stretch forested on either side with ponderosa pines, before descending again into a vast ocean of sagebrush with Navajo settlements—a few so-called towns, but mostly lonely Navajo family camps—along the way.

Far off the highway flat-backed mesas rise here and there in the distance, and occasionally one sees a flock of sheep poking among the scrub, tended by an old woman or perhaps a man on horseback, or even merely a dog. Less frequently, one sees a band of horsemen galloping urgently along a dirt track, headed for a squaw dance where the Navajos will dance into the night around a huge bonfire and, also during the proceedings, identify a witch. Navajo witches, who sometimes take the form of wolfmen and who operate at night, are often reported along this long stretch of Route 264, and Navajos drive there at night only if there is a compelling reason.

Or, Connie Barnes thought, if they've been out drinking. For such reasons, it is a dangerous road, but also the most direct approach from the east to the Hopi Reservation, which is an island within the enormous, impersonal Navajo Reservation that spreads across most of the northeastern corner of the state. As planned, Connie had left Santa Fe early enough to pass through this territory with plenty of light left in the day.

The sun was low on the horizon when the road began its winding descent into Keams Canyon, the small military-style collection of government buildings that is the local headquarters of the Bureau of Indian Affairs, and where the Indian Service hospital is located as well, along with an old school, a trading post, and a gas station. Like most Indian people, the Hopis have ambiguous feelings about the Bureau of Indian Affairs, for it is the vehicle for both a good deal of deserved government funding and a lot of bewildering bureaucratic foolishness. Nevertheless, arriving there from the east is always something of a relief, since one can put the Navajo Reservation and its spooky and dour presence behind. The easternmost of the twelve Hopi villages is only minutes away. One is, essentially, home.

As accustomed as she was to the rational and witchless world of the dominant society, Connie nevertheless always felt uneasy driving through Navajoland. She shared, as well, the longstanding Hopi grudge against the Navajos for turning up in their lives a few centuries earlier and crowding them ever since. But her uneasiness had been compounded during this trip by the increasingly ominous sense she had that she was going to be too late.

Instead of continuing east toward her village after she reached the bottom of the descent into Keams Canyon, she turned right, and moments later parked the old Ford pickup in the hospital's dusty lot. Inside the glass doors of the old yellow building, the reception area was empty. No one was at the desk. The walls seemed to close in on her; so much sadness lingered here.

Here, her grandfather had passed away, in a room down that long corridor. Here, too, her youngest brother had died—a sudden difficulty breathing, a panicky, recklessly high-speed race to Keams, a hubbub, the boy on a gurney, his chest heaving, him turning blue—gone in an instant. A sudden and inexplicable asthma attack, they said. Here, in these halls with the smell of antiseptic and sickness, these things couldn't be forgotten. Even after the ceremonies and the grieving, and the knowledge that they have gone on as they should into the other world, after all the things brought to bear to assuage these passings, the hospital always brought back the immediate horror of loss.

Halfway down the corridor now, Connie heard someone coughing. Then a low sighing. From somewhere came the tinny sound of a katsina dance—drums, bells, a song. A tape recording. Connie saw a nurse emerge from one of the doors along the corridor. A young white woman. She had seen her before, a pleasant-faced woman with short red hair. What was her name? Doris.

"Doris, it's me, Connie Barnes. I'm looking for my— I'm looking for Marvin Tongvaya. He had a heart attack?"

The woman, Doris, turned and smiled. It looked like a sad smile. What did it mean? She knew what it meant. Did it mean . . . ?

"Oh, they took him home. This afternoon," Doris said.

Dead? Did they take him home for . . . ?

"The doctor said he'd be just as well off at home as here if he stayed in bed and took his medicine. His son said he'd make sure of that. Are you . . . well, of course you're going to see him. You can take his hat to him. You know, the one that says 'Big Shot.' They left it here in all the excitement."

An hour later Connie stood in the doorway of the two-room stone house on the outskirts of her village where Marvin Tongvaya and his wife lived. Behind her was the room that served as both kitchen and living room. Besides the old iron cookstove and an oil drum of water fetched from a windmill-driven tank a mile away in the desert, the room contained a kitchen table and three chairs and, in one corner, a cot. On the whitewashed plaster walls were several framed and fading color photographs, mostly of the Tongvaya sons, posed in their military uniforms, but one was of Connie in the robes and hat she had worn at her graduation from the University of Arizona.

Marvin Tongvaya's son Milford now sat at the kitchen table behind her, nursing a mug of thin coffee. His mother stood beside Connie, one old, gnarled hand holding Connie's elbow. Before her now, the second room contained an old double bed with a brass headboard. Beyond the bed, part of the room was curtained off by way of a closet where the old couple kept their few sets of clothes and other possessions, including Marvin's ceremonial paraphernalia. Marvin lay on his back in the bed, tiny under a thick pile of blankets. It was very hot in the house, and Connie felt almost suffocated.

The old man's face was gray, and his white hair was mussed. His deepset eyelids were closed, his mouth slightly open. The face was relaxed, as if in death, but a light wheezing of air—in and out of the open mouth—said otherwise.

"He's sleepin'," said the old woman at her elbow. "He looks a lot better now. That hospital . . ."

Connie stood in the doorway and watched. Her mind

was flooded again with relief, and with old pictures, old scenes in which she played a part. Marvin in his cornfield out north of the village, showing the little girl how to pick the ears of sweet corn from the stalks. Marvin holding the little girl on his lap in his ancient pickup, letting her steer as the truck rattled over a dirt track. Marvin, standing in her mother's house, explaining the role and destiny of a married woman, as Connie, fully grown now, stood in her white, woven robe beside her young husband with whom she lived two more years until he died in a crash on the Winslow Road.

Now the old man stirred and one eyelid fluttered open. Connie grinned, and the other eye opened. He looked over at her and said her Hopi name in a thin whistle of a voice.

"I brought your hat," she said, holding it up. "You forgot it in the hospital."

"That's good," he said almost inaudibly. His eyes closed but he was smiling. "I'll be needin' it when we go pick the corn. Later on. It's growin' real good." His eyes closed and he seemed to be asleep again. "When you gonna marry that white man Mo?" he whispered.

"Mo says you'd better quit chasing the girls so much. It puts a strain on your heart."

The old man giggled. His eyes popped open and he glanced over at her. "He gave me my hat, you know." He nodded and closed his eyes. She heard him begin to snore, a reedy, regular sound, and turned away.

"See," his wife said. "He's gonna be okay."

Tucked away in a niche formed, perhaps accidentally, when a previous owner had added a room onto Mo

Bowdre's house, was an old wind-up Regulator clock that hung on a nail driven into the plaster. Nowadays it gave forth an internal wheeze as it developed the strength to chime, and Mo Bowdre heard it wheeze as he lay in bed. Eleven, he knew already, and listened to the clock's soft *bing-bong* sound eleven times. He had been lying on his back for a half hour, ever since the clock's single *bing-bong* had signaled ten-thirty. He was wide-awake. Several counting tricks had done nothing to create a state of drowsiness.

Upon returning from the restaurant with Conrad, Mo had picked up the message on the answering machine. Connie, calling from the Indian Health Service hospital in Keams Canyon, reported that her uncle had been taken home to the village to recuperate, the crisis evidently over. She would call again, probably not until tomorrow sometime. There was no phone, Mo knew, in either Marvin's house or in Connie's mother's house. She could always call out by using the pay phone at the trading post. Some of the other Hopis had private phones and she could also use one of them. But for him to reach her was entirely another matter. Leaving messages with the other Hopis, asking them to ask Connie, if they saw her, to call him, was about as effective as casting a message adrift in the sea in a bottle.

At such times, Mo felt a bit adrift himself, and given to bouts of hypochondria. A twinge in his leg could, if he allowed his imagination free rein, become a clear-cut case of phlebitis, a sudden clot of blood taking lethal form in his thigh and beginning to move inexorably north where it would soon enough muscle its way into the aorta to sit there implacably while his poor, dear heart, starved of oxygen-rich blood, would heave and struggle in a great spasmodic throe, and he, Mo, in a great agony . . .

And what now was that numb feeling in his arm, his *left arm*?

There was nothing to do but get up and walk around at such times, get on with something, anything. Mo arose from his bed, crossed the room, and wrapped himself in a kimono-style bathrobe. He made his familiar way down the narrow hall, past the guest room where he could hear Conrad breathing deeply in sleep, past the clock, into the living room and out onto the patio, where the temperature dropped about ten degrees and distantly an owl hooted. The patio ran half the length of the house under a portal, and to his left a hammock elaborately handmade of cotton string by Ecuadorians hung from the overhead beams. Connie occasionally napped in the hammock's voluminous folds, and once, Mo recalled vividly, he had heard an odd sound while standing on the patio early one morning and lunged for it, plucking Connie's hungover Hopi cousin from the hammock, to both of their surprise.

Now he listened to the night sounds, thinking it was good that an owl had somehow managed to survive in urban Santa Fe. He did not share the widespread Indian notion that an owl hooting was a bad omen, even a harbinger of imminent death. A dog barked halfheartedly somewhere in the night, and he could hear traffic far off.

Tomorrow he and Conrad would return to Rhiannon Sharp's hacienda, and John Franklin's stables. Kokapelli Arabians, he called the place, after the hunchbacked flute player that was a favored icon in these parts from

Anasazi times right up to the gallery-mediated present. Kokapelli was politely described as a fertility figure, and the actual fertilizing of pueblo ladies was surely something the old flute player thought about, but probably only secondarily, in the manner of a by-product of his main preoccupation. At least, that's how Mo saw it.

There has been times, of course, when the pueblo-dwelling Indians' best weapon against the ravages of drought, or raiding, or other catastrophes such as the onslaught of disease, had been the very fertility of their women, the ability to repopulate their world. How strange, Mo thought scornfully, to think of it in such functional terms—it was the curse of the anthropological mindset, the scholar. But then who was he, Mo Bowdre, to be scornful of a functional approach to such intimate and personal matters? He had, after all, supplemented a meager income at one point in his life by making regular donations to a Denver sperm bank.

Everyone involved in the clinic, he recalled, had been earnest and dreadfully polite, but he had never thought it anything but hilarious that he was now getting paid—not much, mind you, but paid cash money nonetheless—for what his parents in Ruidoso and the fire-eating pastor of the church they attended had so thoroughly disapproved of. *Onanism,* the scrawny old hypocrite would bellow from his pulpit from time to time, as if the very label alone was enough to make its Satanic proportions plain to a twelve-year-old boy whose voice was beginning to change.

Of course, Mo could not know what had been accomplished by the contributions he had made over that six-month period, but he occasionally wondered how many young people who looked a little bit like him might now be seen in the Denver area. It had occurred to him, also, to wonder how he should feel about the possibility that two such beings might meet, fall in love, marry and have children—totally unaware that they were half brother and half sister. This worried him a bit.

At the same time, the implications of his anonymous but widespread sowing of wild oats suggested that he should look upon all children as potentially his and treat them as such. And that reminded him of Conrad. His mind now moving wildly along, but happily no longer in the trough of hypochondria, he wondered what the odds were of John Franklin's first wife having been one of the Denver ladies who applied themselves to the clinic where he ... Had he not heard that Franklin had arrived in Santa Fe after a highly successful career in finance in Denver?

Never mind. The thought was too appalling.

He crossed the lawn, the grass cool on his bare feet, and sat down on the concrete bench where Connie often perched to wait for the morning sun. Marvin, her "father," was still alive. That was a relief. At least a temporary relief. Mo was suddenly struck by the similarity of the Hopi system of having a host of clan fathers and the notion that came to him that all men should be sperm donors, anonymous sires. It suggested a universal male adult responsibility for all children: How would you know if some kid wasn't yours? And at Hopi, virtually every kid was—in some sense—yours.

The owl hooted again, and Mo's mind veered off from

total sentimentality into thoughts of horses and clay. He was aware of the sound of his own relaxed breathing and the distant barking of the dog someone had left out in the yard. He heard a rustling of leaves and felt a breeze on his cheek that came and went like a lover's sigh. The dog stopped barking, and in the night's silence Mo heard yet another sound, nearly imperceptible, less a sound than a rhythm, a regularity. As best he could tell it arose from somewhere to his right, somewhere in his yard, somewhere near Conrad's big Dodge Ram pickup.

He held his own breath and listened for a moment. He opened his mouth and tilted his head back and, with his throat open, tried to mimic the sound, the nonsound in his yard. Again he listened. The rhythmic sound was no longer, but again a breeze sighed overhead, and the dog began its distant barking again. Mo put his hands on his knees.

"Who are you?" he asked quietly in the blackness.

A voice with an oddly familiar timbre, the breathy sound of someone playing the flute, said, "I'm your daughter."

six

Once, years earlier when he was a few years older than Conrad, who was now asleep in his house, a car that Mo Bowdre was driving threw a rod. It had happened without warning, of course, as he started it up after a pause along the highway to take a leak. It was a sudden loud report, part explosion, part the crack of metal on metal. And then a terrible stillness, a terrible silence. At the time, Mo had no idea exactly what had happened, what might have gone wrong under the hood of the car.

Something similar had just gone off in his head, followed by a gargantuan silence. He wondered if he'd had a stroke. But no, he'd heard the voice. It had said, "I'm your daughter."

One of the myriad half clones, maybe? One from the unnumbered array of half brothers and half sisters now roaming Colorado, fruit of myriad female loins artificially inseminated like livestock with the full-strength sperm of the Great Bull of the Rockies, young Mo Bowdre in his very prime, twenty-five dollars a shot in a little paper cup and surely offered on the market at a larger price—a stud fee of grand proportion? But that was all anonymous. The women, he was assured, could never find out who he was. And of course the offspring couldn't. And he would never know, either. It was guaranteed in solemn contract. But the system could have broken down. They might have lied. Or the clinic could have been hit by a freak tornado scattering its records to the winds, the crucial document having been picked up, against all odds, from where it fetched up against a barbed-wire fence miles away in a small East Colorado prairie town, by . . .

"What's your name?" Mo asked into the darkness, unable to think of a more appropriate line of questioning.

"Annie Harper." Breathy, like a flute. Calm. "I met you in the restaurant."

"Your voice doesn't sound right. It sounds different."

"I'm not scared anymore. I was then."

"And you say you're my daughter. Maybe you'll understand that this idea is about as comfortable as a porcupine quill in my—"

"I'm Millie Harper's daughter, too. Remember her?"

Mo's mind skittered into blankness.

"Leadville?" the voice went on. "She lived in Leadville, worked the cafeteria at the Climax mine? I brought my birth certificate."

"How old are you?" Mo asked, his mind suddenly working again. "Exactly."

"Twenty-one. On March eighth."

March. So she'd been conceived in June? Twenty-two years ago, in nineteen . . . damn. That was the summer. The accident. Pictures began to flock into his mind, including a picture of a young woman in a white uniform, kitchen whites, doling out an unrecognizable piece of meat covered in thick gravy, plopping it on his plate, a young woman with brown hair cut short and blue eyes that were like . . . blue eyes like flames in gleaming white, the eyebrows with a special curve to them, a dangerous curve, brazen eyes looking right at him as he held out his plate.

Millie Harper. He had found out her name before being pushed on down the line with his tray.

"People say I look a lot like my mother, just taller," the voice in the night now said. "I've got pictures. But you can't . . . they won't . . . do any good."

"Not for me they won't."

The voice—Annie Harper—sighed.

"Well, now. Just what do we do about this?" Mo asked out loud into the night. He exhaled mightily. "Maybe you should come over here a bit closer. Where are you? Hiding behind that Rambo truck? It's not every damn day in a man's life that he's sitting in the dark in his backyard and someone he never heard of just pops up from behind a damn pickup truck and announces that she's kinfolk. Not even a long-lost offspring, because he never heard a word of such a thing, never knew anyone was lost. What the hell is someone supposed to make of something like this? Suddenly I got a grown daughter? Twenty-one and one-third years old? Why should I believe it?"

"I found you. I found you."

"Well, Jeezus double-H Kee-rist, it's not like I been hiding for twenty-one and a third years. What the hell does that prove?"

"I knew you'd be angry. I guess you hate this. Hate me."

"Hate you? Hell, no. I don't know you from Adam. Or Eve. How could I hate you? That's a personal thing. And I'm not angry. I'm just—this is—well, damn it, I am angry. I need to think."

He heard Annie Harper laugh, hardly more than a whisper. Then she said, "I'm standing right in front of you, about two yards away. There's a near-full moon, and I can see you sitting there with your hands on your knees. I'm going to sit down on the grass." He heard her do that.

"It's wet," he said. "The ground. The lawn gets watered."

"It's okay. Do you remember my mom? Millie?"

Yes, he remembered. He remembered Millie Harper, and also Johnny Budd, whom he saw only the one time, Budd the local hero, the skier. He remembered the fascination of her blue eyes, the billowing urgency of pursuit, the certainty that he, by dint of superior devotion, natural charm, and sheer will, would prevail.

By the time the day shift ended in the mine, the sun had gone down behind the mountain to the west. And they trooped off into the mine each morning before the sun appeared above the mountain to the east. For six days a week they didn't see the sun.

At four-thirty each day his shift was over, the whistle sounded, the little trains hauled mud-covered men, silicon-dust-covered men out of the spiderweb of dank tunnels called drifts and hauled another shift in, the swing shift, which was followed by the night shift. The burrowing never paused.

Shedding heavy rubber boots and hard hats with miner's lights mounted in them, they would trudge out of the main drift and downslope to barracks located here and there on dirt crossroads in the ramshackle unipurpose town erected by the Climax Molybdenum Company right on the slope of the mountain they were gutting. Utilitarian buildings of wood were laid out on a grid, around the huge industrial installations—mills, power plants—it was a study in perfect ugliness. Off to the north and well within sight lay a small sea of poisonous-looking, greenish-white tailings, utterly flat, utterly dead.

In the barracks, Mo showered, shaved, put on clean clothes, and proceeded downslope again to the huge dining hall where, the night before, he had discovered Millie Harper behind the counter with her ladle and her shining and dangerous blue eyes. It was only his third day at the mine. Everything seemed alien, otherwordly, disorienting. His very breath came hard at eleven thousand feet. Everything was strange but this wonderful-looking girl upon whom he immediately hung his dreams.

As he approached in the line, shoving his plastic tray along the metal bars, she looked his way, spotted him, and her eyes lit up with a mirthful gleam. She was glad to see him!

He kept his eyes on her, and she would glance up at him and away from her ladling chore, suppressing a smile, which opened up when he arrived before her station, her metal tureen sunk into the counter, filled with amorphous lumps of meat labeled Salisbury steak. He made a joke, a silly country-boy joke, she laughed, he added yet another silly remark . . .

They danced. That night they danced. He was no dancer, but they danced—a wild, athletic swirling around the empty room, bare floor, bare walls, only a tape deck plugged into the wall, a cooler of beer in the corner. Her place. A local, she evidently had the pull to get one of the company "apartments," two small rooms, one with a railway kitchen. She'd get some furniture later, she said. For now, she had a thin mattress on the floor, her clothes in the closet in the other room with the railway kitchen.

She was no dancer either, but they swirled and tripped, and laughed, his boots clomping on the wooden floor, the hell with anyone below, and sat sprawl-legged on the floor against the wall to get their breath and drink a beer, and with his eyes he devoured her, her short brown hair the color of burley tobacco, the blue eyes, a small sharp nose over full red lips with a mischievous upturn, the full bosom in a loose white shirt, the nicely packed jeans. He committed every detail to memory, and they told each other stories about themselves, the wonderful stories that make one laugh.

Sometime around midnight it became time for him to go, an unspoken mutual recognition. He stood in the doorway, a little unsteady on his feet, and she reached her face up and gave him a soft kiss good night. He stood as still as a post, and the kiss continued, two faces reaching across a narrow gap, touching. After what could have been a minute, or three minutes, they reached for each other, tentative hands on each other's waists, and he stayed on another hour while they kissed and groped in storm-driven desperation, on their knees on the floor, facing each other, not a word spoken, only gasping and laughter, until she had to squirm and, as if in pain, said, "Oh, no, oh no, oh God. I can't. We can't."

And so they parted sometime thereafter, unslaked, and Mo made his uncertain way in the ugly streetlight along the dirt roads and upslope to his barracks with an excruciating ache in his groin misnamed lover's nuts, and the certainty in his soul that he, with this new love—he, with this light of his life—he, with unfaltering devotion and irresistible charm, would surely, one of these nights before long, score.

And he did. They did. In rapturous abandon, the very next night, they scored, she overcoming whatever it was that had held her back. They never danced again. Instead, for five straight nights, they headed directly, purposely, voraciously for the narrow mattress on the floor in the other room, and Mo was convinced that it was going to last forever.

Some of the men in the mine were locals, too—most were out-of-staters, Okies, hardly up to the rigors of the work and the altitude—and the locals knew of Millie Harper, and they knew of Johnny Budd, the local legend, the skier, the downhill racer who was Millie's betrothed and had gone off—somewhere like Europe—for the Olympic trials, a daring, reckless boy, they'd seen him go flat-out sixty down a vertical slope. The boy was fearless, they explained to Mo.

And indeed, Millie went quiet one night when they lay sweaty on the narrow mattress, then spoke of him, confessing how guilty she felt. For she was waiting for

Johnny Budd to return from Europe and surely a triumph on the slopes. They had talked of getting married before the actual Olympics, so she could go with him, but he'd been out of touch now for a month and was late coming back, and he, Mo, was just ... well, it was too overwhelming, and she clutched him around the shoulders and wept, and he comforted her, knowing the rightness of things. He had prevailed over the local boy.

Then on Sunday afternoon in early July, in a privately owned hamburger place next to the post office, the highest post office in the United States, located across the highway from the Climax installation, the local hero appeared. He was just returned from the slopes of Austria, now a chosen member of the U.S. Olympic team, one of eight who would carry the American flag in the downhill racing event the following year. He was famous, famous. He'd come home to claim the glory he was due from the people who lived in the area, and thus to put this remote outpost on the map. He also returned to reclaim the embrace of Millie Harper. Mo saw him in the hamburger place—it was his day off, and Millie had said she needed to spend the day with her mother in Leadville. Johnny Budd was a kid, maybe twenty, twenty-two—younger than Millie. He was of middle height with a shock of blond curls, a small and wiry Adonis with a smirk, standing amid his friends with the belligerent grace of a big fish in a small pond, and Mo felt equal to the challenge.

But he'd already lost. Millie had quit the job in the cafeteria that morning. Her empty apartment was already taken over by a sour-faced mining engineer. This was the

Fourth of July, Independence Day. Without so much as a word, Millie disappeared. His entire grand passion had lasted but a week, and by the next day Johnny Budd was gone as well. They said he'd whisked her off to northern Idaho, where there was still snow.

Bewildered, Mo stayed at the mine, slogging in and out of the mountain six days a week, drinking hard with the reckless men of the mine at night in the Silver Dollar Saloon in Leadville some fifteen miles away, lost in the jocular despair of men who toil underground, when the accident happened and the world went permanently dark. For a long time, all that had come before—the world when it had light and color—disappeared from Mo's purview, and with it the momentary swelling of his soul that had been Millie Harper.

Oh, yes, he remembered her. Now he remembered her. And now it struck him that never had he seen her in the light of the sun.

"I've never seen anyone sit so still so long. You're like a rock."

The flutelike voice. He could hear this voice talking softly in his ear, Millie's voice, the mother's voice as they clung in the dark on the thin and narrow mattress.

"Whatever happened to Johnny Budd?" Mo asked.

"My mother and him—they got married in Idaho where he was practicing. Then he threw her out when he found out she was pregnant."

"Why?"

"Because he knew it wasn't—I wasn't—his."

"How'd he know that?"

She laughed. "Johnny Budd shot blanks." She paused, and Mo let it sink in. His grand, passionate week in June. Live ammunition, sandwiched in (no doubt) between sterile fusillades—the thought struck him that he *had* won in one sense, beat the smirking little hero at his own game.

He felt ashamed at the thought.

"He broke his leg after he sent Mom off, never did get to the Olympics. Served him right. He started drinking after that, and killed himself in a car crash somewhere up north."

"And what about Millie? Your mother?"

"She came back. To Leadville. By then everyone could see she was pregnant and everyone figured it was Johnny Budd's kid. She didn't let on otherwise. Maybe she thought it would do me some good, being thought of as the daughter of the fallen local hero, I don't know."

"Did it?"

She laughed, a snort. "Not that I know of."

"And Millie? Your mother?"

"She married a guy when I was about three, an engineer in the mine. I don't remember him. He left in two years, went back to Louisiana, she told me. He was kind of rough on her and she was glad to see him go. Then she married another guy, ran the drugstore in Leadville. He was a lot older. He had some disability pay from the mine, too—silicosis. He helped raise me when I was a girl, but he died. Lungs gave out. I was fifteen. So Mom and I lived there by ourselves till now."

Mo crossed his arms over his chest and breathed

deeply. He was, all of a sudden, exhausted, tired to the very bone.

"She used to talk about you. About how dumb she'd been, going off that way, not even saying anything to you. Somebody sent her a clipping from the newspaper, when you had that sculpture show at the Amex place, and she kept it in a box of hers, full of souvenirs. And she had some later clippings, too. I've got 'em here."

"And you say you look like her," Mo said.

"Yeah. People say that. Same hair, but mine I wear long. Same eyes. Blue. But I'm a lot taller. Five-ten. I guess I got my height from you."

Oh shit, Mo enunciated to himself.

"Frankly . . ." he said out loud, and started over. "To be perfectly frank and plain here, I don't know what the hell I—I mean we—are supposed to do about this. I don't mean to be insulting or anything, but this is a shock and a half, and if it's true, it really changes things."

"Yeah, I guess it does."

"And I don't . . . I haven't had much time to . . ."

"My stepfather, his name was Joe, Joe Griffin. He used to say that if there was something you couldn't handle, sleep on it." She laughed again. "He used to sleep a lot."

Mo wondered why that was, but didn't ask. He wanted to put some kind of end to this, at least temporarily.

"Oh, well, it *is* late. Where are you staying?"

"Uh . . ."

"Oh. There's this kid, Conrad, in the spare room. He's staying here to help me out while Connie's gone."

"Connie's your wife?" The voice sounded eager.

"For all intents and purposes, yes. We got a big sofa in

the living room. You can roll up in a blanket on that. We can get all this straightened out in the morning."

"When does Connie get back?"

"Don't know exactly. A few days. Why?"

"I want to meet her. She's sort of my stepmother."

Oh shit, Mo said again to himself. How was he going to tell Connie about all this when he couldn't even get a proper phone call to her? Oh, hello, honey, your step-daughter just arrived . . . No, mine . . . Well, you see, a long time ago . . .

Great. Just great.

Mo stood up abruptly. He strode across the lawn and into the house with the girl. Woman? His daughter? Annie Harper following close behind. In the hallway he fetched a blanket from an open shelf, returned to the living room and dropped it on the sofa.

"So, is that going to be okay?" he said.

"Fine."

"Okay."

He turned, took a step toward the archway that led to the hall and stopped.

"Good night," he said. "I'll see you in the morning."

"Good night," she said. The fluty, breathy voice. Jesus. He padded down the hall, hearing Conrad snoring from his room, and got into bed.

His mind was in a turmoil. He could almost feel a physical swirling in his skull, and then a single thought presented itself, like an idiot tugging at his sleeve: I never did turn on the lights for her in there.

seven

At eight-thirty on Monday morning, Anthony Ramirez appeared at the door of his superior's office. Lieutenant Ortiz was a long thin man with a sorrowful look permanently etched into his face, a look that a drooping black mustache did nothing to gainsay. He looked up at Ramirez's tap on the door frame. The sergeant was holding a few sheets of fax paper in his hand.

"M.I. report?" Ortiz said.

"Yeah." Ramirez entered the office and sat down in one of the two chairs in front of the lieutenant's desk. "You want to read it?"

"Later. Tell me about it. Who were they?"

"No ID yet. We're running the dental. Maybe something there. Fluoride in the water, in toothpaste—it really messes things up, you know? Look, Ma, no cavities."

"Yeah, yeah. No cavities, no dental records. So . . ."

"And no arrests, no fingerprints." Ramirez put the fax papers on Ortiz's desk and sat back. "Okay, the male was an Anglo, late teens, maybe twenty. No identifying marks. The female was the same age about, three months pregnant. Indian."

"Oh, man. Pueblo? Navajo?"

"No, India Indian. Like from India, or one of those places. Pakistan, Bangladesh."

Lieutenant Ortiz's tongue darted out and teased his mustache. "And of course we're not so lucky that there's been anyone like that reported missing." He paused. "Cause of death?"

"Like they said yesterday, those nails in the ear."

"You ever heard of anything like that?"

Ramirez shook his head.

"Like some kind of ritual thing," Ortiz said. *"Merde!"* He leaned back in his chair, put his hands behind his neck and looked at the ceiling. "What about marks on the bodies?"

"You mean besides the eyes and genitalia? The M.I. says that had to have been scavengers. Buzzards on the eyes, probably a coyote on the genitalia. Maybe dogs. Besides that, no marks."

"No signs of a struggle? No rope marks or anything?"

"No."

Ortiz sat forward abruptly. "No one's just gonna sit there and let someone drive a nail into his head, for Christ's sake."

"No, they were high. Maybe out. The M.I. found stuff." He reached for the fax papers and lifted up the first page. "They both had this stuff in their blood, some in their stomachs. It's called a psilocybic fungus. A mushroom. You ever heard of that?" He looked up, and Lieutenant Ortiz simply stared at him. "Psychoactive. It's called, let's see, *Stropharia semiglobata*. The book on it says the incubation period—like after it's ingested—is a half hour, maybe an hour. Then it gives you visions, hallucinations for four to six hours. Kids use it. It's real easy to get."

"How so?"

"It grows on manure, cow manure, horse manure in the spring and into summer. M.I. says the amount these kids had in 'em would have made 'em almost comatose."

"What, do they eat it? Chew it?"

"I guess. This stuff was apparently mixed in with something else. Lunch, or dinner. Meat—lamb, they think. Rice. They hadn't metabolized it all."

"Like Pakistan," Ortiz said, "or one of those places."

Ramirez shrugged.

"So, do you figure these kids were in some cult or something? Psychoactive mushrooms, ritual stuff? It looks that way, huh?"

Ramirez told him about the petroglyph that Conrad Franklin thought was new, and about his conversation with Dr. Anjou.

"An altar?" Ortiz said.

"Maybe an altar. With a flame on it. Or maybe a football, Anjou said. You can read anything into these things, she said. You remember those assholes from New Jersey with the Satan stuff? Saw it everywhere? One of their observations was that these people use symbols that sort of mock the Christian symbols. Setting fire to an altar . . ."

"You going to call them?"

"The assholes?"

Ortiz nodded.

"I guess so," Ramirez said.

Ortiz leaned back again in his chair and it squeaked. "So what are we doing about suspects? You said that Franklin kid hangs out there at the site, snuck back when you were—"

"He's the one says the petroglyph is new."

"So what? Is he a member of a cult or anything? Maybe he's playing games."

"There aren't any tracks around the site, but he left his in plain sight the night he snuck out to look. . . ."

"So he was careful one day, careless another. Maybe he lost it. You gonna bring him in?"

Ramirez looked at the wall to his left, where the lieutenant had a new poster encouraging personal safety and not acting like a victim. IT'S UP TO YOU, the poster said, which Ramirez thought was bullshit. It's up to us. The cops.

"It's a little early for that," he said. "I'm hoping for an ID."

"Okay," Ortiz said. "Any great ideas about that?"

"I asked the APD's artist to reconstruct a face on the woman. Maybe someone will recognize her. Put it on TV, maybe."

"What about the male?"

"Him, too. But he's Anglo. Half of everybody in New Mexico is Anglo. But there can't be many people from India. There's only fifteen thousand people in the state who aren't Anglo, Hispanic, Indian, or black. Most of them are Chinese and all those places. Probably aren't more than a thousand people from India, if that."

"Okay, good luck," Ortiz said. "And, aside from that,

the police are not making any details available at this stage in their ongoing investigation, right? Blah, blah."

Ramirez stood up. "Yeah. No details beyond what was already on the news last night—two bodies, male and female, discovered in an arroyo within the city limits. Nothing more to say until further notice. We should put that on tape. Play it to the press over a loudspeaker every four hours."

Mo Bowdre smelled something delicious. It was wafting through the little window high up in the gray stone wall of his cell where they had put him after the arraignment. He couldn't remember what he was in for, something awful he had done. The cot he was lying on was too narrow, too hard. Was that coffee he smelled?

He woke up, in his own bed, yes, and turned on his side.

"I brought you some coffee. I thought you were already awake. You were talking."

It was that woman, his . . . Annie. Annie Harper. He hoisted himself up on his elbow, reached over to the bed table, found his dark glasses and shoved them quickly on his face.

"I talk in my sleep sometimes."

"I didn't see any sugar near the coffee machine so I figured you take it black. Here."

Mo held out one big paw and took the mug she put against his fingers, thinking that this Annie Harper was a regular little detective, wasn't she? He felt a little bit hemmed in, naked as a mule under the covers with a strange woman in his room who said she was a daughter.

"I'll make some breakfast," Annie Harper said. "Bacon,

eggs, toast? It's all there. Conrad is still zonked. Shall I wake him up? Yeah, why not? It's almost nine o'clock."

Mo heard her walk to the door, the sound of bare feet on tile, and the door closed.

Well now, he thought, you just make yourself right at home. Don't let me get in the way or anything. And, he asked himself, what the hell am I going to do about all this?

Rhiannon Sharp felt like the most appalling sneak thief, invading Conrad's privacy like this. But she'd always had success following her instincts, those sudden insights or thoughts that appeared in her mind. She was filled with several kinds of dread now—dread at seeing yet again all the ghastly decorations Conrad put up in his room, the posters with violent rockers or rappers or whatever, photographed to look like one of those awful science fiction movies, the death's heads and the other morbid iconography of the teenager's culture. They do grow out of it, don't they?

She dreaded also having to see what an unholy mess the place was—it was so *typical*. But she dreaded most what she thought she might find, what she had come in to see about. And there it was, among the handful of science fiction novels, mostly paperback, on the shelf of the table beside his bed. A thick paperback, a bit taller than the surrounding ones.

She walked over to the bed, pulled the covers up over the three mussed pillows and sat down. A pain shot through her hip and down her leg, the sciatic nerve acting up again. She straightened out the leg, lifted it, bent the knee, and straightened it out, lowering the leg to the ground. It was no use.

She reached for the book and slipped it out from the others. A magazine that had been resting on top of the books fell behind them. Probably *Playboy* or *Penthouse* or one of those . . . yes. She glowered for a moment at the perfectly tanned fanny that peeked out from between the books where the one she held in her hand had been. Testicles, she snorted to herself, and shook her head. They shouldn't drop until age thirty.

She thumbed through Conrad's paperback copy of Crowley's *The Book of the Law*.

She had seen it in bookstores, shelved among the other books by New Age prophets—Madame Blavatsky, Edgar Cayce. Those she had read, even enjoyed and found comfort in, but she was more inclined to focus on her own personal connections to the spiritual world than take anyone else's prescribed path.

She hadn't read the Crowley book, but knew what it was: the book that laid the foundation for the modern Satanists, awful ravings in convoluted language. She couldn't imagine Conrad plowing through its turgid prose. She thumbed the pages again. At least there were no underlinings. No marks. But it had been read. The spine was crinkled.

She wished she hadn't come into Conrad's room. Wished she hadn't seen this book, touched it, made her sudden thought real, true. Of course, it didn't necessarily mean . . . It didn't mean anything.

That police sergeant seemed to discount the idea of a cult involved in those murders. The mutilations were the work of predators, scavengers, he said. God, I hope so, she thought. I hope there's nothing . . .

"Now what do I do?" Rhiannon Sharp said out loud. It made no sense whatever, bringing it up with the boy's father. John had pretty nearly totally disassociated himself from his son. There was no telling what he would do. Probably just wave a hand in irritation, even contempt. Maybe she should find a way to mention it to Mo Bowdre when he came out to work on the horse. But why do that? She squeezed her thigh and answered her own question. "Nothing. I'll do nothing."

She slipped the book back in its place on the shelf and painfully arose from the bed. It was Monday, one of Flora's days to come. She would make sure Flora stripped the bed, put the sheets and all these damned clothes into the washer. Maybe dust the place. God, what a mess.

With a small and annoying shudder, she looked around the room again, looking for exactly what, she wasn't sure. Strange objects? Bizarre ritual paraphernalia? She looked again at the shelf in the bed table. As if acting on its own, her arm snaked out and she snatched the book from the shelf. With it in her hand, she left the room and closed the door behind her.

Marvin Tongvaya's eyelids had fluttered open once more, perhaps to take in the beams in the ceiling above him, perhaps seeing nothing. He had been humming one of the katsina songs for almost ten minutes, lying on his back in the middle of the double bed. He hummed so quietly that the song would have been inaudible to anyone farther than a few feet from the bed. Then he stopped humming, his eyelids opened, and the dark brown irises, dull with the years, seemed to gleam. They closed and he stopped breathing.

His wife watched this last moment and her own eyes filled with tears. She sat motionlessly on the slat-backed wooden chair for a long time, her lips moving soundlessly, looking at the old face half sunken in the pillow. In its creases and crannies, its sunken jaw and almost transparent skin of his temples, she could see as well the face when it had been young, rounder, with a defiant chin and a dazzling white smile, always at the ready: a half century it had been, even more.

She heard a knock on the door in the next room and began to rise from the chair, pushing downward on the seat with one hand.

"Come in," she said, and realized that no one could have heard her. "Come in, come in," she said, loudly this time. She reached the doorway to the next room and saw Connie coming toward her, saw Connie's face register what had happened, and held out her arms. The two women embraced and burst into tears. Long, drawn-out moans filled the house, and soon neighboring women had heard them and come to the house and joined the sorry chorus. In due course, as if on some exterior signal, they all took a deep breath, the moans subsided, and the women allowed the welcome array of practical measures, now called for, to take over their minds.

He would have to be buried within four days, of course, so that his spirit could successfully move away, move on to join the katsinas, perhaps to become a cloud.

This meant, among other things, that his son who lived in Phoenix and his daughter, who taught at the Indian school in Riverside, California, would need to be notified immediately so they could return for the vigil. The night before he was returned to the earth, he would be put in the same position in which he had dwelled in his mother's womb. Wrapped in a shroud of blankets, he would sit through the night while his family waited with him. His nephews and others, including Connie, would feed him cornmeal—spirit food—and tell stories, and when dawn arrived, they would take him to the cemetery. All these things would have to be arranged, and there were, as well, some of the white man's requirements— proper notification of the proper offices. The details of such a thing were known to everyone, and following them with great care, with prayerful precision, was part of the procedure by which one came to say goodbye with gladness and appreciation.

Connie drove the old pickup through the village to the tribal headquarters. There she reported the death to a woman in the tribal secretary's office and borrowed one of the office phones, reaching the son in Phoenix and leaving word for the daughter in California. She hated that the daughter would have to learn of this via a message, but the young woman at the other end of the line said the news would be broken gently and probably would not come as too great a surprise. The school had been praying for the old man for two days at all its assemblies.

Then Connie dialed her own number, which rang three times.

"Hello."

"Mo, it's me."

"Ahh. How's Marvin?"

"He . . . He's gone. This morning."

"Oh, Connie—"

"He was singing."

"Singing? Well, that's good. I'm real sorry, real sorry."

"We're going to bury him as soon as his daughter can get here from California. Probably Wednesday. Or Thursday."

"Yeah."

"Maybe you can come?"

"Don't see why not. Where are you calling from? This connection's free of the usual rodent attacks."

"The tribal office."

"Are you okay?"

"Oh, yes. I'm okay. I feel kind of orphaned, you know? How are you doing?"

"Fine. I miss you. And . . ."

"And? What? Conrad any trouble?"

"He's fine. You're okay, right, Conrad? Yeah, he's fine."

"He's right there."

"Yup."

"So you can't really talk. Is he driving you crazy?"

"Oh, no."

"You sound a little, you know, upset."

"Well, we're all fine here. I'm sorry about Marvin."

"You can't talk about it now?"

"Uh, no. Best not."

"Mo . . ."

"Nothing I can't handle. Don't you worry. You just take care of things there. I guess there's a lot to do. You think you'll be able to call later?"

"I'll try around five."

"Okay. Give my condolences, and all."

"Okay, 'bye."

"I love you. 'Bye."

Connie put the receiver down and stared at it. Mo hardly ever said that. Neither did she, of course. Two totally different traditions—Hopi and redneck—but both similarly reticent about expressing such things.

"Hey," Annie Harper said as Mo hung up the phone. "You didn't tell her about me."

Conrad Franklin, who was standing in the doorway to the hall, looked over at her. She was sitting cross-legged and barefoot on the red sofa, piling her long brown hair up on her head. She had a barrette in the corner of her mouth like a toothpick and was staring at Bowdre with bright eyes that seemed almost on fire. Conrad had a hard time not looking directly at her breasts, which pressed against the front of a plaid lumberjack-type shirt. The big sculptor sat like a block of stone in a huge chair that had been made from what looked like dozens of pieces of tortured silver driftwood.

"Her father just died," Mo snapped. "She's got plenty to mull over already." Then he softened, relaxed his body in the big chair. He explained the Hopi clan father connection and concluded, "She and this old man were 'specially close. So this is a 'specially bad time for her."

Annie had secured her hair on top of her head, all but

one long piece that hung down beside her cheek. "Sure," she said. "I understand." She twiddled the strand of hair in her fingers. "I just would have felt better if you hadn't said I was unimportant."

"I didn't say you were unimportant," Mo protested.

"Well, you didn't include me in the things that *are* important. She lost a father of some kind, sure, but I just found mine. After twenty-one years. I think that's important." Annie's eyes burned bright against the whites, and even Conrad was distracted by them.

"Our first fight," Mo said with a laugh. His weird staccato burst sounded to Conrad more like a growl than laughter.

"I'm not *kidding*," Annie said. "I mean this is scary for me, and—" Her eyes watered over. "—and it makes me feel lousy to have you . . . I know you'd rather not even believe it."

"Now, let's hold it right there, Annie, I don't have any intention of making you feel lousy. I don't want to make anybody feel lousy. Not you, and not Connie, either. I can see this would be scary for you, and maybe you can see it would be, well, confusing for me. . . ."

Suddenly, Annie uncoiled from the sofa and was on her knees beside the big man's legs. She put a hand on his knee, withdrew it, and put it back, saying, "Oh, oh, I hate it that I'm making a mess of things, I just *hate* it. . . ."

The big man lifted his hands and gestured indecisively, as if he were waving flies away. Then one hand slowly descended and he touched her hair. "This ain't a mess. It's a—well, it *is* a bit of a mess, isn't it? Like a ball of yarn the cat got to. So we just have to straighten it all out, one strand at a time . . . See?"

"I *need* you to understand. . . ." Annie pleaded, almost a wail. Her grip was tight on Mo's knee and her eyes were watering, and Conrad, not one to suffer emotional outbursts with anything but horror, fled into the kitchen and out the back door onto the lawn. He walked across the grass, beyond the stone mill house that was Bowdre's studio, and paused beside the bank of the narrow stream that slipped by in the shade.

Weird, he thought, discovering you had a father when you're as old as Annie. A new father anyway, a real one, not a stepfather. Weird, not knowing who your real father was all those years, thinking it was someone else, some dead guy. What was she going to call him—Daddy? Pop? She didn't call him anything right now.

Watching the water slip by, the rippled patterns in the sandy bottom clear as ice, Conrad contemplated Annie's situation as an extension of his own. Naturally enough, he felt more comfortable thinking about himself. He, too, had no idea what he was supposed to call him— Mr. Bowdre? Mo? Conrad realized that he didn't even have any name or label for the man in his thoughts. Just him. He could ask him. He could say, what should I call you? He could do that, but he probably wouldn't. What difference did it make?

He thought about his own father dismissively. An asshole. A perfect asshole. Conrad recalled a joke he'd heard about some guy who gets hemorrhoids and his friends hear about it and say, oh, really, I thought he was a perfect asshole.

Conrad smirked and watched the water slip by and thought it might be cool to find out your father wasn't your father, some other guy was.

"The National Crime Information Center? That sounds a bit—well—drastic, doesn't it?"

"It's just routine," Tony Ramirez said. "One of the sources you check. There's the motor vehicle division, the state cops, the vital records division . . ."

"Vital records?"

"Get a copy of the birth certificate."

The two men were sitting at their customary table in the bar at Maria's. The place bustled with patrons, and the sound system was giving forth with its third instrumental version of "Maria" from *West Side Story*. It was barely audible over the bubbling of conversation and the clatter of dishes being served.

Earlier, deep in perplexity, Mo had called his friend at the police station and suggested lunch. Ramirez, who often liked to review the details of some of his cases with the big sculptor, accepted. Mo Bowdre's mind worked differently than most, maybe because he was an artist, and it was often helpful to see where a few details might lead him. Maybe also it was because he was happy to be a bullshitter.

Mo had asked Conrad to give him a ride to the restaurant—business, he explained, something he couldn't get out of—and the three of them had ridden through the traffic in Conrad's Rambo pickup, which Annie said she thought was cool, really cool. They dropped him on the sidewalk in front of Maria's and headed for the shops off Guadalupe Street, not far from the plaza, where, among other things, Annie wanted to find some shoes to wear instead of her cowboy boots. Her little emotional storm had passed as quickly as a June cloud across the sun, and Mo had listened to her talk about her life in Leadville, Colorado, for about a half hour.

Pausing on the sidewalk outside the restaurant for a moment, Mo had his own cloud pass over. He wasn't being totally straight about all this. He had avoided telling Connie about Annie's arrival in his life—their life, for it was Connie's life, too. And he avoided telling the kids he was meeting Ramirez. Conrad, who had been pretty badly mortified by Ramirez's questioning, would surely have found it seditious, and Annie in her fragile state would no doubt have been upset to think he was going to check up on her with the help of a cop. So he had avoided saying who he was meeting, and now he felt gritty about being deceptive.

But, goddamn it, he said to himself, and without completing the thought, went inside and found Ramirez. After ordering a beer—Ramirez was sipping ice tea in a burst of professional propriety—Mo explained about Annie's arrival and her contention that he was her father. The timing was right, Mo said, but how did one find out the truth in such things? How did one know?

Ramirez had, of course, explained that all Mo needed was a strand of her hair and a DNA analysis could be arranged. It was expensive and took a few weeks but it was as conclusive as one could get this side of consulting God.

Yeah, well, maybe, Mo had mumbled, thinking of yet further deceptiveness, him plucking a strand of hair from her while—what?—pretending to comfort her with a paternal pat on the head? Or groping around the place on the sofa where she had sat, trying to feel a loose hair? Or actually saying, okay, Annie, let's do this DNA deal, just so we both can be certain about this, um, wonderful new possibility in our lives?

What else can you do? he asked, and Ramirez mentioned the National Crime Information Computer as one of the numerous places where the county, the state, and the national governments kept track of people.

"She has her birth certificate," Mo said. "Brought it with her."

"She give it to you?"

"Why would she do that? She knows I can't read it. She seems perfectly comfortable about me being blind, by the way. A lot of people don't know how to act."

"She could give it to you so someone could look at it for you."

Mo took a long drink from his beer.

"Okay, so what do you find on the birth certificate?" he asked. "That she was born at the right time, like she says, about nine months after the middle of June. My guess is that the mother put down the name of that skier, Johnny Budd, as the father. That was the deception at the time. Anyway, if there's no father around, don't they just take the mother's word for it? She could put anyone down."

"It's just part of the way you confirm that someone's telling the truth—about the timing, in this case. You see if there's a pattern of truth there. You see if she's got any traffic convictions, any minor infractions, any big ones, arrests. If she's one of these wild kids, you can be doubtful. If she's not, if she's been real tame, maybe she's legit, believable."

"What else?"

"You check out the high school, get her transcript, college, too, if she went, talk to her teachers. Places of employment. All that."

"She didn't go to college. Worked for a couple of years waiting tables at the Silver Dollar Saloon." Mo shook his head. "That's where I used to go drinking years ago. Swinging doors and all." He shook his head again. "She doesn't seem to have gotten out of the mountains much. A real local girl. And she could turn out to be a model kid," Mo said. "Goody-goody-two-shoes, and still be wrong. She could have been misled."

"Right. Ideally, you talk to the mother—is she alive?—and her doctor, you know, the OB-GYN. Even the mother could have been misled. Like how does anyone know this skier guy actually was sterile? That could be checked. He must have had a lab test somewhere or how would he know?"

Mo leaned back and laughed. "Hah. Hah. So this is what you police dicks do all day? I thought you led a life of adventure, action, stuff blowing up in the streets, rushin' up staircases shouting 'Freeze!' "

Conversation at the nearby tables stopped for a moment. Mo looked around blankly and smiled.

"Doing the people's work," Ramirez said, "is very rewarding."

"What, do I hire a private detective?" Mo asked.

"I can get some of it for you. DMV, all the criminal checks, vital statistics. Take a day or two. It's a start. Hey, are we going to eat? I'll flag down Viola next time she wiggles through this way."

"I'm in your debt."

"So buy lunch."

"The chief won't mind?"

"The chief is playing golf with the archbishop and their friend the real estate developer."

"Bless them."

Viola the waitress arrived at the table, with a tray under her arm, her little pad in the other hand, and a goofy smile on her face. She was short, with a wondrously round figure and a gold wedding band, and Ramirez thought in an abstract way how lucky some guy was to roll himself up in all that every night. She took their orders—green chili stew, Mo asking for "a double"—and bustled off.

"So how do you feel?" Ramirez asked.

"About what?"

"Being a father."

"I don't know that I am. That's what we're talking about."

"Sure, but if you are . . ."

"I don't know yet."

"You don't know what?"

"How I feel! What do I know about being a father, for God's sake?"

"You had one."

"No, actually, I was born by parthenogenesis. An immaculate conception. You are looking at—"

"Okay, okay," Ramirez said. "I withdraw the question. You want to hear about my little problem?"

"What? Acne? A yeast infection? See, now that I'm in charge of these kids, I think about stuff like that. Hah. Hah."

"One of your kids is my problem, as a matter of fact." Ramirez told him about Lieutenant Ortiz's suggestion that they pull Conrad in, that maybe the kid was playing a weird game with the petroglyph bit, maybe he'd lost it the other night and left tracks where he hadn't before. Maybe he was one of these spoiled rich kids who get so bored they get into bad stuff like dope, hallucinogenic mushrooms, cults.

"That boy could be all of that," Mo said. "But I don't think he's got the gumption in him to do something violent. Got the personality of a rag doll. Raggedy Andy with hip-hop pants and a sour puss. He's probably just as sneaky as any kid his age, but I can't see him playing an ingenious cat-and-mouse game with the police, like one of those Russian novels, taunting you by showing you a clue that he put there. He did me a drawing of that petroglyph, by the way."

"A drawing?"

"Etched in a clay tablet. Like cuneiform. You know, like Babylon. Strange-looking thing. What do you think it is?"

Ramirez told him about his conversation with Dr. Anjou.

"An altar," Mo said. "A burning altar."

"Like mockery. Mocking God."

Viola appeared again, tray on high, and off-loaded three bowls of green chili stew. "Your double, Mo. How are your drinks?"

After she left, Mo asked who the victims were, and listened thoughtfully as Ramirez explained what was in the M.I. report. Anglo and India Indian. The pregnancy. The nails. The remains of psilocybic mushrooms.

"So what do you think?" Ramirez asked.

"And you say they were laid out side by side, all formal like?"

"Like a ritual thing."

"These details get out and everyone in town will be seeing brimstone in it, cloven feet and the stink of goats. Satan right in their backyards, doing obscene things in the night."

"You're telling me."

"And you think old Conrad, the walking noodle, could be one of them?"

"I don't," Ramirez said. "But I'll be checking it out."

"Oh, let's see," Mo said. "You run him through the National Criminal Cult Computer, check the rosters of the local workshops on How to Love Your Antichrist Anima? And the twelve-step programs for coming to grips with your inner evil?"

"Yeah. We have our ways."

Again there was a silence at the nearby tables. Again Mo looked around and grinned. "My friend here," he announced, "writes horror movies for the teenage market. Very spooky. Any of you folks see 'The Reebok Werewolves'?"

eight

"Maria, I got a job for you," Ramirez said. He had returned to the station on Cerrillos after dropping Mo Bowdre off at St. John's College. Partway through their lunch, Mo had made his way to the pay phone in the restaurant, and returned a few minutes later with a predatory smile on his face, asking Ramirez if he would give him a ride to the campus when they were through with lunch. He needed to see an old friend.

"An old friend?"

"Yeah."

"The person you just called?"

"That's right. What's it to you?" Mo asked.

"You just came back from the phone with the smile of the Chester cat on your face, like you ate the bird."

"Tony, I'm going to have to tell you about cat things. It's a Cheshire cat, not Chester. It's from *Alice in Wonderland*, or the other one, the looking glass thing. And the Cheshire cat's smile was always vanishing. Not eating birds."

"Okay. So your smile isn't vanishing. What's up?"

"Maybe a wild goose egg, Tony."

147

"Okay, okay."

So Ramirez dropped Mo off outside the main building, where a tall Anglo with a close-cropped white beard apparently was waiting for him, and drove to the station, wondering what peculiar line of thought his friend might be pursuing. St. John's, wasn't that where they didn't study stuff like most colleges but read Great Books instead? Something like that.

Entering his office, he saw a folder in the middle of the desk with a pink routing slip clipped to it. He sat down, opened it, and drew out two pieces of white paper. From each, a face stared intently at him. The APD police artist worked in colored pencil, and the electronic transmission from Albuquerque to Santa Fe had evidently lost little, if anything making the colors a little more intense.

The Anglo guy, blond, had a narrow face, thin lips, and a prominent nose. Instead of leaving the eyes blank—there was no way to tell what color they were, or really what shape—the artist had given him medium blue eyes, close together, sort of generic Anglo blue eyes, Ramirez thought. The whole image looked generic, in spite of the artist's best effort to put some character into it. He put the drawing aside and looked at the other, the female. It was a looser drawing, as if it had been done more quickly.

A person, a distinct human being, looked back at him from widely spaced, black eyes under thick black eyebrows. Shiny black hair was pulled back behind her head. The bridge of her nose was narrow, the nostrils flared. Her mouth was full-lipped but not especially wide, set in a soft, round jaw. Her skin was light brown, but with a hint of black behind it. The artist had captured an expression—or more to the point, created an expression—of calm, of serenity. The dark eyes stared back at him as if saying, I am at peace. It is you now who are not.

Ramirez was still gazing at the portrait when Maria came in and peered over his shoulder.

"She's beautiful, huh," the chunky policewoman said. "She *looks* pregnant."

Ramirez looked up at the woman, thinking, How the hell do women know when a woman's *face* looks pregnant?

Maria kept staring at the portrait. "How old did they say she was?"

"Late teens," Ramirez said. "The Anglo's about a year older than her. You'd think someone their age would be reported missing."

"Maybe they're strays."

Ramirez sighed. There were probably more stray kids in the state on any given day than the entire population of India Indians. "Okay," he said. "I want them faxed to the high schools. And I want you to take this one—" He touched the female portrait with his forefinger. "—around to the Indian community."

"The India Indian community."

"Yeah."

"Is there one?"

"I don't know. There can't be too many people here from India. Maybe a thousand in the whole state, who knows? Maybe they stick together."

"Tony—"

"Maybe they have a church or a meeting or something. Maybe there's some importer, you know, silks, madras, that type of thing. Try the yellow pages. We got two Indian restaurants here and there's some in Albuquerque. They got any in Taos, anywhere else? Check 'em all. See if anyone working there recognizes her. Find out if there are any associations or whatever where people from the old country . . . Hey, isn't there one of those guru types out near Pecos?"

"Yeah," Maria said brightly. "The guy with all the ems and bees and aitches in his name. Drives around in a brand new Land Rover. I think he only gurus Anglos."

"Is that what they call it? Guruing? Anyway, check him out, okay?" He picked up the portraits and handed them to her. "Let's give it a day or two, see what we get. If it comes up dry, we'll make copies for the media, put these faces on TV. Get going."

The face of the Indian girl stayed in his mind, looking at him with what seemed to be patience. He checked his watch. Two-fifteen. Time to get those inquiries for Mo started, looking into the paper trail of Annie Harper, twenty-one, of Leadville, Lake County, Colorado, and still make the call to that asshole cop in New Jersey before he left work and went off to some big tent and spoke in tongues, or whatever those people did to keep their phone lines clear to God. He wished he could get a direct phone line into God. He had some questions for Him, and also a few suggestions if He ever got around to making a new set of people.

Forgive me, Sir, but it's not just the knee, though it could use a little design work, too . . .

Ramirez picked up the now empty folder and saw another pink slip with his name on it lying on the desk. It said to call a Sergeant Jackson with the state police. The phone number had a Taos exchange. He punched out the numbers, listened to it ring two, three, four times, and a woman answered. He asked for the extension on the pink slip and it rang another three times.

"Jackson."

"This is Ramirez, SFPD."

There was a moment during which no one spoke.

"Oh, yeah. They asked me to check out this guy Clark for you, Sandy Clark. Sorry I couldn't get to it sooner." The trooper spoke with what sounded like a nasal New York City accent. Maybe one of those NYPD cops who agree to take early retirement and head west and avoid a little departmental scandal.

"Okay. Clark. He works construction around Taos, like day labor. Wants to be a musician. A rocker. Plays the electric guitar. He's got this pickup band, call themselves the Skulking Crossbones, can you imagine that? These morbid fucking kids, jeezus. He lives in a run-down place on the road to Arroyo Seco, Route 150. The three of 'em do, the band members. You want their names? No? Okay, they say that this Conrad Franklin was rehearsing with 'em last weekend—came in Thursday afternoon, went home Saturday. Left about seven, eight. Apparently the band was going out with some chicks— they called 'em groupies. Can you imagine? These nobodies with *groupies*? But there was only three of these groupies, so your boy went home. God, he must be some kind of a creep if he was the odd man out of this crowd. These guys sit around like a pile of dirty clothes, saying, 'Cool, man,' and all that shit. Anyhow . . . Is that what you wanted to know?"

Ramirez thanked him and they chatted for a minute or two and hung up.

The door swung open to his bedroom, and Conrad, sitting on the bed, turned sideways, struggling frantically with his fly. To his horror, Annie was standing in the door, looking at him.

Her hair was wet from the shower, pushed back behind her shoulders, and her eyes were incandescent blue, like there was a gas fire burning inside them. The whites were bright; they were dangerous-looking eyes. She had on a tight white tube top, and her midriff was bare, the navel like a single eye. Jeans. Her feet were bare on the tile floor.

Christ, he thought. Caught. She saw . . . He broke into a sweat.

She stood with one hand on her hip, the other on the doorjamb, just looking at him, and a smile crept over her face. Her eyes narrowed mirthfully.

She tossed her head. "Don't be embarrassed. We all do it."

She took three steps toward him, turned a wooden chair around and sat down, straddling it. She crossed her forearms on the back of the chair and rested her chin on her wrist.

"Did you know that girls do that, too?"

"Well, I guess . . ."

"They do. I do." She shrugged, lifted her head up,

looked off to her left. "What do you think about when you do that? Some girl you've been with? A movie star?"

He couldn't believe she was saying this stuff. But her smile seemed trustworthy, like conspiratorial. Like friends sharing this stuff. She wasn't making fun of him.

He laughed. "Sharon Stone," he said, feeling a strange sense of relief.

"Hey, good choice," Annie said brightly. "Like in that movie where she does it on top of Michael Douglas, and that other guy in the beginning who . . . well . . ."

He felt himself reddening. "Yeah."

"That was where they showed Michael Douglas's butt. When he was walking around her place. Big deal, a guy's butt." She looked around the room, pausing to study each poster on the wall. "Cool stuff," she said, and looked back at him. He felt like he was pinned to the bed. Her eyes didn't blink.

"I'm going to take off my clothes, Conrad. Would you like that?" He stopped breathing. Without waiting for an answer, she stood up and peeled the white top up over her head. Her breasts filled his vision like a camera had zoomed in.

She stepped away from the chair and, with her hands on her hips, moved her chest from side to side like she was admiring herself in the mirror, but her eyes were focused on him, boring into him like lasers.

"Don't you want to get naked, Conrad?" She unzipped her fly and stepped out of her jeans, leaving them on the floor next to her top. She was wearing a pair of white bikini panties. *Zoom.* He was in shock. He realized that he'd shriveled up like a prune.

"Stunned, huh? A little? Don't be embarrassed."

"I'm not."

"Good. Bodies are . . . bodies. They're nice." She stepped forward, between his knees, and took his head in both hands, pressing it against her midriff. His hands fluttered up to her hips. He was trying to breathe and his throat seized up, emitting an involuntary croak.

"We're just playing," she said, reaching down and pulling his T-shirt up. He let her pull it over his upstretched arms, and she threw it aside. Above him, only inches away, breasts, and the smiling eyes beyond.

Holy shit, he thought. It's going to happen. Like out of nowhere, it's going to happen. He felt a tingle in his groin and the blood flowing.

Suddenly she grabbed his hand, stepped back and pulled him up. "C'mon, Conrad." She unzipped his fly with what seemed like a practiced gesture and pushed his jeans down around his hips. His erection, nearly complete now, got hung up in his shorts, and he freed it. She smiled a delighted smile and said: "Oh, Conrad."

She crossed her arms. She was waiting for him, wasn't she?

He sat down on the bed and pulled off his jeans and his shorts, watching her slowly edge her white panties down, turning, giving him a full view of her rear end. The light streaming in the window lit some tiny golden fuzz on it. She looked at him over her shoulder, eyes brimming, as if with a joke.

"Like Sharon's, huh?" She arched her back. He reached for her. His fingers fluttered. He turned her around by the hips and buried his face.

"That's cool, Conrad." She sagged against him and he leaned back, pulled her down on top of him.

Now she was kneeling over him, and he was frantic, trying to touch every part of her. His hands flew. She was holding him! He was *in*, Jesus! She was sitting up ... swaying, glistening. Whoa, whoa, here it comes, my God.

He shut his eyes. Too soon. Too soon.

"Ohh, Conrad, Conrad," she said, like a mother crooning to a baby. "I love that feeling. I can't tell you how I love that feeling." She lowered her chest on him and he felt the sweat between them, their sweat, and her mouth on his throat, her lips moving.

"Conrad," she whispered. "You're my lover now. *My* lover." She laughed, a sound like a flute, like water rippling, and nibbled his earlobe. "Don't move. Just lie there. Do as I say, Conrad, do as I say and this dream will last forever."

Conrad lay still as a rock, and felt this magical creature on top of him breathing.

He couldn't believe it. He could not *believe* it. He, Conrad, had done it. He, Conrad, would be doing it again with this ... this wholly different kind of thing, this woman. It was true. He closed his eyes, breathed deep, holding her to him, feeling the weight of her on him.

I can't believe this, he said to himself over and over. He felt like tears were going to pop out from his eyelids.

"Conrad, you make me so happy."

It had occurred to Mo Bowdre as his friend Ramirez explained during lunch how the couple had been killed

out near Canada Rincón, that there were only two kinds
of people who would regularly kill a fellow human being
in so deliberate and at the same time vicious a manner.
These were sociopaths like serial killers, and religious
zealots. From what he knew about it, the first were
absolutely amoral, without a conscience, without any
redeeming connection to their fellow man: monsters like
that Dahmer guy who ate kids. The second, usually pro-
pounding a moral code dictated directly to them by God
Himself, had proven just as capable of maiming or mur-
dering people, and were far more numerous. He thought
fleetingly of the Roman Church's Inquisition, the Salem
witch trials, the circumcision of young African women,
Muslim terrorism, the Aztecs' priestly cannibalism, Jim
Jones and his poison Kool-Aid—all carefully staged in
the name of God, Yahweh, Allah, Oooga-Dooga, what
difference did the name make if His (or Her) words
resounded in your very ears?

Mo figured he couldn't be much help when it came to
serial killers and your other garden-variety sociopaths—
the FBI evidently knew all about that kind of thing, their
personalities, their modi operandi, and so forth. That left
the juicy realm of religious zealots.

Of course, Satanists were religious nuts of a sort—but
more likely, junior sociopaths using a trumped-up religious cult as an excuse for kinky group sex—and he
didn't think he could be much help finding a bunch of
devil-worshiping lunatics among the population of
northern New Mexico. The police should be able to do
that if they put their minds to it, and if such people
existed. Mo couldn't imagine that there were many of

them, or that they would be hard to pick out from a crowd.

That left for his contemplation only approved, legitimate religious zealotry, which was something he figured he could sink his teeth into with relish. Which was why he excused himself and called his old friend at St. John's College—a man named Detlev Van Eck, a longtime scholar of comparative religions. Which in turn was why that afternoon, when Mo Bowdre might have more usefully been contemplating the implications of paternity that had just been thrust upon him, he learned instead about an old Persian named Zoroaster.

It had taken only a simple sketch by the blind man, using a Magic Marker and a large piece of paper, to recreate Conrad's cuneiform etching of the petroglyph, and Detlev Van Eck had said, "Oh yes, the fire worshipers." He had then launched into a long monologue that began with the early Persian cults of Ahura Mazda, who was God, and his son Atar, who accompanied the sun in his chariot. Atar brought all good things to the earth, it seems, and fought against Evil and the power of demons. These Mazdaians maintained altars here and there around the landscape, some of them stepped in the manner of the petroglyph, with fires burning eternally, a visible symbol of the purity and brilliance of the supreme god. In their rituals, priestly attendants of these altars imbibed a sacred drink called *haoma*, the beverage of immortality, like ambrosia for the Greek gods, and with *haoma* they purified themselves and attained a heightened spirituality.

"You mean," Mo said, "they got stoned." Van Eck

barely paused, and then went on at high speed with his monologue.

In the sixth century B.C. a Persian prophet in the tradition of the fire worshipers, a man named Zoroaster, went on a long spiritual quest, just as Buddha would centuries later, and had various revelations which he committed to writing. Several centuries after Zoroaster was dead, his reformist concepts of the ancient Mazdaism became the basis for the official religion of all the Persians—the great leader Darius was a Zoroastrian, for example. Of course, like priests and theologians everywhere, Zoroastrians elaborated all manner of details and filigrees to the more straightforward visions of the original prophet.

The names of demigods and demons rolled off Van Eck's tongue like liquid silver; stories of titanic battles between Good and Evil filled his small office. By the time Europe, under the influence of the Church of Rome, had plunged into its Dark Ages, Zoroastrianism was as rich, as complex, and as weighted down with priestly baggage as any other major religion.

At about this time, however, the fierce new religion of the Arabs—Islam—was ferociously exported into the old haunts of the Persians, and Zoroastrianism was widely and violently attacked. Before long, in what is today Iran, the puritanical Allah had almost obliterated the more courtly Mazda. A handful of Zoroastrian loyalists held out in mountain fastnesses, but most of the last adherents migrated to India, where they settled in the region of Bombay. There they became known as Parsis, which means Persians, and today they are best known for leaving the bodies of their dead in special temples open to the sky where the flesh is removed by scavengers. The actual burning of human flesh is considered not only a bad funereal idea by the Parsis, but an egregious sin. Less familiar to the rest of the world are many other ceremonial practices and beliefs harking all the way back to the earliest Mazdaian cults that the Parsis have maintained. Over the centuries in India, they have been a separate and separatist element of society, and became highly successful in worldly affairs such as commerce.

After Van Eck's lengthy discourse ended, Mo asked a few questions that struck the religion scholar as a bit odd but which he answered nevertheless. Mo thanked his friend, promised he would explain it all at a later date, and begged a ride to Canyon Road. At four-thirty that afternoon, Mo emerged in front of his house from the confines of Van Eck's Volkswagen bug rather like a large butterfly emerges improbably from a small chrysalis.

A plausible story was beginning to develop in his mind, which had also been plagued since lunchtime with the strains of Leonard Bernstein's "Maria," playing over and over in part of his brain with the idiotic insistence of an advertising jingle. Added now to all of this, Mo was surprised to hear the snarl of a lawn mower from the other side of his gate.

Under Mo's hand the old wooden gate squeaked open, and he heard the lawn mower sputter to a stop and a voice say, "Hi, Mo. I found this in the shed."

It was Conrad.

Conrad was mowing the lawn.

Conrad had taken an initiative here that Mo would not have guessed he could even imagine, much less then

stand up and act upon. Mo allowed himself to think that
perhaps he was exerting by his very presence a benign
and maturing influence on the boy. Or it could be simpler
than that. Sometimes people in a self-absorbed funk, as
are many teenagers, thanks to the very forces and facts of
nature, lurch out of it when confronted in one way or
another with the example of a disabled person. There is
nothing, Mo had been told, like the arrival of a new
employee confined to a wheelchair with multiple scle-
rosis, for example, to put a damper on a lot of office
grousing. Perhaps that's what Rhiannon Sharp had had in
mind all along. "Conrad," he could hear her saying, "you
think you've got problems . . ."

Mo beamed in the direction of Conrad's voice.

"That's great, Conrad. Last time I tried doin' that I
cleared out most of one of Connie's iris beds and my ass
was in a sling for a week."

"I'm almost done," Conrad said, and Mo heard him
yanking the hated cord several times until the old machine
popped twice, coughed, and came tentatively to life. As
he made his way to the house, Mo's nose was pleasantly
assailed with the scent of new-cut grass and gasoline.

Inside, he heard the clatter of dishes, and when he
reached the archway into the kitchen, he found himself
grasped by the forearms and firmly but briefly kissed on
the cheek.

"Hi!" Annie said.

"Whole lot of enterprise going on around here," Mo
said. He realized he was smiling. Grinning like a damned
idiot, in fact.

"Just emptying the dishwasher. Connie sure keeps this

kitchen clean. You like a beer?" Mo heard the refrigerator door open and the lovely click of a bottle cap being church-keyed off, felt the cold, wet bottle touch his fingers. Negra Modelo. Now *that's* ambrosia, he thought. And what did the Persians call it?

"*Haoma,*" he said.

"No, it's Negra Modelo," Annie said.

"Right. *Haoma,* like I said. That's another word for the nectar of the Gods. I thank you. Are you having one?"

"After I get this stuff ready for dinner."

Mo sat down at the kitchen table, thinking, Not bad, not bad at all, having this young woman around fixing dinner, doing . . . daughterly? . . . things.

"And what *stuff* are you getting ready for dinner?" he asked.

"It's a surprise. But don't worry. I don't guess you're a vegetarian." She laughed, a pleasant ripple of sound.

"Fee, fi, fo, fum," Mo rumbled.

"You smell the blood," Annie said, "of a bottle of A.1."

Mo let the picture of a large side of beef fill his mind, aged on a butcher's hook to perfection, then ceremoniously riven into the familiar cuts with the entire filet mignon reserved for him, blue, wrapped in white butcher paper with the name T. Moore Bowdre on it. . . . Oh yes.

"What's got into old Conrad out there?" Mo asked. "He doesn't strike me as the volunteer type. Hah. Hah."

Annie laughed again. "I told him that as long as he was hanging around here, eating your food and all, he'd better move his butt. Mowing the lawn was his idea."

No, this ain't bad a-tall a-tall, Mo was thinking again when the phone rang.

nine

Before the first clangorous ring ceased, Mo Bowdre was on his feet and two steps toward the wall phone that hung near the refrigerator.

"I'll get it," Annie Harper chirped, and Mo broke out into a sweat.

"Mo Bowdre's residence. Annie Harper speaking . . . Yes, is this Connie? . . . Hi, Connie, I'm Annie . . . He's right here."

"I'll take it in the other room," Mo said, and lumbered into the living room as quickly as he could. Standing beside his oversized easy chair, he snatched up the phone in a big paw.

"Connie," he said. "You won't believe what's been goin' on here."

"Who's Annie Harper?" Connie said. Her normally alto voice had dropped even lower.

"That's what I want to explain to you about, but what's going on out there?"

Silence. Then: "We're getting ready for the burial."

"When is it?"

"Thursday."

"Oh. Okay." More silence. "Thursday. Okay. Well, now, Connie?" He cleared his throat. "It seems that we've got a bit of a bolt from the past here. This Annie Harper showed up here, she's from up in Colorado, Leadville."

Silence.

"You know, near that mine where I worked."

More silence.

"Seems like she's kinfolks."

Yet more silence.

"Connie? You there?"

"Yes." Mo figured that Connie, at this very moment, could have frozen a truckload of fish with one glance. The Hopi frost.

"Look," he said, "I never heard of her till last night, she just showed up. Appeared in the backyard." Mo bit the bullet. "She says she's my daughter. Now, ain't that the damnedest thing?"

Silence.

"I suppose you'll want to know just how *that* works, right?"

"You didn't say anything about her this morning," Connie said.

"Well, no, that's right, I didn't. Marvin had just died, is what you said when you called, and I hadn't figured this thing out yet, hadn't digested it. Didn't see any reason to throw this in right with Marvin dying and all. Add to the confusion."

Silence again.

"I should've said something about it, I guess."

"Yes."

"So you'd have known about it before she answered the phone here, and all. That must've been something of a shock. I feel pretty stupid. Are you okay?"

"Okay?"

Mo cleared his throat again. He spoke quietly, just above a whisper. "Back then, when I was in the mine, it was about twenty-two years ago—just about exactly twenty-two years ago, as a matter of fact—there was this woman, her name was Millie, and I spent some time with her. About a week it was in all. Then she went off and I had the accident and everything went to hell. I don't think I even thought of this woman—Millie, I mean—more than two, three times since then. No reason to.

"Anyhow, last night I'm sittin' out in the yard and this Annie Harper appears, says she's my daughter. From Millie, Millie Harper was her name. This Annie's the right age and all that. Twenty-one."

"That's real nice," Connie said, her voice flat as a mesa top. "You've got a daughter."

"Well, yes, I *might*. Tony Ramirez is checking out some details."

"You don't believe her?"

"It could be true. May well be. But it makes sense to check it out. I mean, it does change things."

Silence.

"I mean, me being a father. It's kind of a new thought. I mean, aside from us. *Already* being a father, do you see what I mean?"

"Oh, Mo."

"Well, we could have a kid. It just might have this

older half sister. Damn it, this is all a hell of a big surprise."

"It's okay, Mo. I'm glad if you have a daughter. What's she like?" Connie did not sound totally convincing.

"She's tall, maybe five-ten. Conrad says she's got brown hair, blue eyes. She's kind of, well, emotional. Up and down. Right now she's out there, happy as a clam at high tide, makin' dinner. Even got Conrad off his behind and got him mowing the lawn."

"Up and down?"

"She's pretty jumpy. I guess it's nerve-wracking for her. It sure is for me. I mean, what the hell do I know? Like I said, Tony's checking out things, like birth records, motor vehicle stuff, arrests."

"What will that tell you?"

"He says you look for patterns in all that stuff. I guess he means consistency. Truth. I guess the only way to be totally sure about all this is to have a DNA test. But that seems a tad, well, adversarial."

"So what are you going to do?"

"I don't know."

Silence.

"Mo?"

"Yeah."

"I think it would be real good if you had a daughter."

"You wouldn't mind?"

Connie laughed and Mo sank into his chair. "Mind? Mo, that's silly. I was just thinking you should have told me right away."

"Oh shit," Mo said contritely. "So you wouldn't think . . ."

"So what do *you* think?"

"About what?"

"If she really is your daughter."

"I don't know. I guess we'll just have to wait for Tony's—"

"Mo, that stuff isn't going to tell you anything. You better go up there."

"To Leadville? What good will that do?"

"You're the one always talking about the stories in things. That's where the story started."

Silence.

"Mo?"

"I don't have real good memories of that place."

"This way maybe you will."

"Damn."

"What?"

"You women sure do make it hard on a man. How come you do that?"

Connie laughed.

"Okay," Mo said. "After Marvin's burial we'll go."

"Marvin's already gone. You don't need to come to the burial. Conrad can drive you all up there. Is that woman still alive? Millie?"

"Yeah. Widowed. Living on a pension or something."

"Okay. Up there, you'll know."

"You don't mind?"

Connie laughed again. "If she is your daughter, I'll be glad to meet her."

"And if she isn't . . ."

"Then you can leave her in Leadville."

"I love you, Connie."

"All of a sudden you keep saying that. You must be getting old or something."

"Hah. Hah. Oh, by the way, I think I got Tony's problem figured out."

"Tony's problem?"

"Who killed those people out near Rhiannon's place."

"Who was it?"

"I don't know his *name*. Just who he is. Like what he is. You want to hear . . . ?"

"Yes, but I've got to go. They need to use this phone. So you're going, okay? Probably I'll stay out here till Saturday. You know, help out."

"Then I'll probably beat you back here."

"Okay. Good luck."

They hung up, and Mo leaned back in his chair. Behind his dark glasses his eyelids closed, and for a long while he sat still as a slab of rock. Eventually he shook his head, as if shaking off the cobwebs of sleep. The song was still playing in his brain: *Maria, Maria, Ma-reeee-ya.* He wondered if the song would ever leave.

Goddamn it, Leonard.

He sniffed the air and punched out a number on the telephone.

"Tony?" he said. "You're looking a bit peaked there, boy. Anemic. You don't ever eat right when you got a case. I don't see how you ever solve anything on doughnuts and candy bars, or whatever you snatch up. Now, we got some steaks here, a little dead cow. Brain food. What time can you get here?"

"I'm working," Ramirez said. "Anyway, you got that kid there, Conrad, don't you?"

"So what?"

"He's a suspect. I can't just sit down and eat dinner with a suspect. It wouldn't look right."

"In the first place, no one's looking. In the second place, he's not who you're looking for. You know that."

"Lieutenant Ortiz doesn't."

"He's not invited. And in the third place, I got an idea here, might be useful."

"Okay. An hour. Medium rare."

"See ya." Mo hung up the phone and turned his head toward the kitchen.

"Annie?" he called. "We're gonna need one more steak. Got a guest coming."

"Cool," Annie called.

John Franklin never failed to be amazed by the thought patterns of his wife Rhiannon. She had been sitting quietly in the room she used as an office and private place for an hour late that afternoon. Then she emerged just as he was heading out to the stables. She was carrying a quartz crystal in her hand. She had several in her room, big ones that were probably museum quality, and a bunch of smaller ones. She was carrying one of the smaller ones, and had a determined look on her face.

She was not one of those crystal freaks, Franklin well knew, the sort who clutch crystals to their bosoms and chant mumbo-jumbo about power centers and vibrations and do Celtic dances in the moonlight. But she did find them helpful in some meditative or spiritual way. Franklin didn't understand it at all, but it seemed perfectly benign. She told him that she was going out to the arroyo where those bodies had been found and put the crystal there—some kind of ablution, Franklin supposed. A nice thing to do, not that he believed a hunk of quartz could do much about the fact that two corpses had turned up there, two corpses he'd found, with the flies buzzing around the ugly gashes that had been their eyes and their groins. . . . The picture returned insistently again to his mind, and he shuddered, unable to keep away the scene that continued in his mind like a movie: of vultures taking the eyeballs, their disgusting pink fleshy necks and heads dipping, the long beaks gouging, plucking . . . then gusting up in disarray at the approach of the coyote, its fangs soon tearing hungrily at the guy's balls, ripping them away. . . . He gagged, swallowed, and cleared his throat.

The filly stirred under him, and her ears flicked this way and that like radar screens. After Rhiannon left the house, he'd saddled her up and they went through the piñons toward the western edge of Franklin's acreage. Maybe, Franklin thought now, his wife's little pilgrimage and her crystal would at least help keep such visions from ambushing her this way. He wished he believed in crystals. Being out on a horse, any one of his Arabs, was usually enough to clear his mind, but not now. He wondered if it would ever clear, or whether riding, and particularly riding Flame Gypsy, wouldn't always remind him of . . . No, he wouldn't let that happen.

"Come on, baby," he said, and nudged her with his calves. She stepped ahead smartly, eagerly, in the confines of the reins, and Franklin turned south. He would go to the very spot, confront it, exorcize it, defy it. He would find Rhiannon there perhaps, and they could be together, each washing away this awful event in their lives in their own ways. Then he heard the scream.

Oh shit, his mind said, oh shit, *no!*

He pressed his calves on the filly's flanks without thinking, and she broke into a fast and hazardous trot through the trees.

No, no! Please God, no!

The pink afterglow in the sky over Mo Bowdre's backyard had faded into dusk. Some birds in the surrounding trees were calling it a day with a few tinny bleeps, and a bat had taken to swooping overhead in frantic soundlessness. Without the sun's direct efforts, the mountain air had begun its rapid cooling—in June at seven thousand feet, the temperature could drop more than thirty degrees in a few hours, from the mid-eighties into the low fifties.

Among the flagstones of the patio that lay just beyond Mo Bowdre's covered porch, he had excavated a shallow pit where, on cool nights like this, he liked to put a few piñon logs and start a fire to sit by as the night came on. Just why Bowdre had not burned his house to the ground was a mystery to Sergeant Anthony Ramirez, who had watched the big man on innumerable occasions toss a new log on the fire from a standing position, causing a vortex of sparks to surge upward into the dark. Ramirez figured he must have a guardian saint or angel. He even started the fire in a dangerous way, sloshing charcoal lighter over the logs and tossing in a match, with a resulting *whump!* of ignition. As often as not, Bowdre would laugh his staccato laugh, and Ramirez always wondered why someone for whom a fiery explosion had been so devastating would be so reckless with his own fire. Maybe it was a form of defiance, Ramirez thought.

His blind friend's approach to life sometimes seemed to be an act of defiance. For a blind man to take up sculpture was certainly an act of defiance. To memorize increasing amounts of the world so completely that he could get around much of it without a seeing-eye dog or even a cane—this also had to be an act of defiance. There was an Anglo phrase for it, something about using a bigger envelope.

Right now, Mo sat across the fire from him, the flames from the logs burning quietly and casting an orange glow on the big man's face. He was sitting in a canvas director's chair, a big hand on each knee, quiet as a sphinx. Before long, Ramirez knew, he would launch into some story.

The trouble with television, Mo had once explained in one of his soliloquies, was not that it was utterly vapid and without content, like so many people said. For most people it had plenty of content: car chases, shootings, adultery, rape. The problem with TV was that it handed out all these canned stories and replaced ten thousand years of sitting around an outdoor fire at night spinning your own yarns, trying to make up plausible explanations. How many religions, Mo asked, have been founded in front of a TV set?

And often, Ramirez admitted, the stories that got told around Mo's little pit fire with its explosions of sparks *did* help to explain things, several times even casting a new light on matters that were puzzling to a homicide detective. He suspected that the sudden, almost summary invitation to dinner tonight was planned to be just such an occasion.

Meanwhile Ramirez had observed the comings and goings of Annie Harper with a normal human male's interest. She was, very simply, a knockout. She reminded him a little of that actress who had played Lois Lane in the Superman movie, what was her name? Kidder. She had that kind of smile. But her eyes were something else—a fierce blue that danced like they had their own sun inside behind them. And the whites of her eyes—they seemed to glow, too, from her suntanned face. She was tall, as tall as he was, though it wasn't odd these days to see tall women. Annie Harper also had the kind of figure to make a man goggle, and Ramirez had conscientiously tried not to do that during the evening. She was packed into faded jeans and wore a loose white shirt with a scoop neck, and from time to time she tossed her head by way of resetting her long and shiny brown hair. There are some women, Ramirez reflected, for whom bare feet are a kind of statement, and Annie was one of them.

Of course, Mo Bowdre couldn't see any of this, but he had clearly enjoyed having this Annie, the self-proclaimed daughter, being hostess, serving dinner in the candlelit cave of a dining room, sitting to his right at the square table. Throughout the meal, whether she was seated or popping up to fetch something from the kitchen, she tended to lean slightly toward the big man, as though he were a magnet, and when she looked at him, her eyes shimmered with what could only be taken as adoration.

As captivated as she was by Mo, young Conrad was clearly captivated by her. He was barely aware of Ramirez's and Mo's presence. Whenever she happened to glance at him, he grinned uncontrollably and then looked every which way, like someone had launched a couple of pinballs in his eye sockets. Most of the time, Conrad watched her with an obvious hunger, and Ramirez was amused by this newfound alertness in Conrad's normally flaccid demeanor. He was even sitting up more or less straight, without the usual slump of his shoulders—infused, Ramirez thought to himself, with rivers of grand fantasies. On one occasion, having insisted on clearing away the plates herself, she patted Conrad on the shoulder and Ramirez watched him turn nearly puce from the neck up to his forehead.

Now the two young people were in the kitchen and the clattering of dishes being stowed in the dishwasher could be heard over the sizzle of Mo's fire.

"That Millie Harper must have been a handsome woman," Ramirez said. Mo stirred in the fire's glow and his dark glasses flashed orange.

"Yeah, she was that."

"Because this Annie doesn't—" Ramirez stopped.

"Hah. Hah. You mean she isn't burdened with my particular features? Well, that's a blessing, isn't it? She could have got her size from me—if she really is my daughter. Her mother wasn't very big—maybe five-four, five-five. You find anything nefarious in her past yet?"

"So far," Ramirez said, "she checks out. That skier was listed as the father on the birth certificate, but that doesn't necessarily mean anything, given what you told me. It was only the mother who signed it. And Annie got two speeding violations in the past five years. That's all we know for now."

"You have any sense of it?"

"Me? No. Except that she sure acts like you're her long-lost daddy. You know, body language and all. And Conrad—well, he is a lost soul, making geegaw eyes at her all through dinner." Ramirez laughed quietly.

"Goo-goo," Mo said.

"What?"

At that moment, Annie came through the screen door, followed by Conrad.

"Two grown men talking baby talk?" she said.

"It's *goo-goo* eyes, Tony."

"Oh, right."

"I brought coffee. Decaf. Okay?" Annie said. She held a mug out until it touched Mo's fingers and he took it from her. Then she handed the other to Ramirez with a smile. "You guys talking about me?"

"No," Ramirez said.

"No," Mo said. "Police business. You two got coffee? Sit down. We got a nice fire goin' here. We got bats swooping. You scared of bats?"

Annie and Conrad pulled up chairs to the fire's edge and sat down, Annie taking up a proprietary position on Mo's right. Conrad sat across from her, on the big man's left, and looked furtively at Annie's lap.

"Tony here," Mo began, "has got himself a double homicide, found the bodies over at Conrad's place. Maybe he told you about it."

"Yeah. Weird. And you—" she said, turning to smile again at Ramirez "—think Conrad might have—"

"Of course not," Mo interrupted. "No way in the world Conrad had anything to do with it. It wouldn't make any sense at all that way."

"Mo's going to tell us a story," Ramirez said. "Just like the old days when cavemen sat around the fire, gnawing on bones, inventing myths."

Annie looked quizzically at him, then at Mo, and back to Ramirez.

"In the Santa Fe Police Department, we try and humor him. See, it's still kind of a small town, and you don't want to offend any of the big-shot artists."

Annie smiled ingratiatingly at Ramirez but her laser-lit eyes remained puzzled.

Ramirez leaned toward her and, behind his hand, whispered, "Some people around here call him the redneck Nero Wolfe."

"Who's Nero Wolfe?" she whispered back.

"Hah. Hah. He was a Montenegrin orchid grower."

Annie leaned back in her chair and folded her arms across her chest. "You guys," she said.

"I want to hear this," Conrad said.

ten

"I don't know as I'd call what I've got a story in the conventional sense—you know, a beginning, a middle, and an end. All I got is a middle. And old Conrad here is right in the middle of the middle, aren't you?" Mo turned his head to the left, fixing Conrad with a blank look from his dark glasses. Conrad looked back, looked down and began to turn red.

"Now, as I already told you, Sergeant Ramirez here doesn't believe you did it. Nobody believes you did it. Well, except maybe for the rest of the police department. But don't you fret. Hah. Hah."

Conrad looked up and his eyes went back into pinball mode.

"Okay," Mo said, and cleared his throat. "What just about everyone has come up with is that these murders were a ritual sort of thing. The bodies of this couple—everyone assumes it was a couple, an Anglo male about twenty, and an India Indian woman a little younger, who was three months pregnant—they were laid out nice and straight, side by side, down there in the arroyo next to those big boulders. It's not like they were just dumped out there in the middle of nowhere by someone in a hurry. Sergeant Ramirez—is it okay if I call you Tony in front of these people? Tony says there was something especially innocent-looking about them, lying there. That right?"

"Right."

Mo turned to his right. "A lot of the details of this thing are pretty gruesome."

"That's okay," Annie said.

"Okay. The eyes were gone and so were the genitalia. So your first thought is that it was a cult thing, Satanists out doing disgusting things, like a sacrifice to all the imps of earth and air. That's what came to Rhiannon's mind right off—Conrad's mother. But it turned out it wasn't mutilation by human hand, it was just the local predators and scavengers out doing their usual thing. Part of the natural cycle that the poets don't get all rapturous about, any more than they get all warm and gooey about stomach parasites or athlete's foot fungi. That's nature, too, even though the Sierra Club doesn't put out picture books about it."

"Yuk," Annie said.

"Exactly right. Yuk. I'm guilty of the same thing. Never did sculpt a critter biting at flies. I told old Frazier down at the gallery I was gonna do that once—do a parasite-ridden elk—and he took it seriously. Started hemmin' and hawin' . . . He's a good man, but his sense of humor doesn't run to joking about business. Now where were we?

"The bodies. Here they are all laid out, each of them

sent into the great beyond by a two-and-a-half inch nail someone hammered into their ears."

"Gross!" Annie exclaimed. "Sick. Conrad, you didn't tell me that."

"I didn't know it."

"The M.I.'s—the medical investigators—found the nails," Ramirez said. "Nobody's ever heard of that before. The bodies didn't have any marks on them, like rope burns or anything. So we were wondering how you get someone to sit still while you drive a nail in their ear, but it turns out they were stoned. They had the remains of psilocybic fungi in them."

"Hallucinogenic mushrooms," Mo explained. "Enough to knock 'em out, right, Tony?"

"Right."

"So let's suppose these two were passed out and someone comes along and kills them, drives a nail in their ears. Now why the hell would anyone do that? Why would they even think of it? Tony says that none of the cops at the scene noticed it. You wouldn't, after all. There wouldn't be a whole lot of blood flowing out, would there? So who'd go looking way down in their ears? Anyway, these people were killed in this bizarre way, probably somewhere else, and then brought out into the boonies and laid out. That's all real puzzling, and we can come back to it. Another thing that's puzzling is that there weren't any tracks around the place."

"That's easy," Annie said. "Whoever did it brushed his tracks away when he left. What's so puzzling about that?"

"That's what he did," Mo said. "Or *she*. Exactly. But

how many vultures you know about brush away their footprints?"

"Or coyotes," Ramirez added. "They figure vultures got the eyes, and coyotes did the rest. Maybe the coyotes scared off the vultures."

"This really is gross," Annie said.

"Someone else came out afterward," Conrad said. "And brushed away his tracks. Or hers. And brushed away the vulture's tracks, too."

"You're right, Conrad," Mo said. "And since that was a place you go to every now and then for, uh, meditation, that's another reason why some of Tony's colleagues wonder about you. You went out there the night they were working the crime scene, maybe you went out an earlier time, too. A lot of killers go back to the scene of the crime, right, Tony?"

"Yeah. Those FBI profilers found that serial killers usually do that. It's part of the kick they get. And they're real interested in the police investigation, too."

"Hey, wait a minute . . ." Conrad said, his face screwed up into righteous anger.

"Now, hold your water," Mo said. "No one's sayin' you're a serial killer. Hell, two killings don't count as serial. Hah. Hah."

Annie sat back in her chair and crossed her arms again. "I think you're both being mean." Conrad gazed at her with doting gratitude.

Mo pursed his lips. "Sorry," he said presently. "Just kidding around. You okay, Conrad? So what we've got here is a killer who takes a lot of trouble—probably twice—not to leave any footprints around. He's real careful about that. Obviously, he didn't want anyone to be able to identify him. Now that seems like perfectly normal behavior for your standard thoughtful, premeditated murderer, doesn't it?"

Mo leaned forward in his chair and hung his hands over his knees.

"Then why," he asked in a phony stage whisper, "did he leave that petroglyph on the rock?"

He turned to Annie and said, "See, Conrad here noticed that there was a new petroglyph on his rock. He tell you about it?"

"Yeah. He drew it on a napkin at lunch."

"Good. So we're all on the same page here. Now Tony found out that one of the things that petroglyph could be is an altar, maybe one that's on fire. So here we go, back to Lucifer and his goatish cult. Burning an altar. Mocking the Church. Sneering at Christ. Satanists! But that just doesn't jibe with two important things we already talked about.

"First, Tony's odd feeling, an aura of innocence. Now Tony's no cynic—and he's no romantic, either—but he's seen a lot of dead bodies, and if he gets a feeling like that, it's important.

"Second is the cause of death, the nails. There's plenty of ways you could dispatch a couple of kids who were already unconscious or close to it. You could strangle 'em, stab 'em—lots of ways. Why nails in the ears? What got me thinking was that the forensic people on the scene didn't find the nails, had no idea what the cause of death was. In fact, it was the exact opposite of mutilation. The killer didn't want to put *any* marks on them."

In the pit, Ramirez noted, the fire had died down to a steady glow from three separate embers. "I'll get a couple of logs," he said hastily. He crossed to the other end of the patio where a ragged pile of piñon logs sat under the portal, and brought two which he placed carefully on the embers. Flames leapt immediately from under the dry wood, but no sparks.

"If he had to bring 'em out there from where they were killed," Conrad said, "maybe he didn't want any blood in his vehicle."

"Then why not strangle them? Or suffocate 'em with a pillow?" Mo asked.

"Maybe he was in a place where there weren't any pillows," Annie said.

"And strangling would leave marks," Conrad added.

"Exactly," Mo said. "He wanted these bodies to be free of any visible sign of violence. And he went on to lay them out real carefully. Like the whole thing was done out of respect."

"Respect? Who'd kill someone out of respect?" Conrad looked pained.

"A religious zealot," Mo said. "Every organized religion has its zealots, and they do the damnedest things out of fanaticism. You remember old Abraham? In the Bible? He just about killed his own son, almost sacrificed him on an altar because he thought Jehovah had told him to. There's no one like these true-believing zealots to kill someone for their own good. Make a fine ceremony out of it. I was thinking about that, so I went and talked to an old friend at St. John's College. He's the local whiz at comparative religions, and he told me all about this boy Zoroaster. Conrad? How about you switch us over to beer, and when you come back, we can go on with this little seminar."

Conrad did as asked, and in a few minutes Mo launched into a brief summary of the ancient Mazdaians, Zoroaster, and the Parsis.

"So let's invent a situation here that fits all the weird facts about these homicides. This is just a story, mind you. You've got a Parsi man, immigrated to New Mexico a while back, or maybe he was born here of Parsi immigrants. He's educated like all of them, maybe a businessman of some kind, maybe an engineer or something. A big guess I'm making here is that he got a thoroughly Western education and maybe, even probably, he fell away from the true path of his fathers. Then something terrible happened, maybe his wife died or some tragedy like that, and he goes scrambling back to Parsi-ism or whatever it's called. Basically he gets born again. It happens all the time here, and people who do it are—well—pretty hard to reason with, to say the least.

"Of course, there isn't a whole congregation of Parsis here in the land of enchantment so this fellow's alone with his faith. Far from home. Far from what might be the calm and restraining hand of a Parsi priest. Instead, this boy is hag-ridden, driven, has to reinvent his religion, and its rituals, for himself.

"Then, in the midst of all his fervor, he discovers that his young daughter is pregnant. Three months pregnant. And to make matters worse, she's pregnant by some

Anglo kid. See, the Parsis over in India, they're real exclusive, keep to themselves. Marry within the group and all that. Well, there has to have been some inter-marriage with the other people around there or they'd all be albinos with six toes by now. But generally speaking, they marry within the group.

"So his daughter has committed this awful sin, maybe dishonored his lineage and his god's rules about that kind of thing—you know, Mazda. Here's this guy, seething with the moral horror of it all, the shame of this awful stain. It's got to be redressed, purified. Maybe he hears old Mazda crying out to him: *'Vengeance! Avenge me!'*

"So he kills them both. First he fills them up with this mushroom stuff—not just to knock 'em out or to kill them, but to purify them in some crazy way. *Haoma*, they call it. An elixir made from whatever local stuff they could find, herbs, whatever. Mushrooms. The priests slugged it to purify themselves, and maybe the flock took it, too. So maybe our killer quaffs a little of the mush-room juice himself so as to put himself in closer touch with Mazda. He gets a little stoned, and probably old Mazda comes to him in person, carrying on about the shame of it all, hungering for a sacrifice.

"At the same time, our boy overdoses the hapless young lovers—mixes a killer dose of his bathtub *haoma* in their curried lamb and rice or whatever the hell, and waits for the great purification. But he finds that it didn't actually do 'em in, so he finishes them off with twelve-penny nails. See, this way he hasn't disfigured his daughter, whom he loves deeply even though she's sinned so terribly."

"Sick," Annie said.

"Sick as hell. But logical. At least it's logical if you accept a couple of crazy premises, which is just what religious zealots do all the time, world without end. So now our boy has these corpses, and the Parsi way is to put 'em in a big open temple and let the vultures dispose of their flesh. But they don't have such places here, so he drives around, goes down a dirt road a ways—there aren't any signs there, are there?—and lugs them into that arroyo. He lays them out with great respect and care and then he notices the old petroglyphs on that big boulder right next to them.

"An idea pops into his crazed and feverish mind. Symbolically, he turns the place into a temple by scratching that burning altar into the boulder. That's the ancient altar of the Mazdaians, of the Zoroastrians, and of the Parsis. Fire worshipers, they were called. It's the best he can do."

"And he comes back later," Conrad said, "to see if it's working. If the vultures have come."

"Right, and he sees the empty eye sockets and the genitalia gone. Everything's going just fine."

Annie shuddered. "Gross."

"And that's it. There's the story," Mo said. He sat back in his chair. "So the killer is a guy old enough to have a seventeen-year-old daughter, probably from Bombay originally. He's big enough to lug a corpse over some pretty rough ground for quite a way. Probably well-educated, and I'm guessing westernized. How's that sound to you, Tony?"

"I'm thinking."

"While I'm at it," Mo continued, "I'd bet the guy is one of those India Indian types that work at Los Alamos, or one of these weird science institutes that've been springing up all over the place. There's plenty of foreign scientists around here. I'll bet our boy is a scientist or an engineer of some kind, I'll stake my truck on it. Maybe a technician. That would fit my profile perfectly. Now, Conrad, how'd you like to fetch another round of beer?"

"Not for me, thanks," Ramirez said, and stood up. "I gotta go. Thanks for the dinner. Thanks for the company." He set out across the grass toward the old wooden gate that led out to the street. From the darkness they heard him say, "Thanks for the new mythology, too. Sounds good."

Conrad went in the screen door to fetch the beer, and Annie leaned toward Mo, looking at him with awe.

"That was amazing."

"Hah. Hah. If true," Mo said.

It should hurt, it should hurt. Something should hurt.

John Franklin was puzzled that nothing hurt. You don't get thrown from your horse, even a small one like his filly, and land in the rock-strewn dirt, and have nothing hurt.

He was on his back in the dirt, looking at the sky, now dark, full of little pinpricks of light. Stars. The sky shouldn't be dark yet. It was light when . . . When what? What had happened?

Move. Move your toes. Pull your toes toward you.

Can't.

Fingers, then.

Oh, no. Oh no. Oh Jesus Christ, no.

Can't move.

Stars are fading. Rhiannon?

I'm paralyzed. Nothing. It doesn't hurt.

Rhiannon on the ground, down by the boulder, head at a horrid angle, horribly twisted, oh God. Eyes white, all white, only white, and the teeth . . . a silent scream. Rhiannon. Slam, the jackhammer horse. Why?

Something leapt out. A man running, leapt at us. Out of the trees. Scared, he was scared. He screamed. Slam.

The stars are going. I'm here. Can't move. He killed Rhiannon and I can't move.

Where's Gypsy? Her tack could snag. She could kill herself.

Only one star left. Damn. It's gone, too.

Light. I want light . . . Oh, please. Please?

All too aware of the empty half of his bed, Mo Bowdre lay on his back, thinking about Connie, wishing that it was she who would be setting out with him for Colorado tomorrow. It had been a long time since he'd ventured very far from home without her. Instead he would have to put himself to a considerable extent in the hands of two young people he hardly knew. Conrad, the moping teenager, had shown a few signs of life in the past few hours to be sure, but how long could he sustain it? Maybe he'd be happy enough just being assigned driver of the ensemble in his Rambo pickup-with-everything. Feel like a big shot. I'll work on that.

And Annie—she'd been awful damn quiet when he announced after Ramirez left that they would be leaving for Colorado first thing in the morning. She'd been so attentive, so adoring through the evening, but then he could almost feel her cooling off. Emotional kid. He remembered her outburst of the morning, blasting through like a summer squall. Kid? She's twenty-one. An adult.

Kids reached puberty sooner these days, Mo thought. Maybe they leave the stormy region of teenagerhood later these days, too. Maybe she's just emotional. Maybe, he thought, I'm just being dense. After all, why would she want to go back there? She just left the place, and life didn't sound all that great up there, from what she'd said.

The old mining center was a depressed area now, putting on a few pathetic airs to try and generate a little tourism money. Once awash in money from mining gold, silver, lead, zinc, you name it, all but one of the old mines were now closed. The only jobs for someone like Annie were working in a bar, which she had done, or making beds in the ski resorts like Vail, thirty miles away. People in Leadville, a lot of them, anyway, were scratching out a crummy living on welfare or social security, the surviving old-timers from the mines hacking and coughing and steadily dying off, like the last flies of summer, from silicosis. Everyone there lived amidst the toxics from a hundred years of devil-may-care dumping. Annie's mother—Millie—was apparently just as depressed and run-down as the town itself, behind its brave facade, and the two of them, mother and daughter, had evidently never gotten along. Why would Annie want to go back there? Here, she was in a nice house—

well, on the sofa in a nice house—in a spiffy part of Sante Fe which itself was about as far from Leadville as a lion is from a centipede.

Maybe there was no point in this, no point in going back up there. Maybe he could call it off and just rely on whatever Tony Ramirez turned up, and if things got serious, get a DNA test.

He dreaded going back up there. The big Climax mine itself, fifteen miles north of Leadville right on Fremont Pass, was closed now, a dead hulk. He could just imagine all the old equipment, the tall mill buildings, the whole industrial conglomeration—at one time the largest underground mine in the world—falling apart and rusting like a graveyard of dinosaurs.

And Millie, Millie Harper. He sure as hell didn't relish the thought of seeing her. But she was, arguably, the mother of his daughter. So he owed her something, didn't he? And this Annie—arguably his daughter, his own flesh and blood. He owed her, too. She *thought* she was his daughter, and maybe she was. Maybe, as Connie said, he'd know more once he went back to the beginning, to where the story had begun.

As for Annie herself, Mo found that he liked her. Moody, yes, but who wouldn't be under the circumstances? Otherwise, there was a sparkle to her, wasn't there?

Mo was drowsing off when the door to his bedroom swung open and clattered against the wall.

"What the—"

The door slammed shut.

"You don't understand, do you?" Annie said, her voice

nearly a wailing sound. "You really don't understand." Mo heard a gagging sound, like her tongue had got caught in her throat. "You didn't hear what I was telling you. You didn't listen! Why would you when nobody else ever has? I mean, I was trying to tell you something— something *important*."

"Wait a minute, now—"

"I *have* been waiting. I've been waiting ever since I can remember. I've been waiting for people to be straight, to be honest with me, to . . . to . . . and not to . . . Oh, God."

"Annie, what are you saying here? Why don't you sit down? You want me to turn on a light?"

"Noooo," she wailed, and fell silent. Then in a flat voice she went on. "My *mother* didn't *want* me. She was ashamed. She was living a lie. *I* was the lie. Every time she looked at me . . . I could tell. I could tell. And she didn't believe me. She didn't believe me when I told her what my *stepfather* had done, *her* husband. I was just a little kid, eight years old, and him and his hands . . . Oh, jeez." She sobbed, an ugly catching of breath.

"So they thought I was, like, being a wedge, trying to push them apart. And I caught him once, I caught him in the storeroom at the drugstore, you know, with another woman, and I tried to tell my *mother*, and she . . . and he . . . The same thing. It was *my* fault! *I* was making trouble. Don't you see?

"So finally I find out the truth. I find out *who I really am*. And I come to you, and you . . . *Why* do you have to go back there? Why? I know. You don't believe *me*.

You're another one ... God, when is this all going to stop, when will I ... ?"

Mo found that he was sitting up in his bed. "Annie, come over here and sit down. Let's just talk about this." He heard her step across the room, felt the corner of the bed sag under her weight. She sniffed.

"It's not that I don't believe you," Mo said. "I do believe you. I believe you have been told that I'm your father. And maybe I am. Could well be. And that wouldn't be so bad at all. I like you. And I don't want to go up there, either. The whole damn place has bad memories for me."

"Then why are you going? Why are ... I *hate* that place. Your memories are old. They happened a long time ago. They can't be as important as—" She stopped, and it sounded as if something had caught in her throat, like a bone. She stood up. "You just don't understand. I *need*—"

"Annie."

"I don't know why I expected anything more from ... here. From you. You don't want someone like me just appearing. Out of nowhere. You've got your sweet life here, everything cool, big-time sculptor, get some kicks from helping the cops, you've got *Connie*, you've got *every*thing, so why ... ?" She stood up.

"You know?" she said, her voice suddenly calm. "You know, I've figured you out. You're an iceberg. You're hiding in there behind this big front you put on. The good old country boy. The big bear. And that fake laugh. *Hah. Hah.* That's crap, isn't it? You don't *have* any real feelings. You just say what you think'll work. Keep everyone around adoring you without giving them a thing, a *damn* thing."

Annie's voice had begun to rise.

"You like me. You say you like me. Big deal. You think that's *enough*? You're a big taker. A taker. You're not a giver, *Dad*. Dad. Shit."

"Now, look here, Annie—"

"Look, look. What is there to see? Big selfish faker, treats women like toys . . . not a father, not a loving father. Wham, bang, screw Millie and walk away, like dogs do it, the hell with whatever happens next. Well *I* happened. *Me!* You weren't there then, and you're not here now. Not for me. You just worry about what it means to you and your little life here. You haven't once, *not once,* thought about what this means to me. Have you? *Have* you?"

He heard Annie wrench the door open, and heard it slam shut.

Holy shit, Mo said to himself, and it was a long time before he could muster much more than that. It was like being blindsided by a . . . what? An explosion. He sat there in the permanent darkness of his life, furious.

eleven

At some time in early June in Santa Fe, the City of Holy Faith, which is 7,500 feet nearer to God then sea level is, there comes a day when the weather is so sublime as to qualify for the word *perfect*. On such a day the sun will warm the world up to no more than 79 degrees Fahrenheit, and a few silvery-white clouds will ride across the sky. The humidity will be so negligible and the air so clear that, overhead, it will appear almost blue-black, as though one could see through the atmosphere of earth into the vastness of space. The fondest breeze will ruffle penstemons and other local flowers that nod in sidewalk gardens outside walled homes, and in the crystalline clarity of things, sharply delineated shadows on sunstruck stucco walls make whole and intelligible the beauty of pueblo-style architecture.

Such a perfect day was in store when Conrad Franklin awoke uncharacteristically before the sun had risen above the Sangre de Cristo Mountains and saw a patch of brightening sky through his bedroom window. After a moment spent puzzling out where he in fact was, he sat up in the narrow but comfortable bed, rubbed his eyes, and guessed it was about six-thirty. He checked his watch, pressing the little button that lit up its face, and found that he was close. Six-twenty.

His mind dwelled hungrily on the moments of high passion that had occurred right on this very bed the day before, reliving its juicy mystery. But then, abruptly, he recalled the wailing and the harsh voice that he'd heard last night—Annie clearly upset. He had listened to her voice, unable to make out the words, and heard the door to Mo Bowdre's bedroom slam, heard her stride past his door. It had occurred to him then to go to her and find out what was going on, but his courage quickly shriveled and he stayed put.

Now, however, his courage was back up, his proprietary feeling for Annie returned, and he got out of bed and padded to his door, clad in a pair of orange bikini underpants. Opening the door, he listened carefully, detecting the sound of light snoring from the end of the hall where the blind man's bedroom was. Quietly, he made his way to the living room where Annie was evidently asleep, lying on her side on the sofa, long brown hair in a mass around her face and a bare arm folded over her head at an odd angle. He stood watching her for a moment, unsure now what he should do.

One blue eye opened behind the swirl of brown hair and looked at him. The bare arm moved, and her hand swept her hair from her face. Two blue eyes now looked at him, in fact seemed to look through him.

"You're awake," he whispered. The two eyes blinked. Annie arched her back under the blanket and its upper edge slipped down an inch or so on her chest, filling

Conrad with delicious expectation. He stepped closer to the sofa and Annie's eyes closed.

"Are you okay?" he asked.

"Yes."

"I mean, last night, like—"

"Oh, no, I'm fine."

"It sounded—"

"It was nothing." She opened her eyes and looked up at him.

"I was thinking . . ." Conrad said, and stopped helplessly. He didn't know what to do with his hands, standing there. "Maybe we . . ."

"You better put some ice on that, Conrad. This is no time for that."

"He's asleep. I heard him snoring."

"He can hear a pin drop, but that's not the point."

"Well . . ." Conrad said, his courage again fading.

"Go get dressed, Conrad. We've got work to do before we go to Colorado. There'll be time when we get there to fool around." She smiled at him and sat up. The blanket fell away and Conrad gawked at her breasts. "Go on," she said.

Conrad turned and left, whipsawed by a turmoil of leaden anticlimax and golden hope.

Sometime later, when the sun was above the mountains in the east, Mo Bowdre woke up and took a long shower, hoping it would clear his mind, which still writhed over Annie's surprise attack of the night before. Emerging from the bathroom wrapped in a large towel, he sensed a presence in his bedroom just as Annie said, "Hi. Good morning. I brought you some coffee."

He felt the mug touch his fingers and took it from her. Her voice was cheerful, flutelike.

"It's a beautiful day," she said. "So clear out there it's awesome. I made a bunch of sandwiches for the cooler. That way we won't have to stop."

Mo's mind spun. Didn't she remember? What was going on? What *wasn't* going on?

"As soon as you've finished breakfast, we can go," she said. She touched his forearm and pecked him on the cheek. "I'll let you get dressed now."

He heard the door shut and he sat down on the bed. Crazy as an owl on speed, he thought. Maybe she really is crazy. Do people ever get Alzheimer's at twenty-one? What if I got a daughter who's a head case? What do I do then?

He wished Connie were here, to handle all this, and then realized the cowardice of that wish. Hell, maybe there was some truth to what Annie had said in her tirade. Maybe he was a bit self-absorbed, something of an actor. Maybe he hadn't really thought about it from her point of view. Maybe . . .

Goddamn it, I'm just a sculptor, he said to himself. I do art. I'm not cut out for this relationship shit. Women do that stuff. And shrinks. And . . . Oh, shoot. Fathers, I guess.

What they need, he said to himself, happily letting his mind stray from the bewildering situation at hand, was a father school. A school for fathers.

How the hell is a man supposed to do this right with nothing but on-the-job training?

* * *

Flame Gypsy, the Arabian filly, stood outside the paddock, her head leaning over the white pipe fence, and whinnied, calling out to the other horses. Gypsy was both hungry and thirsty. The other horses, all locked in their stalls, were hungry as well. By this time of day, with the sun up over the mountains in the east for more than an hour, John Franklin would have fed them each a two-inch-thick slab from a bale of alfalfa hay. The other horses, too, were restless, and one of them, an old mare, had begun rhythmically kicking the side of her stall.

Outside, Gypsy whinnied again. For ten minutes after the fall on the night before, she had stood near the rider, now in the utterly strange position of lying on the ground. A few times she had pushed at him with her nose, big nostrils flaring, trying to smell what was going on. Then she wandered off, soon fetching up against the paddock fence, where she had waited, fully saddled, reins hanging down before her front legs. From the round tank about twenty feet from the fence inside the paddock, the smell of water came to her.

A mile or so away John Franklin lay on his back in the dirt. His eyes were closed, and to anyone coming upon him, he would have appeared to be sleeping. His chest rose and fell slightly but with some regularity at a rate of about eight times a minute. Down the incline to the arroyo, about fifty yards away, the flies had already come to Rhiannon Sharp. In the early morning sun, theirs was the only sound.

In the Sharp-Franklin house no one had made the usual morning adjustments of the solar heating and cooling system, and the house would soon begin to heat up inside. By mid-afternoon it would be a furnace. And now the phone began to ring—four rings, until it was intercepted electronically and the low menopausal voice of Rhiannon Sharp said, "John and I can't come to the phone right now. Please leave a message and we'll get back to you as soon as we can."

In his cramped office in the police station on Cerrillos Road, Sergeant Anthony Ramirez sat with his feet crossed at the ankles on his desk, his arms crossed behind his head. A cup of coffee was sitting on the desk losing heat while he explained briefly the profile of the man who had murdered the two young people to Maria, the chunky policewoman only recently assigned to the homicide department. Maria's eyes had widened toward the shape of saucers by the time Ramirez finished his account.

"That's really sick, you know?" She shook her head. "A man killing his own daughter."

"Yeah," Ramirez agreed. "And just because of a roll in the oven."

Maria's eyes widened yet farther, then crinkled up and she laughed. "I think it's a bun they get in the oven. After a roll in the hay. You want to speak Spanish?"

"It's my second language," Ramirez said, thinking that Maria was pretty when she laughed. "Anyway, maybe we can get some help on this from Los Alamos."

"The cops?"

"No, the personnel department. They'd know if there was anyone there who was Indian, from Bombay originally, wouldn't they? And maybe Sandia Labs down in

Albuquerque. Try them, too. All those lab employees have to go through a security check. Check for employees, and recent employees, too. And ask 'em about other science places, institutes, high-tech businesses that've spun off from the labs—all of that."

"What makes us so sure this guy is a scientist?"

"We aren't. It's just a possibility. Anything come in yet from the schools? About the girl?"

"Yeah. La Cueva High School in Albuquerque. The principal's office called last night around six, said they have a student who looks something like the drawing, but she's on a field trip to Alamagordo. To the Space Museum. They checked down there and she's with 'em. Maybe we'll hear more this morning."

"Yeah, maybe. The restaurants?"

"Nothing so far," Maria said. "We could use more bodies."

"Have 'em go back and ask if anyone knows any Parsis. I'll talk to Lieutenant Ortiz, maybe get some guys from Vice to help us out."

"Those creeps?"

"Maria, they're our colleagues."

It was not until another hour passed that the Santa Fe Police Department learned that matters were awry at Rhiannon Sharp's residence out beyond Tano Road. A call came in to the 911 operator, and the dispatcher had the wit to inform Ramirez's office. The 911 call was made by a Pojoaque Indian kid name Joe Tapia, whom John Franklin had hired for the summer to muck out the stables of Kokapelli Arabians six days a week and take care of the other menial chores for six and a half dollars an hour.

Tapia, an unreliable student struggling through high school, reported to work every morning between nine and nine-thirty, having driven the fifteen miles south from Pojoaque Pueblo in an ancient Chevy pickup he kept functioning by the continuing application of spare parts. As good a mechanic as he had to be, he was especially attuned to horses. Within seconds of alighting from his pickup where he had parked near the stables, Tapia knew something was wrong. The horses were carrying on, calling out, and they should have been contentedly munching the last of their alfalfa. Coming around the corner of the stables, he spotted Gypsy across the paddock, tacked up but loose on the other side of the fence. He couldn't imagine what was going on, and he made his way calmly toward her, crooning her name. About twenty feet from her, he ducked under the white pipe fence and approached, still crooning. She stood watching him come, ears rotating like radar screens, and seemed to sag with relief when he took her dangling reins in hand.

Once the filly was safe in her stall, he fed the horses, taking it upon himself to provide them with a bit more than the normal amount. Calm descended in the stalls, and only then did he begin to look around for signs of human life, finding none in the vicinity of the stables. With a panicky feeling in his stomach, he trotted over to the main house and knocked on the front door, knocking three more times in the next minute. He tried the door but it was locked, so he trotted around to the back of the house, the west-facing side, and peered in the windows, seeing nobody. On one of the patios he saw a tall, blue-tinted glass, partly full of colorless liquid and with a sprig of wilted mint hanging over its lip. He went to the patio door, found it unlocked, and entered the house. Five minutes later he called 911, reporting that the owners were nowhere to be found and the horses had been left unattended, which never happened.

Fifteen minutes later the first squad car arrived in the big turnaround area of the driveway, followed closely by an unmarked car from which Sergeant Anthony Ramirez yelled to the two uniforms, Gutierrez and Franco.

On hearing from the dispatcher, Ramirez had burst out of his office into the bullpen, demanding from anyone what the local news broadcasts had said about the murders last night. The *New Mexican* had given the story only a couple of inches this morning, noting only that two bodies, male and female, had been found in a remote area of the city and that the police suspected that they were the result of homicide. Assured that no other details had been announced on yesterday's late afternoon or evening news broadcasts—after all, the department had provided no other details—Ramirez had run from the building to his vehicle, his mind adding the next chapter to Mo Bowdre's story of the night before.

The guy had heard on the news that two bodies were found, male and female. He had to check, to see if they were *his* bodies. Maybe he knew, or maybe he just suspected, that such corpses would be hauled away from the scene and, if unclaimed after some period of time, disposed of. Cremated. God's will wouldn't be done if the work of scavengers was unfinished. And hadn't Mo said something about the burning of human flesh being a major sin among the Parsis? So the nut goes back yet another time to check and, for whatever reason, he runs into Sharp and Franklin.

This worst scenario still boiling in his mind, Ramirez told the cops to follow him and set off over the bumpy ground through the piñon trees toward the arroyo where the young couple's bodies had been found just over two days earlier. Within minutes he found Franklin, supine in the dirt, and ascertained that he was unconscious but still breathing, if only barely, maybe in a coma. At the same time, down in the arroyo about fifty yards away, he spotted the body of Rhiannon Sharp. On his radio phone he called for an ambulance and then for a forensic team.

But there was no doubt what had happened. From the hoof marks in the sand it was clear that Franklin had been thrown from a horse. It was clear that someone, probably a man, judging from the size of the footprints made by a pair of running shoes like Reeboks, had been present, maybe spooked the horse. And it was perfectly clear, even from fifty yards, what had been the cause of Rhiannon Sharp's death. Her head had been twisted almost halfway around on her skinny neck, and her limbs were sprawled this way and that like broken twigs.

"Shit," Ramirez intoned, thinking about the implications of the scene. It was a scene crying out with surprise, panic, carelessness. The guy could be in some other state by now. He waved the two uniforms away from Franklin and knelt down beside him again, listening, hoping against hope that he would keep breathing.

*   *   *

In all, it is 110 miles from Santa Fe north on Route 285 to Antonito, an old Hispanic settlement a few miles across the state line in Colorado. The town is still largely agricultural and with a short growing season, being nearly eight thousand feet above sea level in high plateau country, not far to the east of where the southernmost tongue of the Rocky Mountains reaches down into New Mexico. A so-called Port of Entry into Colorado, Antonito is one of those places that people would only pass through, hardly noticing it, if it were not for the railroad yards that dominate the town and seem totally out of place.

For Antonito is the western terminus of the Cumbres & Toltec Scenic Railroad, one of the last stretches of operating narrow-gauge railways that once laced much of the entire southern Rockies together, transferring the fabulous mineral resources of the mountains to places like Santa Fe and Denver, where they immediately became money. This all took place in the latter part of the nineteenth century, and it was a monumental task, using mostly hand tools and mules, to forge these iron links over mountain passes, along precipitous cliffs and over deep canyons.

But things soon went to hell, as they usually do in mining country, and the railroads fell into disuse. The Cumbres & Toltec, rescued by private citizens from oblivion and still belching raw coal smoke and ash in sufficient quantities to alarm environmental purists, now takes tourists some sixty miles through the glorious high montane forest to the New Mexican border town of Chama. It is the longest and the highest stretch of narrow-gauge railway left.

Were it not for the Cumbres & Toltec, the world would surely take no note whatsoever of the town of Antonito, but it was here that Conrad Franklin had slowed from the steady seventy-five miles per hour he had maintained for most of the drive from Santa Fe, and pulled into a somewhat slatternly gas station and geegaw store along the highway. Precisely as they crossed the state border, Annie announced her urgent need to pee, explaining that she hadn't noticed very many places in this part of southern Colorado where it was possible.

While Annie was inside, and Conrad assiduously washed the corpses of bugs from the windshield of his otherwise still gleaming, black Ram 1500 V-8 Magnum pickup with club cab and six Infinity speakers, Mo Bowdre stood by the passenger door in the dusty lot, his fists balled up in the pockets of his jeans. His hair and beard were whipped by the wind that almost always blows across this high plateau country. The sun was warm on his neck, to be sure, the air itself was cool, and the wind was fresh but for a pleasant trace of coal dust, but Mo Bowdre's spirit was depressed and he'd begun to feel ominous twinges here and there in his frame, the onset of hypochondria. His heart, simply, was not in this adventure.

In his state of mind, even Conrad's spiffy pickup annoyed him. It ran too quiet, for one thing, and it was too plush, for another. It just didn't seem right being in a pickup that felt more like a luxury car with its soft imitation leather seats, and not one, but two handles by which

the passenger riding shotgun could steady himself if . . .
Mo couldn't imagine what road condition might cause
the super suspension of this Rambo vehicle even to
hiccup, much less lurch enough to toss a passenger
around. You were *supposed* to rattle around a little in a
pickup, for God's sake, not sit prim and pretty like in
some pantywaist parlor.

Rambo pickup indeed. Rambo in a tutu maybe.

It was going to be a long day.

They still had about 150 miles to go—another three
hours, given the mountainous roads that lay ahead—and
a cheerless silence had characterized the first leg. Annie,
in the rear seat of the club cab, had chirped about one
thing or another for a few minutes after they set out
and then fell asleep. Conrad had hooked up some earphones to the audio system and disappeared into God-
knew-what noisy place. Whatever music it might have
been, it was audible only as a tinny whine escaping his
tightly clamped earphones. Mo had sat, strapped in like a
huge infant in a car seat, gloomily pondering the nature
of women, and coming to no conclusions. Beneath his
gloomy mood an unresolvable question lay, gnawing like
a parasitic worm: Was he really a selfish person?

He heard Annie's boots crunching across the parking
lot and turned in her direction.

"I got us some lemonade," she said. "Some little kids
have a stand over there in the shade. Really cute. Great
big eyes, all serious when they were counting out the
change. Twenty cents a cup. Did you ever do that when
you were a kid?"

Moments later Conrad, hooked up to his sounds, his

cup of lemonade in his left hand, expertly swung the Ram pickup out onto the two-lane highway.

"What exactly are we going to be doing up there?" Annie asked. She patted Mo on the shoulder and left her hand resting there.

"I don't know for certain. I'd kinda like to buy us a beer in the Silver Dollar Saloon. Old times' sake."

"Cool. But Conrad's under age," Annie said.

"They didn't used to worry too much about that."

"They do now."

"We can get him some sarsaparilla. Hopalong Conrad."

"Huh?"

"You never heard of Hopalong Cassidy?" Mo said. "And at some point, I guess we'll want to go on over and see your mother."

"Yeah," Annie said, and removed her hand. She moved over to the backseat directly behind Conrad and touched the back of his neck. Slowly, as if absentmindedly, she moved it around to the front and snaked it down inside his T-shirt, stroking his bare chest. Conrad wriggled with pleasure, and with her other hand, Annie pulled one earphone away from his head.

"When we get to Salida," she said, "we can change seats and I'll drive. Would you like that?"

It was 10:38 in the morning, the very moment when Sergeant Anthony Ramirez called Mo Bowdre's house on his radio phone to find Conrad and give him the bad news about his parents. The answering machine recorded the message. It said, simply, to call Ramirez.

twelve

"No way, man," the ambulance driver had said, waving his hand impatiently at the surround. "Not over this shit." So John Franklin, carefully trussed and still only barely breathing, was lifted away from his own south forty by helicopter and flown to the University of New Mexico Hospital in Albuquerque, where it would be quickly ascertained that his neck was broken, his body totally paralyzed, and his chances of surviving nearly nil.

Leaning on the roof of his vehicle, Ramirez had watched the chopper swoop away like a big dragonfly, the sun glinting from its bubble cockpit like a big insect eye. He turned to Lieutenant Ortiz, who stood nearby watching the helicopter disappear behind the piñon trees above them.

"What do you think?"

Ramirez had filled the lieutenant in on the Bowdre scenario, adding his own chapter, which explained what might have happened to Rhiannon Sharp and her husband. Ortiz was frowning.

"You want an APB, the only fact we can offer is the guy looks like an India Indian?"

"With running-type shoes and probably in a New Mexico vehicle. What harm can it do?"

"It can make us the laughingstock of law enforcement personnel in six states."

"Right now," Ramirez said, "I don't have any better idea. If I was him, I'd be getting my ass as far from here as I could. His bodies are gone, his ceremony or whatever it is is fucked, and he's killed another person, maybe two for all he knows. Even some religious fanatic would know he was in it deep now."

"If that's what all this is about," Ortiz said.

Ramirez crossed his arms, looked to the west and waited. He had made his case and, under the scrutiny of his superior, the two of them standing in the glare of the sun in this star-crossed arroyo rather than sitting in the dark around a cheerful piñon fire with a beer, it sounded pretty thin. Pretty elaborate, pretty—well—outlandish.

Ortiz sighed. "Okay," he said. "Okay. Do it. And the police portraits?"

"I'll give 'em to the press this afternoon."

Ortiz turned and began trekking up the rise to where his own vehicle was standing. He stopped, turned around and fixed Ramirez with his eyes. His tongue flicked out and probed his mustache, then disappeared back between his lips.

"It sure as hell was simpler when this was the land of only three cultures," he said, and stalked up the rise. "Parsis," he muttered to himself. "What next? What fucking next?"

* * *

I don't want to go there. I don't want to see her. I don't want to go in that house again, listen to her, see her sitting there with her little copper ashtray full of butts, listen to her whimper and moan. Like it wasn't her fault, her fault all this happened, all of it. Her and that disgusting creep, both of them shouting at me, looking at me like I'm an insect or something—no, no, no! I don't want to go there. Well, he's long gone anyway.

Didn't I already cut it off, cut it, *severed the old bag. Not part of me anymore. I left her there. I found him.*

What am I going to do? I can't let him . . . no. I want him for my father. I love him. God, I love him, sitting there, look at him, big, silent. So beautiful. Sleeping again. I want him to love me, me . . . *he will. He does. I can make him happy. I won't let him . . . I won't let* her *screw this up.*

We can't go there.

What am I going to do?

Whatever I have to. And I'll be needing Conrad, won't I? Probably, yes. Poor dumb twit with his bony chest. Look, his ear sticks out when I pull the earphone away.

"Conrad, why don't we trade places now? Wouldn't you like that? Why wait till Salida?"

Mo Bowdre stirred but didn't seem to wake as Conrad pulled over on the shoulder and brought the truck to a stop. He slept on as moments later Annie eased the truck back out on the highway and up to fifty-five miles an hour. Conrad, after furtively glancing over at the sleeping man in the passenger seat, leaned close to the back of the front seat and slipped his hand down into Annie's shirt, entering immediately into a euphoria so great that it was five full minutes before he noticed that cars and even a battered old pickup were passing them.

"How come we're going so slow?" he asked.

"Fifty-five's the speed limit on this road. Colorado cops are murder on speeders," Annie said.

"These guys sure don't seem to know it."

"They do their thing, we do ours, right, Conrad?"

She patted his hand through her shirt, and he said, "Right, right. No problem."

"Good."

The tires made a gentle, rhythmic ticking sound as they crossed each joint in the cement highway, passing through mile after mile of flat farm and ranch country, whitecapped mountains rising on the east and west horizons like giant rows of teeth. The huge landscape around them was cool and bluish, seen through the tinted windows of the pickup, but Conrad was too preoccupied to notice any of it. Part of his mind, however, drifted back to the muffled sound of Annie yelling at Mo the night before. She's just met this guy, he thought, just met her father after twenty-one years, and she starts yelling at him. He had never yelled at his father, just looked disgusted and shrank away whenever they had a disagreement. But Annie—she just went in there and hollered.

I guess she's quite a handful, Conrad thought, and then, under the circumstances, thought that was pretty funny. He smirked.

Yeah. A handful.

Later, a few miles beyond Alamosa on the utterly straight stretch of Route 17, Mo's head jerked and he grunted. He reached up and squeezed the nape of his neck, craning his head this way and that. Annie looked over at him and gently lifted Conrad's arm away from her, sensing that he subsided back into his seat. She turned her head to give him a brief grin.

"Were you dreaming?" she asked, and reached over to put a hand on Mo's leg. "Was it a bad dream?"

"Oh, well, it was a mining dream." Mo shook his head. "Where are we?"

"About an hour south of Salida. Then it's another seventy-five miles."

"You're not into speed, are you, like Conrad?" Mo said.

"I'm going the speed limit. Fifty-five. How can you tell?"

"It's just a sense you get. A feel."

Annie left her hand resting on his knee. "Wow," she said. "Were you dreaming about your accident?"

"Oh yeah. And you're going fifty-five in a state where an ignition key turns everyone into a damn maniac. I guess neither of us are all that anxious to get there, huh?" He patted her hand with a big paw. "Well, we'll be all right. We'll sort it out."

We, Annie said to herself. He said we.

We'll sort it out. Yes.

God, how she loved him.

Santa Fe, while it is the state's capital and a leading world art center and tourist attraction, is a city of merely sixty thousand souls, and supports only a small press corps—a handful of local print reporters, a smaller handful of wire service stringers, and an even smaller handful of reporters from the state's television stations. Except for those among them assigned to specific beats like the art world, most turn up when the Santa Fe Police Department suggests that it has an important announcement to make.

By three o'clock Tuesday afternoon the usual group of press people had assembled in the largest room available in the police department, one designed specifically as a conference room. An attempt had recently been made to make the room a bit less discouraging than the rest of the station decor: the walls were painted Navajo white, and someone had hung six Georgia O'Keeffe posters on them. Three of these showed her familiar, nearly abstract versions of the northern New Mexico landscape, and the others were equally familiar intimate portraits of the innards of brightly colored flowers. The latter had given rise to the oft-repeated sexual jokes until the chief, hearing of them, cracked down with a sternly worded memorandum to the entire staff about sexual harassment.

Of course, the press and the police all knew each other quite well, and a more or less friendly and ritualized relationship existed between them—part adversarial, part collegial. So when Sergeant Anthony Ramirez strode into the room, bearing a thick manila envelope under his arm, followed by the policewoman, Maria, they all called out cheerful greetings from the conference room chairs in which they lolled.

"Hey, Tony."

"Hey, it's Inspector Clouseau."

"Is this a show-and-tell session?"

"Maria, what's he got in the envelope?"

Ramirez took up a position at the end of the room and handed the envelope to Maria.

"Okay, amigos, can I have your attention?" Ramirez said unnecessarily. "Officer Baca is going to hand out to you copies of two police department portraits. These are of the two individuals found two days ago who were determined to be homicides. The individuals were apparently in their late teens, and they are yet to be identified. The Santa Fe Police Department hopes that you people will assist us by showing these faces in the media."

As Maria handed out the portraits, each member of the press stared at them.

"Hey, this girl looks Indian. What tribe?"

"Not that kind of Indian," Ramirez said. "She's the other kind. The subcontinent of Asia."

"Oh. An *Indian*."

"How were they killed, Tony? Cause of death?"

"We cannot divulge that at this time. We do not want to impede our investigation."

"Aww, bullshit, Tony . . ."

"Amigos," Ramirez said, and shrugged.

"So where exactly did this happen?"

"Within the city limits, out in the northwest part," Ramirez said.

"Out where they're building those big estates? Out past Tano Road?"

Ramirez remained silent, as if weighing something in his mind. "Will we have your cooperation with the portraits?"

Voices indicated complete cooperation.

"Very good. There is another development you should

know about. I can only give you preliminary details. This morning, in the same general vicinity as the previous homicides, the police discovered two more individuals, one a homicide, the other severely injured in what appears to be a riding accident."

Ramirez ducked at the clamor that arose.

"Yes," he said, "we know the identity of these individuals, but their names can't be released until the next of kin are notified."

"Christ, it's like a crime wave. Are these all related?"

"We don't know that," Ramirez said.

"Does this have anything to do with the guy they medevacked out of there this morning?" This was the man from one of the local network affiliates. The others all stared at him. He was often ahead of the pack.

Ramirez elected to say nothing about that. Instead he looked at one of the other reporters. "You asked if there were any suspects? The answer is no, not exactly."

"What about the APB, Tony? Isn't that about a suspect, or does some deadbeat owe you some money?"

"We have asked other jurisdictions to be on the lookout for an individual whose origins are from subcontinental Asia. A male. We have reason to believe such a person might be helpful in our investigation. That's all I can say about that."

Again a clamor arose. "The girl's father?"

"Husband? Don't they arrange marriage with young virgins or something?"

"Come on, Tony, give."

"That's all I can say for now, amigos. I am grateful to

you, as always, for your attention, and in this case for your help."

Five minutes later Ramirez was at his desk and punched out the numbers of Mo Bowdre's telephone. He listened until, for the fourth time that day, the fourth ring ended and the answering machine began to click on with the usual message that no one could answer the telephone at this time. . . .

"Damn," Ramirez said out loud. Where the hell were they? Bowdre and his unlikely little family. Connie might know, but she was back home on the reservation. Maybe he could get the Hopi police to find her, have her call. But then . . . Ramirez smacked his hand down on the desk. *Yes!*

Two minutes later he and the big cop Gutierrez were listening to the tape-recorded messages from Rhiannon Sharp's answering machine, which Gutierrez had routinely collected. There were two messages, the first from a woman who was evidently a neighbor, hoping that Rhiannon had learned some dirt about the killing of the couple on her property. The other was from Mo Bowdre.

"Rhiannon? This is Mo. It's Tuesday morning. Look, I got me some business up north, and Conrad is going to give us a ride up there. Everything's just fine. And, oh yeah, the police don't think old Conrad here had anything to do with that couple out there. So don't you worry yourself none about that. We'll be back in a coupla days, call you then."

In another five minutes Ramirez was talking to a sergeant in the Lake County, Colorado, sheriff's department.

"Yeah," he said. "A new one. Black. Got a rack of

searchlights mounted on it, New Mexico plates." He read off the number. "We got a homicide investigation down here . . . No, no. The truck's owner is this kid Conrad Franklin, seventeen years old. He's next of kin and we want to . . . Right. No, no, there's nothing dangerous about these people. We just need to . . . Yeah, right. The other guy is big, blond, got a beard, always wears dark glasses. Bowdre, Mo Bowdre. He's blind. You can't miss him. And they probably have a girl with them. From up there in Leadville. Annie Harper . . . You don't know her? Brown hair, blue eyes. About five-nine. Twenty-one . . . Him? I don't know exactly. Maybe late forties? Okay? I really appreciate it."

Conrad had never seen such a dump, such a depressing place. Of course, in his relatively carefree life growing up in the happier parts of Santa Fe, he hadn't seen very many truly depressing places. So the countryside alongside Route 24 leading into Leadville struck him as utterly blighted, not just a few crummy and run-down homes here and there like in parts of New Mexico, but a whole area dying if not already dead.

They had been climbing mostly for more than an hour, and Annie, who was still driving, had broken her silence only a few times, once to point out the huge white-topped mountain to the west, saying it was Mount Elbert, highest place in Colorado, and adding that Leadville itself, at more than ten thousand feet, was the highest incorporated city in North America. She had explained these things in a flat voice, almost like a recording, and lapsed again into a tense-jawed silence. They entered a high valley, and the signs of what must have been mining activity blotched the landscape, big piles of dirt, black piles, orangish piles. Slag heaps, Conrad guessed.

This must have been a real beautiful place once, Conrad thought, this high valley between the mountains with those two big ones, Mount Elbert and another one, dominating the sky. Probably lots of forests, elk, deer, all that stuff. But now it was pretty much denuded, just some scrubby-looking woods around, here and there, and these slag heaps. More and more he began to see great ridges of black slag, and old abandoned foundations like little cemeteries. A few industrial-type buildings made of wood and falling down. Mills, he guessed. A few isolated shacks and abandoned mobile homes sprinkled along the road, and then some kind of settlement—a bunch of little houses, mobile homes, shacks of dry, unpainted boards, garages about to topple over.

"Is this Leadville?" Conrad asked in disbelief.

"Stringtown," Annie said. "Like a suburb."

Conrad shook his head. Good, he thought. There's better things ahead. A better part of town. He assumed that Annie came from a better part of town, and not a dump like this Stringtown. But then if this place was a suburb, maybe Leadville itself was a dump, too. To the extent that he had ever been close to poor communities, with the people looking tired, half dead, they made him edgy, filled him with apprehension, even fear—like what he felt when confronted by strange dogs or, once, by three Hispanic guys about his age who crossed an empty street in Santa Fe seemingly to intercept him. They had snorted about gringos and gone by laughing, leaving him feeling drained.

"Leadville's right up ahead," Annie said, but she slowed down and turned right off the highway onto a dirt road full of pits and rocks jutting out of the dirt. The Ram swayed and bounced and she slowed down to a mere five miles an hour. Mo Bowdre sat erect in the passenger seat, grinning.

"This must be one hell of a road if it's got this baby swaying."

Conrad peered past Annie's hair and through the windshield. They rounded a hill of black slag and ahead he saw an old mobile home sitting on cinder blocks in a patch of bare dirt. A few pieces of junk, maybe parts of engines, littered the ground, along with a clothesline that had fallen over and an old blue tarp that had got caught under it and flopped in the wind like a big mollusk taking its last breaths. The mobile home's windows were mostly broken, a few covered over with cardboard, and the door hung open, swaying back and forth through a small arc. The place was obviously abandoned, and Conrad couldn't imagine what they were doing here.

Annie brought the truck to a stop and opened the door. "It doesn't look like she's here," she said. "Car's gone." She stepped out and added, "My mom."

"But this place—" Conrad blurted, and Annie's fierce blue eyes fixed him, skewered him, with a scowl. She drew a finger across her throat. Conrad sank back into the seat, wondering again what the hell was going on. This couldn't be . . . no one had lived here for God knows how long. He watched Annie go to the door, hanging open on its hinges, and saw her knock on the door frame. She stood motionlessly before the entrance and then returned to the truck, climbing in behind the wheel.

"Not home. She might be over at the clinic. We better go find a place to stay. There's a motel the other side of Leadville that isn't too expensive."

"First, the Silver Dollar Saloon," Mo said. "Put a little courage in our veins. Hah. Hah."

The Silver Dollar Saloon was a lot more promising, as far as Conrad was concerned. Even classy. The main street in Leadville had given him a lift, lined with multi-storied, colorful old buildings of brick with stone trim like gingerbread. Some of them were falling apart, abandoned-looking, but a lot were restored. One of them, a big hotel, looked like something out of the movies, and so did the Silver Dollar Saloon, with its highly polished old bar and the lights designed to look like gaslights. It was a dark place, lots of gold-framed paintings on the walls, along with other stuff.

Two men sat at the bar, on stools at the far ends of the bar. They looked ordinary enough, guys in western shirts and jeans, old guys with bellies. The bartender was younger, with a shock of blond hair he wore the same way Robert Redford did, but that's where the resemblance ended. He had a pinched little face, with dark eyes so close together they almost touched. He looked up as they came in, Annie walking about a half step ahead of Mo Bowdre, the blind man keeping pace with her and looking like just another person with dark glasses.

"Hey, Annie. Back so soon. Where you been?"

"These are my friends," Annie said unsociably. "Mo and Conrad. Phil."

Phil came around the bar as they pulled the chairs back from the table nearest the entrance and sat down.

"What's on draft?" Mo asked, and Phil rattled off some familiar names. "Actually, I think I'll have something a little more courageous. You got bourbon? On the rocks."

"Coors," Annie said, glancing up at Phil with what appeared to be an unfriendly look.

Shit, Conrad thought.

"Same for you?" Phil said.

Conrad nodded and scratched his jaw the way guys with two days' growth of beard do. He looked at Annie and shrugged.

"I used to work here, nights," Annie said to Mo. "And you used to come here, too, huh? That's really something."

Conrad stood up. "I'll be right back. I got to use the men's room."

"It's back there," Annie said, gesturing with her head into the dimly lit rear of the saloon. Conrad made his way around the tables into the gloom, looking appreciatively at the naked woman lounging above him in a gold frame.

Moments later, checking himself in the mirror over the little basin in the men's room, he was startled by the door opening, and more startled to see Annie step in and stand behind him.

"Conrad," she said, putting her hands on his shoulders and turning him around. With her in her cowboy boots, they were the same height. A slight frown wrinkled her forehead.

"What's wrong?" he asked, wondering what he would do if one of those old guys at the bar chose this moment to take a leak.

"With us? Nothing." She put her hands on his waist and pulled him a step closer. "We're fine. We're lovers. But this is a very important time. There are some things here, some things I've got to do you might not understand at first."

"Like what? Like that place, the mobile home? There wasn't anybody—"

"Put your arms around me. Good, like that. See, this whole thing is very complicated, and I've got to see that we all come out okay." She pressed her stomach and hips against him. He couldn't imagine what she was talking about, except that she was pulling a few numbers on Mo, the blind man, her father.

"I don't get it," he said.

"You will. It'll all get clear. Soon. But I need you, Conrad. I totally *need* you, need your help. Will you give it to me?" She put her arms around his neck and pulled his head toward her. "Will you?"

"Yeah," he said.

"Do what I ask?"

"Yeah, no problem."

She kissed him on the lips, and he felt her tongue flitting in and out, then felt her rotating her hips against him. Then, abruptly, she stepped back, holding him at arm's length, smiling broadly at him. Her eyes brimmed. "Oh man," she said. "It's going to be good. Real good."

She turned and left Conrad standing in the middle of the men's room, filled with grand visions. When he returned to the table, Phil had delivered the drinks and Mo sat with one big paw wrapped around a glass of ice and bourbon. Annie was nowhere to be seen.

"Annie's still in the can," Mo said. "Women can find any manner of things to do in the bathroom."

thirteen

What had until recently been known as the El Moro Motel on Cordova Road in Santa Fe, now served as the offices of an organization called Complex Forecasts, Inc. In its days as a motel, it had never amounted to much by way of the tourist business, but it eked out an existence over the years by not overcharging transients and not undercharging hookers and making sure the rooms were clean, the bedding fresh, and the satellite TVs operational. The family that owned the motel made most of their money running a combination saloon and sandwich shop next door, and were all too happy to bail out of the motel business when they were approached by a realtor representing a new-start business, something about applying mathematical theory to complicated events. Now the family were landlords, a far more carefree role.

The building was little more than a long rectangular box of one story approximately in the middle of a gravel parking lot. Under the big plastic sign that spelled El Moro in neon was a large room that had been office and lobby, and sixteen bedrooms, each with its own bath. These had been renovated at the renter's expense into a reception room, fourteen separate offices—each still with its own bathroom—and a large room, made by knocking out a wall, where the company had its storage files and Xerox equipment.

The family had watched the old sign come down with some sadness, and the rest of the work with some puzzlement, wondering what sort of business it was that wanted its employees isolated like that, each in a separate compartment like a cell. And they watched with some amusement as the new tenants moved in, as strange a group of human beings as they'd ever seen. Several looked for all the world like those hippies that used to be around, longhaired and wild-looking, a smaller group wore business suits like bankers, and the rest looked like a delegation from the United Nations—diminutive Orientals, anthracite blacks in robes, people of varying skin color and costume, including one who was Anglo but always wore a white turban and white clothes, like those Sikhs who run the car-parking service for the rich people.

These oddballs would arrive at various times of day or night and each disappear into his or her cell, not to emerge for hours at a time. The only one who ever came into their saloon for any reason was one of the business suits, a man named Edward Jans, who apparently was the big boss. Dr. Jans arrived at noon on the last Friday of every month, ordered a double Canadian Mist on the rocks, drank it, and handed over the rent check for the following month.

The family was fairly well convinced by all this that they were renting out the former El Moro Motel to an international gang of thieves bent on lifting secrets from

Los Alamos National Laboratories. Hadn't these people also moved into each cell a lot of expensive-looking computers and God knew what other sorts of electronic equipment? And they had no visible clients, either, did they? No one but the employees ever showed up and parked in the gravel parking lot.

Thieves, or maybe CIA. But they did pay the rent.

As suspicious as Complex Forecasts, Inc. seemed, however, it had been brought into existence by virtue of an enormous grant by the third largest bank in New York City along with smaller go-along grants from two mid-western foundations. With these gobs of money, Dr. Edward Jans, who had been an administrative type of some clout at Los Alamos, assembled thirteen of the brightest mathematicians and computer nerds in the burgeoning new field of Complexity Theory, several of them leaving Los Alamos with Jans before being laid off in the federal government's spasm of firing its most intelligent employees. Complex Forecasts, Inc. was one of several institutes and businesses that had sprung up in and around Santa Fe in recent years, spinning off from the national labs and into the promising new money trough of cyberspace.

In the former El Moro Motel, the thirteen odd geniuses set to work developing the means to forecast such things as the behavior of the New York Stock Exchange and NASDAQ, and the climate, especially the climate as it affected—*impacted* was the word of choice—the long-term ups and downs of the commodities market. Had they known all this, the landlord family might have snickered, there being no vehicle even approaching a

BMW or a Lexus in the parking lot. But the bankers in New York had promised funds covering half the operating expenses for five years of research and development, not a great deal of money considering the payoff if this long shot were to bear fruit.

Edward Jans, a theoretical physicist himself before turning to administration, spent most of his time these days fund-raising and listening with increasing incomprehension during the loosely organized seminars when his troops met to exchange ideas, which usually took place twice a week. Jans always found himself in a bad mood when the nerds drifted off after such a seminar— they were operating in a dimension where he could only grope his way—and he was feeling typically irritable when Myrna, the pretty new receptionist they'd just hired, told him there was a Sergeant Ramirez waiting to talk to him, evidently a policeman. He looked at his watch. It was four-thirty.

Jans did not stand up when the door to what had been room 1A of the El Moro Motel opened and Myrna stood aside on the concrete sidewalk to let the policeman in. He was a compact Hispanic with sad, almond-shaped eyes and black hair that looked like it was made of iron, and he wore a blue blazer jacket over a pair of tan slacks. He reached in his jacket pocket and produced a wallet as he said, "Dr. Jans, I'm Sergeant Ramirez with the Santa Fe police." He flipped open his wallet to show the badge, and put it back in his pocket. "Thank you for seeing me. I'm sorry to interrupt your, uh, day."

"What can I do for you, Sergeant?" Jans said, remaining in the chair behind his oversized wooden desk. He

watched Ramirez's eyes flicker around the sparsely deco-
rated former bedroom.

"We understand that you have an employee here
named—" Ramirez stumbled briefly over the name.
"—Raymo, Rammho, uh, Ramohan Singe."

"Yes, Dr. Singe," Jans said, keeping his face
expressionless.

"Until recently he was employed at Los Alamos?"

"Yes, that is correct. He began here in January, when
we all did."

"And we understand that he came to this country from
India."

"From Oxford, but yes, he is originally from India.
May I ask—"

"From the west coast of India, around Bombay?"

"I believe that is so. Now, again—"

"We have reason to believe he could be helpful to us in
an investigation. A homicide investigation. Is he here?"

"Good God!" Jans said, and felt sweat pop from his
forehead despite the hyperactive air conditioning. "Is
he—is he—"

"We would like to ask him some routine questions. He
has a daughter?"

Jans, unaccustomed to such rapid-fire questioning, was
suddenly outraged. "Sergeant, this is one of my employees we are discussing, and a friend. I really need to know
more—"

"Does he have a daughter?" Ramirez repeated.

"Yes," Jans said, just as suddenly subdued. The policeman's eyes had neither blinked nor looked anywhere but
into his eyes for as long as they'd spoken. "Ray—Dr.

Singe—brought her here several months ago. From England. In February, I think it was."

Ramirez smiled thinly and nodded. "Have you met the daughter, Dr. Jans?" He reached into his jacket pocket and removed a sheet of paper which he unfolded and slipped across the desk faceup. "Could that be her?"

Jans studied the portrait, frowning. "I met her once. Ray brought her by here. This could be her, but I can't be certain. What—"

"If this is Dr. Singe's daughter, she has been missing from home since Sunday morning, or earlier. We are trying to establish her identity."

"Then it couldn't be Ray's daughter. He would have said something about her being missing. Yesterday. Monday. He's very devoted."

"Is he here?"

"Uh, no. He works at home on Tuesdays and Wednesdays. On a separate contract with his government. He works here the other five days."

"Seven days a week?" Ramirez said, suddenly all sympathy. "That must be a terrible strain. Has Dr. Singe seemed under a strain recently?"

"These are all very driven people who work here, Sergeant."

"Yes, of course. Can you tell me about Dr. Singe's religion?"

"Religion? Good God. I wouldn't think he had a religion. You know, like Hinduism or whatever. He's a mathematician, a mathematical physicist. And he's a very private person."

"He never mentioned the Parsis?"

"Not that I can recall, certainly. What are Parsis?"

Ramirez stood up. "You can give me Dr. Singe's address?"

"Of course," Dr. Jans said, and spun around his chair and opened a drawer in a gray filing cabinet. "He moved out near Cerrillos somewhere. Sergeant, is he—"

"You know," Ramirez said, looking around the room again, "I made an arrest here a few years ago. It was when I was with the vice department. I believe it was this very room. One of our state senators was here with a . . . well, it was a great embarrassment." He smiled conspiratorially, took the piece of paper on which Jans had written an address, and touched his finger to his forehead in a mild salute.

Jans watched him open the door and disappear into the late afternoon glare.

"Cerrillos," Ramirez said to Gutierrez, the big cop behind the wheel of the unmarked police car. "We're in a hurry."

Gutierrez slapped the light on the roof and sped out of the parking lot with the siren blaring. Cars ducked and swerved out of their way as they sped down Cordova, turned on St. Francis, and turned onto Interstate 25 south.

"Okay," Ramirez said, and Gutierrez shut off the siren and turned off the flasher. "Tell the sheriff's department we are proceeding to Cerrillos to talk to a potential witness." Gutierrez thumbed the radio, and Ramirez slumped down in his seat.

This guy Singe—he sounded like the one. Surely was the one. And he could have lit out almost twenty-four hours ago. He also could have blown his brains out. No telling what they were going to find.

Cerrillos was located in the low foothills of the Ortiz Mountains, about ten miles south of where the state penitentiary brooded in ominous isolation over Route 14 and, distantly, the interstate. Once a small and sleepy settlement, Cerrillos was now a growing residential place—not a town, a place—with adobe-style homes springing up like tumbleweeds among the sagebrush and piñons. Increasingly, it served as a bedroom community for Santa Fe, with real estate and construction prices climbing accordingly. The pay for a mathematical genius at Complex Forecasts must be pretty good, Ramirez thought. Dr. Singe's street address was on a new road punched through the scrub to the east of Cerrillos's new suburban sprawl. It wound through more jagged country that had once been a cattle ranch.

The house, reached by a rough dirt driveway, was smaller than Ramirez had expected—a trim one-story adobe with the usual features, vigas protruding from the walls at roofline, the covered portal, the sinuous wall forming a gated courtyard in the front, and a row of clerestory windows jutting up above the roofline. What could be thought of as the yard was bare dirt extending out around the house about twenty yards to the sagebrush scrub. The nearest house was a few hundred yards away to the west, nestled into a low rise. Under a carport a white Isuzu Trooper sat in the shade, a promising sign.

Ramirez waved Gutierrez around to the back and went through the gate, knocking with his left hand on a thick wooden door fitted with black wrought-iron hinges, while with his right hand he drew his service revolver from its holster under his jacket. Noting a doorbell beside the door, he rang that, hearing it chime inside. Hearing nothing further, he knocked again and rang again and again heard nothing. He tried the door and found that it swung open into a small but high-ceilinged hall with a tile floor. On the wall between two archways hung an elaborately wrought circular piece, probably brass, showing what looked like a priest and the head of a bull.

The archway to the left led into a spacious living room that was sparsely furnished, its white hand-plastered walls mostly bare of decoration. At the far end of the room a large leather easy chair, the kind that rocks back into a lounger, faced away from Ramirez toward a rounded bay of floor-to-ceiling windows. A man's head—black hair—was visible above the back of the chair.

"Dr. Singe?"

The head didn't move. Ramirez glanced nervously around the room again. It was spotless. On the ledge below a voluptuously rounded kiva fireplace were two picture frames. From each, a serious face stared back in black and white—one of them a girl who looked much like the portrait in Ramirez's pocket. The other was a boy, almost a dead ringer for the girl.

Ramirez picked up the picture of the girl and approached the chair.

"Dr. Singe? Police."

The man didn't move, but as he came around the chair, Ramirez noted first that his chest rose and fell. He was breathing. His eyes were open, staring straight ahead, as though he were studying the desert landscape outside the tall windows. Beyond the scrub, the Ortiz Mountains glowed in the low sunlight. Huge round clouds rose up behind them, tinged with gold.

The man's skin was brown, a little darker than Ramirez's, but with an underlying pallor. He had full, wide lips, now compressed together, a long narrow nose, and intensely dark eyes that blinked once but took no notice of the policeman standing now before him. Ramirez guessed that he was a six-footer, maybe one seventy. He wore a white shirt, khaki pants, and black sandals over white socks.

"Dr. Singe. Ramohan Singe?"

Slowly the nearly black eyes moved to Ramirez's face, at the same time seeming to return from an unimaginable distance. The whites were a sickly yellow, and a small glob of mucous clung in the corner of his right eye.

Ramirez held out the photograph and holstered his revolver. "This is your daughter," he said quietly.

The man blinked again.

"And the other one?" Ramirez said. "Your son?" The man's eyes watered. He stared out the window. Ramirez stood patiently in front of him.

The man's lips parted, sticking together in the corners. Finally, in a barely audible whisper, he said, "Cancer."

"And your daughter?"

The man, Dr. Singe, glanced at Ramirez and blinked again. "Yes," he whispered. "I . . . She . . . It is . . ." He fell silent.

Gutierrez's large bulk appeared in an archway.

"He's a do-it-yourselfer," the big cop said in a voice

that seemed far too loud. "He's been adding a room on out there." He held up a hammer and unfurled the fingers of his other hand to reveal a few large nails. "Twelve-penny."

"For his daughter, I guess," Ramirez said. He looked back at Ramohan Singe, who was again staring blankly at the window.

"You'll be wanting to come with us, Dr. Singe," Ramirez said slowly. "Isn't that right?"

The lips opened, sticking at the corners, and then shut. Ramirez wondered how long the man had been sitting here, staring out the window. Fasting? Maybe fasting was an acceptable form of suicide among the Parsis. Ramirez reflected on the particular madness that could drive human beings. A man's son dies for no reason, dealt some unreasonable blow by fate. Then his daughter—pregnant with a mongrel. Instead of grasping at . . . instead of reaching out for life, for living, he looks for *purity* in some ancient . . . what? Magic? For a moment Ramirez permitted himself to dwell on the profound sadness of it. There was no one left, was there, to whom one might pray?

"Get him a drink of water," he said to Gutierrez. "Then we'll go."

fourteen

It was snowing.

In June. Lightly, to be sure, but snowing. The flakes drifting down, few and far between, were visible in the pale light from the parking lot of the Frontier Motel, where two one hundred-watt bulbs presided on poles at each end inside what were supposed to look like hurricane lamps. The motel, a long, low building made of dark wooden planks and a wood shingle roof, was designed to look old, like a frontier building. There was a log railing around the front of it, like hitching rails.

The sky had begun clouding over that afternoon, and by early evening the cloud cover was complete. Leadville, the highest incorporated city in North America at 10,200 feet above sea level, was completely shrouded, hidden away from the stars. As the night wore on, the temperature dropped thirty degrees, reaching the freezing point.

The cold struck Conrad Franklin like a slap in the face when he stepped out of his motel room and ever so quietly closed the door behind him. He was wearing only a pair of undershorts.

"Jeez," he said in a whisper, and lit up the dial on his watch. Twelve-forty. The blind man was asleep in there, breathing these amazing long breaths. He'd been asleep for a while, maybe an hour, but Conrad had to be certain he wouldn't wake up. Clutching his bare sides, goose bumps all over him, he trotted barefoot down the wooden walk under a narrow overhang toward the end of the long row of rooms outside of which one of the two hurricane lamps glowed weakly, snowflakes falling past it like dying moths. At the far end he stopped outside the door of room 8 and pushed it. It opened. He stepped in and closed the door behind him.

"Annie," he whispered. In the dim light that came through the window next to the door, he could see her. She was sitting on the bed with her knees pulled up, her arms wrapped around them. The whites of her eyes gleamed.

"It's snowing," he hissed. "Can you believe it? It's *freezing* out there."

"You don't have to whisper," Annie said. "Come here. I'll warm you up." He peered at her as he approached the bed, watching her unfurl her legs and lie back on her elbows. In the shadows, she appeared to be wearing a short nightgown, barely hip-length.

"Lie down here," she said. "We have to talk." He lay down beside her and she said, "No, no. On top of me. There." She wrapped her arms around him, pulling his head down to her neck. Her hair smelled fresh. Beneath him she was soft, firm, strong. He was riding on top of the world, he thought.

"Talk?" Conrad said.

"About us." She laughed. "But I see that'll have to wait." Underneath him, Conrad felt her legs open, her hands reaching down his back, and for a moment he had the pleasant sensation that the world was dropping away beneath him, that he was going to float. . . .

"Here," she was saying. "Here. Let's take our time."

He realized he had slept. Dozed off. He was lying on top of her again, his full weight on her. His face was buried in the pillow, next to her head, his chin touching her shoulder. There was hot sweat between them. Somewhere in the melee, the miraculous writhing, they had shed their bits of clothes. When had that happened? He lifted up his head.

"You're a wizard," Annie murmured. "A fucking wizard." She giggled and tightened her arms around him.

"It was . . . ?"

"It was awesome, Conrad." She wriggled his body from side to side on top of her. "Awesome."

Conrad let his face fall into the pillow again. He was grinning. He felt like he was glowing, like he was lit up like a big neon sign. A big sign blinking FUCKING WIZARD. Yes! There was a pleasant shrunken feeling throughout his groin.

Annie sighed and let her arms fall away to her sides. Slowly, Conrad slid off and lay next to her on his side, his head resting on his hand. With his other hand he traced little circles around her navel. Her skin was still sticky with their sweat. He couldn't believe it. Again, like the time before, he could not believe it was him, here, her, them, lying here, doing it, having done it. He was in a state of pure ecstasy and already anticipating the next . . . He flopped happily over on his back and something under the other pillow hit his head. Something hard. He stuck a hand up under the pillow and touched metal.

"Holy *shit*!" he exploded, and was sitting up, staring down at her. "What's that?"

"That's what we have to talk about, Conrad. Part of it."

"It's a . . ."

"A gun."

"A . . . a . . ."

"A thirty-eight, like the police use." She stretched, arching her back, elbows tight over her head.

For a panicky moment Conrad's mind flashed to the Sharon Stone movie, the guy getting killed in the middle of . . . Was Annie planning to . . . ? No. No. That didn't compute. Suddenly nothing computed. A gun?

"What's it for?" he asked.

"Control."

"Of what?"

"Of the situation."

"Annie, I don't understand this."

Annie rolled onto her side, facing him where he sat cross-legged. She put a hand on his knee. "It may be hard for you to understand, but maybe you can because of the way you and your father are. The way he has no respect for you, like you said. Always fed up with whatever you want to do. That sort of thing."

She paused, then resumed. "So he's a big problem for you, an obstacle. I mean, you're not really going to be yourself until you get free of him, right?"

Conrad was silent. That was all certainly true.

"Look, I'm going to be straight with you," Annie said, and her fingers tightened on his knee. "If I say something that hurts you, it's because I love you, see? Your father's got you on a string. He's got all this money and you can get stuff you want, like that pickup. But you can't get his respect. He doesn't *want* you to get out on your own because then he loses control over you. And you get stuff like the pickup and feel guilty about it. You resent it, and him, but you need it. And he won't respect you because you need him. It's a vicious circle. Until you're on your own, free, he's got you by the balls. But you *should* be free, Conrad. You deserve to be free. Nobody should have you by the balls."

She giggled and touched him. "Except me."

"I guess you're right," Conrad said, trying hard to concentrate on what she was saying. Things were beginning to make sense to him. In his mind's eye he saw his father looking heavenward in contempt. He hated that.

"My situation is different," Annie said, "but the same. I never had a father. There was my stepfather, but he was a creep. An old guy, just hung around my mother like a servant, a wuss, you know? And he was always trying to grab me. It was disgusting. Can you imagine? This old guy with wrinkly elbows and a wrinkly neck trying to feel me up? I was glad when the old fart died.

"The guy who's *supposed* to be my father, who I always thought *was* my father, the skier—he was dead before I knew him. She lied about that. To everyone, not just me. So then I find out about my real father. Mo Bowdre."

She flopped over on her back and put her hands behind her head.

"All those years," she said, her voice turning harsh, "all those years my mother didn't tell me. *Kept* it from me. Who my father really was. And he turns out to be this totally cool guy."

"Why did she lie about it?"

"She's vicious. She always hated me. This was one way she could get back at me, you know? I mean I came along at a time when she'd already fucked up her life, and I guess I just made things worse by being born."

"Jeez, that's awful," Conrad said, and put a comforting hand on her stomach.

"She even thought it was *funny* when I finally told her about the creep, her husband, grabbing at me. Said it was good there was some life in the old guy, or some crap like that. Told me to grow up. Can you believe it? Well, I don't give a shit about *her*. She doesn't bother me. My whole life has sucked because of her, but now I'm free of her. And now I've found my father, my real father. My whole life can begin. My whole life *is* beginning. It's like a dream come true. It's like a miracle."

She fell silent. Conrad looked down at her in the dim light from the hurricane lamp outside the window. The whites of her eyes gleamed. Were those tears? Her body was a magical terrain, stretched out before him, so beautiful, so incredibly *new*, an altogether new world, but so intimately, openly here. For him. *That* was the miracle for him—this woman body here. She. Her.

"I don't want to lose him," Annie said. "I'll really die if I lose him, Conrad."

"Why would that happen?"

"My *mother*. He's decided he has to go see her. I can understand that. Yeah, I can understand that. They had an affair. Then it was over and she went away. And he . . . he never knew about me. Never knew she was the *mother* of *his* kid. So now, he has to see her.

"But she hates me so much she'll try and screw it up. Somehow. I know she'll screw it up. She'll lie again, make him think he isn't my father. I know her. She's a disgusting old drunk, let herself go completely to hell, but she's . . . shrewd. Yeah, shrewd. She'll blubber and carry on, but underneath it all she'll be sabotaging this whole deal."

"So are you going to shoot her?" Conrad asked, trying to sound like he was making a joke.

Annie laughed. "No. But we have to be in control of the situation, Conrad. Whatever develops, we have to be ready. No, the gun is . . . I always carry it in my bag. Like it's for protection. But I wanted you to know I had it. We shouldn't have any secrets between us, should we? You and me. We're like one."

She put her hand out, touched his cheek. "You're it for me. Do you see how lucky I am? You *and* a father. All at once. I just don't want that old bag to mess it up. So maybe we'll have to push her, you know? Be strong. And I'll need you. I'll really need you."

"Uh . . ."

"And I can count on you," she said.

"Yeah. Yeah, sure."

"Oh, thank you, Conrad. Come here. Come here and do me again that same way, will you?"

* * *

In room 1, Mo Bowdre was awake. He didn't know where he was but he was awake. Something had wakened him.

Yes, he was in a motel a few miles north of Leadville. The kid Conrad Franklin was in the other bed. It was dead silent in the room.

Conrad wasn't in the other bed.

That was what had wakened him. Cold air, the door closing. What was he doing? It must be about one o'clock, maybe two.

Oh no.

Annie. Him and Annie? Could they . . . ?

No.

Mo couldn't imagine it, didn't want to think about it. A wimp like that? With *his* . . . ? No.

The little . . . He'd strangle him. He'd march down there to Annie's room and strangle the little bastard, snatch him up in the air and strangle him.

Mo sat up.

Wait a minute, he said to himself, wait a minute. Think. First, she's twenty-one. An adult. She can do what she wants.

But with . . . ?

What she wants. And anyway, what's it to me? She may be my daughter, but maybe she's not. And even if she is, that stuff is none of my business anyway.

Christ, is this how fathers feel?

All right, what if she is my daughter? What does that change? Nothing really.

Everything. It changes everything. Why do I feel like

I've left everything behind? I haven't. It's just that I'm here in Colorado, in Leadville. With these two ... without Connie. How will it be with Connie and a daughter, this Annie? Two women in the house who hardly know each other? Both there because of—well, me. Does that work? She doesn't have to stay there with us. She's an adult, ought to be on her own.

She's strange, strange as a snake with three ends. Carrying on like that the other day, this sudden tempest, turning the sky dark green and black, *bam!* And then, sunshine.

Maybe she's crazy.

The little girl with the curl? Horrid—but then she's very, very good? What do they call that, manic depressive?

They got pills for that. Lithium or something. We can take care of it.

And when she is nice, she is very, very nice. A real sparkle to her, isn't there? And that fluty voice. Like her mother had.

Do I want this?

Do I want a daughter now? Her? This one?

Not my choice, is it? It just happens. Some things just show up, unbidden, and the nifty little plans you've got ... What have I left behind this time? How much do I have to ... ? What do I owe?

I owe, I owe, it's off to work I go. *Stop* that! Mind's turning to oatmeal ...

Too bad I can't see her.

Where's the fun in this?

Mo Bowdre flopped back on the bed and sighed. It was

like there was a safe, a strongbox somewhere deep down inside him, and it was locked and his fingers were all fumbly.

A man shouldn't try to think at two o'clock in the god-damn morning.

At three o'clock that morning, Sheriff's Deputy Hensen "Beau" O'Brien pulled into the parking lot of the Frontier Motel, the headlights of his patrol car sweeping the vehicles parked there. There were five, including one pickup that he recognized, a new Ford belonging to the mayor of Salida, evidently up to Leadville again on what he would later list, on his expense account, as business. The story was that the mayor and that Yolanda from Twin Lakes Cafe with the receding chin and the awesome mammaries did it in there with leather straps and hand-cuffs. But Beau O'Brien knew that might just be a story—the leather and cuffs part, anyway—the sort of tale that breaks the boredom. Yolanda's old Bronco wasn't in the lot, and Deputy O'Brien, who was as bored as anyone in Lake County, speculated that she and the mayor might have had an argument in there over who gets spanked first or some damn thing, and she grabbed up her straps and shit and went home in a huff.

Beyond the mayor's pickup, down at the far end of the lot, was an enormous Winnebago camper, forty feet long if it was a damned inch. No black Ram with floods like they'd been told to be on the lookout for.

Deputy O'Brien glowered at the camper. He hated those big motherfuckers, lumbering up the high country roads in low gear, blocking off any sense of the road for anyone behind. Oughta tax 'em by the amount of sky they cut off. People get crazy behind them, do stupid things, and Beau O'Brien had to scrape their sorry guts up off the pavement. Oughta outright ban them goddamn campers from most of these roads around here, he thought for what might have been the twelve hundredth time.

He backed up, turned around, and parked in the entrance of the lot, nose out. This night shift duty sucked. About as exciting as watching turtles fuck. Another week of it. And another five hours to go tonight. He yawned and scrunched down in the seat. Maybe he would just steal a few z's.

fifteen

The brief snow flurry the night before had not amounted to anything on the ground locally, but the mountains east and west of the valley where the Arkansas River has its origins and where Leadville sits had received several inches, perhaps the last they would see this summer. Mount Elbert and Mount Massive presided over the skyline as always, glowing even more purely in the thin sunlight this morning, like two eternally perfect twin goddesses.

Taking advantage of the early morning cold—the temperature, not yet forty, would soon enough climb well into the high sixties, even seventies—mountain bikers in shiny skintight sheaths were already heading bravely off, singly and in small swarms, for the even thinner air of the roads up Fryer Hill or Mosquito Pass or, less challenging, the loop around Turquoise Lake. Leadville had recently become another premiere site in the West for these hardy souls, and their care and feeding brought much needed tourist dollars into the city coffers, as did the hikers and others of the new outdoors class. But there were those in Leadville who noted sourly that such low-budget people don't drink much, if at all, and booze is where the real money is. There were still plenty of old-timers, many given to coughing up phlegm from their dust-coated lungs, who knew that the good times of the Old West were over, gone forever with the closing of the mines, but who didn't see a worthy future either in pandering to all these goody-goodies who filled up their little plastic bottles with Gatorade and ate bean sprouts and goat cheese. Damned if they didn't already have sections in the restaurants where you couldn't smoke.

Annie Harper tended to side with the old-timers in such matters, when she thought about it at all. It had never struck her as much fun to imagine Leadville, still pretty raw and ready for a boisterous good time even if it was falling apart, becoming a bush-league Aspen or a second-rate Telluride. But she didn't want to think about Leadville, past or future. She didn't want to be in Leadville, and she was having a hard time covering up her bad mood as she left her motel room and walked over to the black pickup.

During the night, someone from Illinois with an enormous Winnebago had parked right next to the pickup, and it looked like it was going to be damned hard getting backed out and turned around between the Winnebago and the phony hitching-post-type railings. Inconsiderate fat-asses.

She dropped her green canvas bag in the back of the truck. Conrad's and Mo Bowdre's duffel bags were already there. Conrad had banged on her door earlier, saying they were going to breakfast. Through the door she said she would be along, but instead she stood in the shower for fifteen, twenty minutes. She wasn't hungry.

Along with the rush of hot water, the shower emitted a sound that was something like the ring of a distant telephone, and for a moment she feared it might turn into the voices again, the ones that came from far off and always ended up screaming at her. High-pitched sounds often did that. But she fought it off, cranking the water's heat up almost past the bearable and scrubbing her body hard with a coarse motel washcloth. Later, standing naked in front of the mirror in her room, she saw how red and splotchy her body was and frowned. Hurriedly, she dressed so she wouldn't have to look at it.

Now, standing by the pickup, she stared out at Mount Elbert. It seemed closer in the crystalline air. When she was a little girl, the big mountain had been something serene, full of promise, a place where maybe wonderful things could happen. She reflected now that she had never climbed it, though it was little more than a long uphill walk to get to the summit. And she never would climb it. These mountains, Leadville and its slag heaps of memory—this place was not part of her plans. She'd escaped once. The blind man had brought her back, but . . . never again.

Across the lot, Conrad and Mo Bowdre exited the motel's coffee shop and walked in her direction. Conrad, walking a step ahead of the big man, had put on a pair of blue jeans instead of his baggy black pants, but he still looked nerdy. He walked with his feet turned outward like a duck. They both looked different somehow, not quite themselves, the way someone does whose reflection you see in your mirror, or in a storefront window.

Conrad was looking at her with a sappy grin as the two men approached. If he had a tail, it would be wagging, Annie thought. Bowdre put a hand on the pickup's tailgate and followed the edge of the truck bed around to where she was standing beside the driver's window. She touched him lightly on the arm to let him know where she was, and was surprised when he put a big arm around her. It was like being in the grasp of a bear. She looked up at him.

"Don't you want any breakfast?" he said. "Breakfast is the most—"

"Most important meal of the day," Annie said and laughed. "But I'm not hungry."

"It's just as well. All that stuff they got in there is bad for you. Eggs. Bacon. Biscuits with gravy, flapjacks with butter . . . Terrible stuff. They should rename the place, call it Cholesterol Corral. Well, are we gonna be off now?" He squeezed her shoulders and let her go, making his way back around the rear of the truck.

Conrad scrambled into the club seat, Mo clambered aboard after him, and Annie backed fast and expertly out from the shadow of the Winnebago, missing the wooden rails by no more than an inch and causing an involuntary intake of breath on Conrad's part.

"Don't be such a little old lady, Conrad. A pickup isn't real till it's got a few scratches and dents." In the rearview mirror she saw his face fall. "Hey," she said. "Hello? Conrad, it's like making love. After the first one, you stop worrying about it."

Mo Bowdre's blond eyebrows rose and fell over his dark glasses and he said nothing.

They drove through town, where some of the stores were just opening hopefully. A small gathering of mountain bikers still lolled around the little tables on the sidewalk outside a new coffee shop that catered precisely to such folk—coffees of various exotic types and homebaked things. Annie peered past Mo out the passenger side window at the unisex cluster of bikers and said, "The new West."

Soon they were out of the town proper and Annie accelerated, almost immediately slowing down and turning left onto the dirt road with its deep depressions, sharp rises, potholes, and ruts. The truck swayed and slowed further.

"Your mother's place, it's in the foothills," Mo said. "Up near all those old mines."

Annie glanced over at him. He was sitting erect as a post, his dark glasses facing straight ahead. He seemed to be impervious to the swaying and the jolts of the truck underneath him.

"With all these bumps you can tell that?" she said. "Yeah, we moved into the trailer up here after old snotface died. Rent-free. All she had was social security. She got a job cleaning up at the clinic, but the pay stank."

In the rearview mirror she saw Conrad's eyes widen. She caught his eye in the mirror and glared at him. He shrugged.

"We tried to grow some flowers outside, you know, make the place nice, but I guess the ground was ruined by all the slag. Stuff leaching out and all. They came up, the flowers, but they turned yellow almost right away. We had a well but I wouldn't drink the water. No telling what was in it. Millie did. She didn't care."

"You call her Millie?" Mo asked.

"She hates it when I call her that."

"Then why . . . ? Oh, yeah."

"I don't know what you're expecting," Annie said. "Maybe you remember her like she was. You're in for a surprise, a shock. I still don't understand what you expect to get out of this. I mean, Millie started to go to hell five, six years ago."

"Well, I guess I'm just old-fashioned," Mo said, his dark glasses fixed straight ahead.

A moment later the truck crawled around a conical black slag heap and stopped in the dirt twenty yards from the trailer. The ragged blue tarp lay still on the ground among the rusted auto parts. Around the side of the trailer, plastic cord was tangled on the collapsed clothesline, its two-by-fours now silver with age. Without the breeze, the trailer door hung partly open, inert. The wooden steps up to it were silver, the bottom step sagging almost to the dirt below it.

"Home sweet home," Annie said, and shoved her door open. "Maybe you want to wait here, huh, Conrad?"

"Okay."

Annie stepped out of the cab and plucked her green bag from the back. Then she walked around the front of the truck, and when Mo reached her near the fender, she took his arm.

"You just go ahead," he said. "I'll follow you." He sniffed the air loudly. "Acrid damn business, mining," he said and walked behind Annie toward the trailer.

He heard wood creak, and Annie said, "Watch out for this first step." He heard another creak, a metallic one—the door opening. He put out his foot and felt the step. It sagged under his weight, but the next one was firm. The side of the trailer had already begun to warm up in the sun. He stepped into the trailer, took two steps, feeling a carpet under his feet. It was dead silent. The only sound was that of Annie, breathing a few feet away. He sniffed again.

"Annie," Mo said. "Why have you done this?"

"Done what?"

"This place is abandoned. No one has lived here for months."

Annie said nothing.

"I can smell it, Annie. Where is your mother?"

He heard her move across the trailer.

"She's not here, is she?"

"Oh, she'll be along," Annie said bitterly, her voice rising. "Millie'll come and screw everything up."

"Annie, how is she gonna do that?"

"She lies."

"Annie . . ."

"She never wanted me to know. . . . She kept you a secret from me. She wanted me to be—to be like her. *Slut!* Drunken slut! On her back, spread her fat legs for anyone in a pair of pants. Not me. Not *me*. I don't do that. She's a liar. But I tell the truth. She hated that, hated that I told the truth."

"Annie, maybe we could—"

"I always tell the truth," Annie said emphatically. "I always try and be good. And I always wanted my father to know that. I *need* my father to know that. I love you, can't you see that? I love you. And you weren't there. How could I tell you when you weren't there?" She gasped, a rushing intake of air.

A horrid yellow flash filled his head, a sharp pain shot deep through his skull into his neck. He was on his knees on the floor. He felt nothing.

Outside in the pickup, Conrad heard Annie's voice, and then a heavy thunk. He pushed down the seat and bolted out of the truck just as Annie appeared at the trailer's door, her face ashen. There was a blob of what looked like blood on her shirt.

"Conrad!" She jumped the steps and rushed over to him.

"Conrad, he fell. He fainted or *something*. Hit his head on the corner of the sink."

"Jesus, is he—"

"He cut his head. Look, you go to the drugstore back in Leadville. Get some of those big gauze pads, some tape, you know, like bandages, and some disinfectant."

"Disinfectant . . . ?"

"Oh Christ, Conrad, ask the druggist what to use. Say a man's cut his head. Now go, *go!*"

"Should I get a doctor?"

"No, it's just a cut. Go on, will you?"

"Where's your mother?"

"She's late, I don't know. Will you *go*? The man is bleeding."

Conrad raced around the hood and jumped in, and Annie watched as he spun an enormous spurt of dirt and dust into the air before slewing around and lurching down the dirt track past the black slag heap that loomed up over the trailer. Once he was out of sight, Annie trotted over to the broken-down clothesline and began undoing a knot on the plastic cord that was tangled there. It resisted, and she tore at it with her fingers, finally undoing it.

Coiling up the cord, she glanced around the yard as if looking for something among the bits and rusted tatters. Her eye fell on a rusted piece of chain partly buried in the dirt, and she crossed over to it. On the end that showed, there was an iron hook. She gave the chain a tug. The rusty old links scraped against each other as it straightened but it wouldn't budge. Buried too far. She dropped it in the dust and went back to the trailer.

Mo Bowdre had sunk to his knees with the force of the blow and fallen over on his right side. He lay now in a near-fetal position on the floor. A small gash was visible about two inches above his left ear and blood ran from it through his blond hair to the back of his skull, where it was forming a small pool that the already badly stained carpet soaked up with reluctance.

Annie stood over him, looking down at his face, which was in repose, like he was sleeping. For a moment she saw him as a gigantic baby, curled up in sleep. There *was* something naked about him. She saw his dark glasses lying a couple of feet away and reached for them. With the edge of her shirt, a plain gray sweatshirt, she buffed the lenses and carefully slid them on over his eyes. Reaching up, she skimmed her shirt over her head, lifted the big man's head, and put the body of the shirt under it like a pillow. Next she wound the arms of the shirt around his cranium and forcefully tied them in a knot. She stood up, fetched her green bag, and took from it a folded red bandanna handkerchief, which she jammed under the knot of sweatshirt arms, covering the gash in his head. Leaning forward, her naked breasts against his shoulder, she took his head gently in her hands, pressing her head against his, and wept. She didn't want to hurt him.

After a minute while her shoulders shook uncontrollably and salty tears ran from her eyes into his hair, she heard him groan underneath her, a low rumbling that seemed to come from a deep cave. Quickly she straightened up, got to her feet, and took him by one wrist, heaving his vast bulk over the carpet a couple of feet closer to the sink. A crude cabinet had once been built under the sink, but one of its doors was now gone, and the other hung awkwardly from its lower hinge. Inside, the old pipes were beginning to rust, and a plastic bottle of detergent lay on its side, covered with dust.

Grunting with the effort, she pulled his arms toward the pipes and picked up her coil of plastic cord. In a matter of minutes Mo Bowdre's thick wrists were trussed tightly together and lashed in turn to the rusting pipe under the sink. She stretched the remaining few feet of cord from the pipe toward his ankles, finding it too short to wrap all the way around them. She let it lay and bent over to examine the handkerchief tied to his skull. The bleeding seemed to have slowed. At least it wasn't dripping onto the floor. Head wounds, she knew, even relatively small ones, always bled a lot. This one couldn't be too bad.

Something made her shudder, and she thought to look under the sink. Peering up beyond the pipes, she saw a white ball about the size of a pill, tangled in a messy cobweb. Beyond it, legs furled tight, a black widow sat unmoving in the tangle. Annie craned her neck to see if she could spot the red violin-shaped mark on her shiny body, but it was obscured. No mistaking it, though—a black widow. It seemed early in the season for her to be around, Annie thought, and mentally shrugged. They didn't bother anyone unless they were bothered. She heard an engine whining and growling in low gear. She rustled around in her green bag, found a T-shirt and put it on. And she heard her mother's voice, distantly, complaining.

"No, no, *Mother*." She shrieked. "Millie, you fat hog, *no*. Don't start all that shit again."

Conrad grabbed the bag of first-aid supplies off the seat and headed for the trailer door. Bursting in, he said, "Here's the stuff you . . . What the . . . ?"

It was totally insane. Totally unhinged. Mo Bowdre was lying on the floor, unmoving, with a sweatshirt tied around his head and his arms reaching under the sink, where they were apparently tied to the pipe. Annie was kneeling on the floor across the trailer, bent over, her head in her hands. She was moaning, a high-pitched sound. She looked up through fingers that clutched her face. Between her knees, lying on the dirty carpet, was the pistol, black and gleaming like a living thing.

"*Jesus,* did you shoot him?"

Annie looked up at him and blinked.

"No. No, I didn't shoot him."

"What is this?" Conrad said, his chest tightening with fear.

"I'm not going to let him go," Annie said, a new calm in her voice. She picked up the pistol and stood up. She held the weapon loosely by the grip. She backed up against the wall and put the gun down on top of an empty set of bookshelves made of unfinished wood. It rested there next to a yellowed paperback book with no cover.

"Annie, this is . . ."

"He said . . ." and she paused, her eyes widening as she stared at the form on the floor. "He said he didn't think I am his daughter, that there was some mistake. He said he was going to leave. He said there wasn't any way but one to find out if I was his daughter and that was a DNA test. So I said, okay, let's have one, and he said he didn't have to. It was me making all the claims, not him, and he wasn't interested. He didn't want a daughter."

Conrad was silent, and she suddenly spun around to face him.

"*Don't you see,* Conrad? I'm screwed. He's all I have." She was openly crying, and Conrad wished he could simply vanish, disappear.

"He can't do this to me," she said, looking back at him. "He was my new life, my way out, my . . . Now I'm alone again."

"What about your mother?"

"That bitch? She's been dead for six months." She

glanced over at him. He was staring wide-eyed at the pistol on the shelf. "No, no. She died of lung cancer."

"Well, I don't under—"

"Conrad, we're in this thing together. You and me. Like two orphans, right? And we *can* get something out of it. I've figured it out. Here, give me those bandages."

She took the paper bag and knelt down beside the blind man on the floor, slipping the sweatshirt off his head. She prodded his hair gently with a finger, and then opened up the bandages, tearing away the packaging. She squeezed the tube and rubbed the stuff into the wound, placed a gauze pad over it and wrapped it, tying a knot with the gauze strip. Throughout the procedure she crooned in a barely audible voice. Conrad watched her fingers work, so gentle. It didn't compute. It didn't make any sense. His own hands were shaking, and he thrust them in his pockets.

"There," she said, sitting back on her heels to admire her work. "He'll be okay." She stood up and wiped her hands on the seat of her jeans.

"Annie, this is . . . this is crazy."

She turned on him, shrieking, cobalt-blue eyes searing him. "No! No! *No! Not* crazy! This is *not* crazy, Conrad, goddamn it."

"*What is it, then?*" Conrad was appalled to find he was shouting, too. "What *is* it? What are we *doing*? Why is he tied up?"

Annie turned her back and picked up the pistol from the top of the bookshelves, fondling it in both hands before setting it down again. "He sired me, Conrad. He rammed his *seed* into my mother and then I happened.

But he was gone by then. Long gone. Now I found him, twenty-one years later I found him, and he *owes* me a life. So I'm going to get it. If he won't give it to me, I have to take it."

"I don't under—"

"Ransom," she said, and turned, smiling fondly at Conrad. She stepped over to him and placed her hands on his shoulders, squeezing him gently, and licked her lips. Her hips pressed against his groin. "Like an advance on my inheritance."

sixteen

Into a dense thicket of despair, Mo Bowdre clawed his way upward, seeing again the yellow flash, knowing his vision was gone, that he couldn't see, wouldn't see again. He was caught in the fuses, tangled, couldn't move. The world had gone crazy, and he heard someone saying, no, no. *No. Not* crazy.

"—this is *not* crazy, Conrad, goddamn it."

Someone else shouting. "What are we doing?"

He couldn't see. Lie still, don't move. Pain, pain in the head.

That was a long time ago, the dynamite. Where was he? In the mine?

Conrad? The voice had said Conrad.

He was in the trailer, on the floor. Annie and Conrad.

"—and he *owes* me a life. So I'm going to get it."

That was Annie. Listen.

Ransom? He was kidnapped? Kidnapped?

Tied, his wrists were tied. He was lying on his side, his arms were extended, wrists tied, something besides the cord biting into his arm. An edge. Move a finger. What's that? Metal. A pipe. Tied to a pipe? A sink. He was tied to the pipe under a sink.

"—this morning, while you guys were eating. On his answering machine. I said you and I have him and we want two hundred and fifty thousand dollars. I said we'd call again to tell 'em where to take it."

Silence. Someone is breathing loud.

"Hello? Conrad?"

"You told them who it—who we are?"

"They'd know that anyway. Relax. Hey, you're all tense, all knotted up here. Let me—"

"Annie, this isn't—"

"Hush."

The flutelike voice saying hush. Hush. So soft. His head hurt where it was ringing. Kidnapped? Two hundred and fifty thousand dollars?

Mo Bowdre slipped out of consciousness.

Conrad Franklin sat in the driver's seat of his black Ram 1500 pickup-with-everything. He'd told Annie that since they were simply waiting around, he would go sit in his truck and listen to some music. He had the earphones clamped on his head, but there was no music. Conrad was thinking.

Clouds had appeared earlier over the mountains that hemmed them in east and west, and now the sky was totally gray. The wind had started again, and across the dirt yard it was making the tattered blue tarp rise and fall, like a living thing. He wondered if it was going to snow again. Snow in June. At home it was always sunny. Almost always.

Conrad was trying to think what he should do, how he was going to extricate himself from this, make it go away—all of it.

He'd been crazy to go along . . . but had he gone along? Well, of course, he'd gone along with the screwing. Who wouldn't? Who'd turn *that* down? But then all this other stuff—hadn't it happened without him knowing? She had slugged Mo Bowdre while he was waiting in the truck. She'd tied him up while he was getting the bandages. *She* had hatched the idea of kidnapping him. Kidnapping, for Christ's sake. Didn't they execute people for kidnapping? It wasn't him who had done this.

He said it over and over to himself, but he knew that he *had* gone along. Gone along with all of Annie's little deceptions. All that crap about her mother and this trailer, how this was her mother's place. And now . . .

Now his name was on the answering machine in Mo Bowdre's house. Annie's partner in crime. In kidnapping. He was trapped. It was a terrifying thought. He couldn't stop yawning.

Again Mo Bowdre became aware. Again he puzzled his way into recalling where he was and what had evidently happened. She had slugged him—with something, God knew what—and tied him to the pipe under the sink in this abandoned trailer somewhere between Leadville and that place, what was it called? Stringtown. In the foothills. She was crazy, absolutely crazy.

How did that happen? How did someone get so crazy? Why had that happened to her?

What was it, Wednesday? Five days ago, Saturday, he and Connie had been at his opening in Frazier's gallery. It seemed like a lifetime ago. Maybe it was. Only five days ago the world had been normal. And Sunday, that was normal, too. Well, Tony Ramirez had his homicides and all. But life was going according to plan. Then Sunday night, he thought, in the middle of the night in my backyard, this lunatic explodes like a neutron bomb into my life, like she's been waiting out there around some corner I didn't know I was turning. . . .

He heard breathing.

"Annie," he said. "Is that you?"

"Yeah."

"This isn't going to do you much good, you know."

He heard her walk across the trailer toward him. She was standing directly over him.

"What else have I got?" she said. "You say you don't want a daughter, you don't want me."

"Annie, I never said that."

"I heard you. I *heard* you say it."

"Maybe you were hearing things. I know this is—"

"*I'm not crazy!* I don't *hear* things. Don't call me crazy. People talk to me. I hear their thoughts. I've always known what people are thinking. I know what you're thinking. You can't fool me."

Her foot scrunched on the carpet and he heard her walk away, heard her slump to the floor. He pictured her sitting with her knees up, leaning back against the wall. He wondered what she looked like. Maybe she did look like her mother. He tried to picture her mother, but all he could remember now were Millie's exciting blue eyes.

"I have a gun," Annie said.

Jesus, he thought. She hit him with the gun. His head hurt, and he felt the bandage tight around his head. How do you deal with a lunatic with a gun? A lunatic who says she's your daughter, and maybe she is, God help you, and she's kidnapped you and is holding a gun on you? How had this nightmare happened? *Why* had it happened?

He had to get out of here. How was he going to do *that*?

"Where's Conrad?" he asked.

"Listening to music in the truck."

"And we're just waiting."

"We're just waiting," she agreed.

He moved his fingers, felt the pipe he was tied to. His wrists were tied together and then to the pipe. It was the P-trap, the drain. He could feel the coupling, the ring. The cord was tied to the drain. Annie was sitting on the floor, maybe ten feet away. He was on his side on the floor. She couldn't see his hands over his bulk. Or so he figured.

"So how long are we going to wait?" he said, and wrapped his fingers around the ring coupling.

"As long as it takes."

He tightened his grip on the ring and twisted. It didn't move.

"Connie won't be back until Saturday, you know." He tightened his grip on the ring coupling again and strained. It moved. Okay, okay. He let it go. "Nobody's going to miss us till Saturday," he said.

"Shut up." She was crying.

"Oh, Annie, we should—"

"Don't 'Oh, Annie' me. You don't give a shit about me."

"That's not true—"

"Shut *up*! Just shut up!"

He knew he would get only the one chance, and that he'd have to take it when it arrived.

It was sometime in the late afternoon, maybe a little later. His usually unerring sense of time was gone— probably from being slugged and out cold, he thought. Conrad had entered the trailer, accompanied by cold air, and said, "We got to eat."

Annie agreed, and told him to drive into Leadville and pick up some hamburgers and fries.

"And some beer," she said.

"Um . . ."

"Oh, yeah. Coke, then. Whatever."

She evidently gave him some money. "Okay," he said, "I'll be right back." Mo heard him push the door open.

"Conrad?" Annie said.

"Yeah."

"If you're not back in a half hour, I'm going to shoot him."

Mo heard the door close and Conrad clump down the wooden steps, then the truck starting and moving off down the dirt road.

A half hour. If I were Conrad, he thought, I'd haul ass out of here, out of Leadville, go home and deny everything, while Mo Bowdre lay dead and rotting in an abandoned trailer and Annie went off raving and ranting into the landscape, maybe find some other innocent soul whose life she could turn upside down. She was like a string of tornadoes.

But she was alone now, alone with him. He had a half hour to get the hell out of here. Something had to happen.

And it did.

Annie approached, and he felt her bend over him. Her hand touched his wrists, and she pulled this way and that on the cord that bound him to the pipe. Then she stood up, evidently satisfied. He heard her walk across the trailer and push the door open.

"Where are you going?" he asked.

"To pee."

He heard the door close, and grabbed at the ring coupling, grasping it tight, turning it. Sideways motion he could do, but up-and-down motion—he didn't know. Would he be able to shove the damn ring down? It turned freely in his hand. It was unscrewed. He pressed it downward but it didn't move—stuck. Again. The edge of the cupboard was hard and sharp against his wrist. He pressed again and the ring popped downward.

Now. The hard part. He pulled his knees up toward his chest, put his foot against the cupboard and yanked his arms back toward his chest.

Nothing but an agony in his wrists where the cord cut tight.

Again.

Nothing. A third time, and the U-shaped drain gave a little. He pulled again, pain shooting through his wrists and forearms, and it gave again. He worked the cord down the pipe and pulled free. He was panting, gulping air.

On his feet, he groped around in the sink, hoping to find something, anything with an edge, but there was nothing. To his right there should be a back door. He had felt a nearly imperceptible draft on the floor coming from there. He reached out, felt the door! He found the latch and pushed it open. He put one foot out and down, searching for a step, holding onto the doorway with his two hands tied together. Nothing. He put his foot down farther and felt a step.

Putting his weight down, he guessed it had been a minute since Annie went out to pee. How long did it take to pee? This was a no-hoper, he thought, and began to move away from the trailer, holding his tightly coupled hands out in front of him.

The ground underneath him was smooth, a dirt yard probably, and it inclined up. He moved faster.

Keep going till you trip over some goddamned thing. Then on your knees. Scramble.

He gasped the thin air and pushed forward, step after step. His foot hit something, a rock, and he veered slightly to the side, still moving up, still gasping, cursing the altitude. The Okies couldn't stand the altitude here. It had been eleven thousand feet at Climax. More. The Okies arrived at Climax looking for work, and quit the next day. That had been the standard sneer.

Jesus!

He hit something else, another rock, and lost his balance, pitching forward in terror. A no-hoper. No hope. How could he escape? He was blind, for Christ's sake, and his wrists were tied together. Fumbling around in the permanent goddamn darkness in the middle of . . . She'd be done now, she'd come roaring out the back door. With her gun. Would she use it? She was crazy. He waited for the sound of the shot as he scrambled to his feet.

The ground under his hands was loose. Tailings. A slag heap. He scrambled up with his hands and feet like an ape, then down the other side, crashed into something else, something low, and pitched over on his side on the ground, saying *Shit* over and over in his mind. He lay on the ground, his chest heaving. It was a big timber he'd hit. An old timber like a railroad tie they used to hold up the mine shafts.

Somewhere near there was a mine shaft. An old mine shaft, abandoned, caving in like all of them, full of noxious shit and no oxygen, and he didn't want to go in a mine shaft. Not ever again. He wanted to be in sunlight, feel it on his neck, feel it warming his body.

In a mine shaft it was dark. Without light.

She couldn't see in a mine shaft. They would both be blind.

He groped forward, hands out in front. It was too much to ask, wasn't it? That the scavenging bastards had left the rails, the rails that would lead him to the shaft.

From below, Annie's voice came, piercing.

"Don't!" she was shrieking. *"Don't!"*

Then a shot crackled in the thin air.

The smell, the familiar greasy smell of hamburgers and french fries, was making him crazy with hunger. They were sitting in the paper bags on the seat next to him. Why did he have to wait? He didn't. There was plenty of time. Ten minutes. He'd pull over and eat the first of the three hamburgers he'd ordered for himself—two each for the others. On the side of the road, he'd just pull over and have a hamburger and think some more.

He took his foot off the accelerator and looked up into the rearview mirror.

"Shit."

A police car was back there behind him, maybe a hundred yards back.

Be cool. Just drive. He put his foot back on the accelerator and brought the truck back up to speed.

What speed? He looked wildly around for a speed sign. He was going forty. He slowed to thirty-five. He looked back at the police car. It was closer now.

I'm going too slow.

He sped up to forty-five, glanced up and saw the light go on, the red light.

Oh God. No, no, no, no, please—I'm caught, I'm caught. How do they know? Someone heard the message on the answering machine? I'm going to jail, death row. They're going to execute me.

Conrad thought he was going to throw up.

The flashing red light was closer now. He could see the cop through the windshield, big dark glasses. He saw the cop's gloved hand come up and point him toward the shoulder. He could barely breathe. The pickup drifted off the road onto the shoulder and rolled to a stop. Conrad sat slumped over the wheel. He didn't think he could move. Accessory. The word kept running through his mind like a tape.

He heard the cop's boots crunching the gravel along the side of the road. He heard the crunching stop. He turned his

head to the window. The cop's face was huge, looking at
him, frowning behind the big shiny shades. He had a darkly
tanned face and a jaw like a tank. His teeth showed when
he spoke—teeth like a shark. I'm dead, Conrad thought.

"Are you Conrad Franklin?"

"Yessir."

"From Santa Fe, New Mexico?"

"Yessir." Conrad was confused. The cop's voice had
softened.

"There's a message for you, son," he said. "From
home."

When they didn't have anything better to do, and that
was often, some of the guys at Climax would use their
day off to explore the old mines that honeycombed the
mountains and passes, poking around in the old mills,
checking out the old drifts and shafts, imagining the old
days. Even into modern times, some of the old mines in
the area were small, primitive, worked by old machinery
and by hand up until the exhausted men and the exhausted mine decided to give it up.

Groping his way from the entrance along the rough walls
of the tunnel, Mo recalled those days, remembered the
typical configuration of these old mines, even the terms. He
was maybe twenty feet into the drift, the horizontal tunnel
in which, somewhere, they had sunk a shaft down, like a
well. They'd send men and equipment down the shaft in
big buckets or cages that hung on the end of cables that ran
around a sheave wheel and to an engine of some kind to
raise and lower it. Some of the shafts were hundreds of feet
deep. It was where most of the mining accidents happened.

Mo wanted to get past the shaft.

The sound of the gunshot still reverberated in his brain, and his mind screamed at him: *Go, go, go!* But the place had been stripped. No rails leading in and out meant the rest of the machinery had probably gone too, maybe reused somewhere else, maybe sold for scrap. He had no idea what kind of collar there might be now around the shaft. None, probably. So he groped his way cautiously, keeping an elbow against one wall, feeling the timbers every ten feet or so, shoved into place long ago to keep the drift from falling in. There was rubble underfoot, meaning that the drift was deteriorating, rock had fallen. The second set of timbers he encountered sagged low enough that he struck his head. He crouched down lower and went on, step after cautious step into the interior.

It was dank, the mountain over him leaking as they all did once they had been violated. Here and there he felt water dribbling down, icy on his neck. The soles of his boots were wet through, cold. He kept his coupled hands low, hoping to encounter a railing or something that would signal that he'd reached the shaft. He saw himself plummeting down the shaft, turning and twisting, descending into hell.

Between steps he listened.

He wanted to get beyond the goddamned shaft, he wanted to get out of direct range of the entrance, he wanted there to be a turn, a bend, he could get around. He thought of bullets ricocheting around in the drift— baa-*zingggg* like in the old Westerns—and he thought of rock falling.

Mainly what he heard was rock crunching under his

wet boots and his own lungs sucking in the poor air. And water running over rock.

These old mines leaked all kinds of toxic gases, too, everyone said, and this place stank. He didn't know what he was smelling in the acrid air that assaulted his nose. He knew you can't smell some of the gases that kill you.

His foot struck something and he lost his balance, threw his hands up, righted himself and crouched down. The shaft. A vacuum of blackness in the dark.

What a foul and awful place, this mine. All of them. People got all warm and gooey, Mo thought, talking about caves and the protective womb of Mother Earth. For a miner, that was purest bullshit. This was her horrid maw, filled with fangs and acid.

He crept around the shaft, the great emptiness, the black hole that sucked up lives, and kept going. He wondered how many men had died down this one hole, blown up or simply plummeting in an iron bucket, gone to hell flailing and screaming. He hugged the wall of the drift, feeling the slickness of the snowmelt lubricating the rock. It widened, no, not widened, turned! Turned slightly to his right, a large protrusion of rock marking the turn. He squatted down on his heels behind the protrusion. Water trickled between his boots, icy cold to the touch. He felt the rock, found what passed for an edge, and began sawing back and forth on the cord that bound his wrists.

It was no use. No time.

He stopped, listened. She'd be coming. Soon. He'd left a trail plain as a highway through the tailings. Water was falling somewhere behind him and in front, between him and the entrance—meltwater dripping off the rock. Had the sound changed? The notes of the dirge, had they changed to a higher register?

She could wait him out. That would be the sensible thing to do.

But she was crazy. She might just come roaring into the dark in a fury, blasting away. Or she might sit out there at the entrance, crying . . . or laughing, for Christ's sake, no telling what. She probably didn't know what she was doing, probably thought all her stories were true, that all the things she made up had actually happened, probably thought she was perfectly sane. She didn't believe she was a nutcase, couldn't admit that her whole sorry head was wired up wrong, every bit of the tangle in there capable of short-circuiting at any moment. God, how did that *happen* to a person?

And with all of that, she could be his daughter.

But she suspected, didn't she? Suspected she was a lunatic. And she hated the idea with utter terror. He had to count on that. It was all they had going for them now.

He listened.

From the direction of the entrance came the sound of a foot on loose rock.

"You're in there," Annie's voice said.

Silence but for the dripping and the click of a pebble falling to the floor.

"It's stupid, going in there."

Silence.

"You want to know why?"

"Annie," Mo said, and his voice sounded altogether

different to him, the way it sounded on a tape recorder—
someone else's voice. "We need to talk—"

"No, no. We've done the talking. There's nothing else
to say. You betrayed me. Twice. *Twice.* You weren't there
for me from the start. And now you're denying me.
Aren't you? You don't want me, you don't want your
own daughter. Isn't that right?"

"Annie, we can—"

"I hate you. I *hate* you."

He heard her boots crunching. He counted the steps,
guessing she was now about ten feet into the drift. Fifteen. Now twenty.

"You want a father?" Mo said. "And you think I'm
your father, you think I owe you? I heard you say that,
Annie. That I owe you."

"Yeah, you do. You owe me." She had stopped.

"I owe you the truth. You want to hear the truth?"

Silence.

"You told me," Mo said, "you always try to tell the
truth. You want to hear it, too?"

"Shut up. Shut *up!*"

"No, I won't shut up. I'm going to tell you the truth.
You're not going to be able to stand the truth, Annie."

"I'll kill you, I'll kill you."

"The truth is, Annie—"

"Shut *up!*"

"The truth is you're crazy. Crazy, Annie. Looney
Tunes. A nutcase."

"No!"

"Even if you were my daughter, I'd disown you. You're

a mess, a nutcase. Who'd want to put up with that, huh, Annie? Who?"

Annie was screaming, her voice shattering the air, and the gun went off—once, twice—a violent assault on his eardrums. He crouched down, hands and elbows in the icy water, the explosions ricocheting in the dark.

"I'm coming, you bastard, you fucking bastard, I'm coming, I'll *kill* you, I'll hurt you, I'll *hurt* you." She was shrieking, her voice trailing off into a high-pitched howl in the drift. She was coming closer.

"You're sick!" Mo shouted. "You're sick, sick!"

"Damn you, damn you!" The gun fired again, the awful noise swallowing the air. Three shots? Five? The ricocheting of the blasts, how many? It had to be empty. They kept echoing, farther off, lower-pitched, now closer, merging into a growl. Oh no.

He lunged forward.

The world was falling, the rumble now a roar. A stream of dirt and pebbles and then rocks hit his shoulders, his head. There was a scream, Annie screaming, and another, a searing scream of wood breaking, and Annie again: "Auugh, no!"

The shaft. She was at the shaft. He dove forward, arms out in front, wrists cinched tight, felt her falling into him, snatched, clutched her, hit the ground—no, her, fell on her legs . . . grabbed at her shirt and pulled, yanking her torso up, out of the shaft, and crawled away from it, scrambled, hauling her over the rock. It was pounding on his back, his shoulders. Another. Shit. Shit. The mountain falling in. The noise, Christ, the noise was awful, all this rock, this rock . . .

seventeen

Unfamiliar fingers held his wrist. It stank of hospital, of antiseptics and sickness. He hated hospitals.

The fingers put his wrist down. On the stiff clean sheet of the hard mattress of the hospital bed. He hated hospital beds. People died in hospital beds.

"Who're you?" he growled.

"Ah, Mr. Bowdre," said a male voice. A male nurse? "You're with us." It was a cheery voice, like a lot of staff people use in hospitals, trying to make you feel better, like maybe you won't die of gangrene or whatever you've contracted from being in the hospital. "I'm Dr. Billings. Jeff Billings. You took quite a beating there."

Ha, ha, fella, you took quite a beating there. We all have our fun, huh?

"But you'll be okay. A lot of cuts and scrapes. Bruises. Nothing broken. You've got a good skull. It was under a pretty good-sized rock when they got to you."

"Got to me?"

"They dug you out."

"Who?"

"The sheriff's deputy and your friend, that kid, Conrad

Franklin. They got to you first. Called for assistance. You're awful lucky the whole damn place didn't fall in."

"Conrad?"

"Yeah. Poor kid. The deputy spotted his truck, gave him the bad news—"

"What bad news?"

"About his parents."

"What about them?"

"The police from Santa Fe asked the sheriff to be on the lookout for the kid. His mother was killed, murdered. His father was attacked at the same time, they say, got thrown. From his horse. Apparently paralyzed, but maybe he'll get his arms back. They caught the guy. It was on the news."

"Jesus."

"Awful. So anyway, the sheriff's deputy spotted the son driving out of town, told him the bad news. The kid seemed like he was in shock already, they said, even before he heard the bad news. And then, even afterward, he didn't say much, just begged the deputy to come with him. He needed help."

"What day is it?"

"Friday . . . After they got you out, the kid said he was driving home to see his father."

"I'd like to get home, too. By tomorrow. Saturday."

"No way. You got a pretty good concussion from that rock. You got a thick skull, but it's not indestructible."

"What about the girl? Annie."

"Poor Annie. She's going to be all right. Physically anyway. She got banged around pretty good, just like you. What a life. You know her well? What were you doing in there anyway?"

"She's a . . . We go back a ways. I spent the last few days with her. She was looking for her father."

"Oh, God. Poor Annie. And she picked . . . ? She's had the worst kind of life here, you know. I've known her since she was born. I delivered her. Her mother—Millie Harper, you know her? She died a couple of years ago. Lung cancer. Millie tried to be a good mother, just didn't have it together, as they say these days. And there are some things I guess you can't overcome."

"Like what?"

"Annie's strong as an ox physically. Healthy. Big girl . . . and that's sort of surprising considering her birth weight. Only weighed five pounds. But that kind of benign neglect, I don't know. The human psyche is so damn fragile. Anyway, this stuff didn't begin to really show up until she was in her late teens."

"What stuff?"

"They call it borderline personality disorder. It doesn't sound like much, but . . . It's a cross between paranoia and schizophrenia. Nobody knows where it comes from. Or how to treat it. I don't really know much about it, not my field. I do know that most of the shrinks won't touch it. It's an awful fate, like the old Greek fate. It just reaches out from nowhere and fingers someone."

"Where is she? Annie."

"We sent her to a hospital in Denver. She's in the psychiatric ward. They can patch her up there physically, and maybe help with the rest. I don't know."

"You said she weighed five pounds?"

"Yes. A preemie. Two months early. We had to keep her here for more than a month."

"So she was conceived in . . . ?"

"Well, that makes it August, I guess. Yeah, sometime in August. Why?"

"I wasn't here then."

"Oh. I see. Okay, well, Mr. Bowdre, I've got to see some other patients here. I'll look in on you later. This evening."

Mo heard him walk toward the door, where he stopped.

"You saved her life, you know."

"Yeah? That's good. I owed her *something*."

"Who knows? Who knows? Oh, there's someone waiting to see you. An Indian woman. Got here a few minutes ago. Shall I send her in?"

"Now that would be just what the doctor ordered."

acknowledgments

Among the many people who advertently or inadvertently aided the author in writing this book, special thanks are due David Leeming of Albuquerque; Martha A. Nelson of Denver; Bazy Tankersley of Al-Marah Stud; Lindsey Truitt of Washington, D.C.; and Steve Accardi, Manuel M. Romero, and Michael Claire of the Albuquerque Police Department.

The author also offers his sincerest condolences to anyone who is afflicted by or who is—for one reason or another—close to someone afflicted by the tragic madness called (with such deceptive mildness) borderline personality disorder.

Don't miss the other Mo Bowdre mysteries by Jake Page . . .

THE STOLEN GODS

Mo Bowdre, a powerfully built wildlife sculptor, is blind—but that doesn't stop him from pursuing the truth when a major dealer in Native American art is murdered.

THE DEADLY CANYON

Mo Bowdre's newest sculpture is commissioned for a remote desert research station rife with conspiracy and smuggling. When the corpse of a woman who was both a scientist and an FBI special agent is found, Bowdre goes into action.

THE KNOTTED STRINGS

A controversial historical movie, being filmed on tribal land, is interrupted when the leading man is murdered. Blind sculptor Mo Bowdre believes that the solution to this crime is more complex than it seems.

THE LETHAL PARTNER

Santa Fe is caught up in the death of a gallery owner's lover, a string of unsolved murders, and the discovery of previously unknown Georgia O'Keeffe paintings. Mo Bowdre thinks he knows who has committed the crimes—but he must act before it's too late.

Published by Ballantine Books.
Available at your local bookstore.

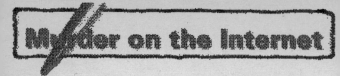

Murder on the Internet

Ballantine mysteries are on the Web!

Read about your favorite Ballantine authors and upcoming books in our monthly electronic newsletter MURDER ON THE INTERNET, at
www.randomhouse.com/BB/MOTI

Including:
- What's new in the stores
- Previews of upcoming books for the next three months
- In-depth interviews with mystery authors and publishers
- Calendars of signings and readings for Ballantine mystery authors
- Bibliographies of mystery authors
- Excerpts from new mysteries

To subscribe to MURDER ON THE INTERNET, send an e-mail to **srandol@randomhouse.com** asking to be added to the subscription list. You will receive the next issue as soon as it's available.

Find out more about whodunit! For sample chapters from current and upcoming Ballantine mysteries, visit us at
www.randomhouse.com/BB/mystery